DEAR LIFE, YOU SUCK

DEAR LIFE, YOU SUCK

SCOTT BLAGDEN

HARCOURT

Houghton Mifflin Harcourt

Boston   New York   2013

Harcourt is an imprint of
Houghton Mifflin Harcourt Publishing Company.

www.hmhbooks.com

Text set in Garamond

Library of Congress Cataloging-in-Publication Data is available.
ISBN 978-0-547-90431-3

Manufactured in the United States of America
DOC 10 9 8 7 6 5 4 3 2 1
4500397132

To Connor & Madison
Follow your dreams

Crickets, like all other insects, are cold-blooded.
They take on the temperature of their surroundings.
—Wikipedia

CHAPTER 1

The shrinkadinks think I have a screw loose. Ain't playing with a full deck. Whacked-out wiring. Missing marbles.

Oh, wait. I live in the north of Maine now with the moosikins and lahbstahs.

The shrinkadinks think I have a bent prop. Knots in the net. Sap in the chain. Am thin in the chowda.

A danger to myself and others. That's what my file says. I've read all my files. And believe you me, that's an avalanche of reading. It's friggin' *War and Peace*. War, mostly. Required a hefty dose of criminal rapscallinity on my part, but no big thing. Ain't an office or file cabinet I can't *entrez-vous* with my city-boy ingenuity. I ain't always lived in Flanneland.

But I gotta tell ya, I think it's the brain ticklers with the bats in the belfry. There ain't a damn thing wrong with me. They just label me mashed yams on account of I mess with their heads. To me it's funny. To them it's insanity. *Potayto. Potahto.*

A danger to others. They think that 'cause I've been brawling since I've been crawling. But that's only self-defense. Brawling for a binky don't make a toddler touched. Makes him human. It's instinct. Just 'cause P. H. Deed, Mind Mangler, never had to wrestle anything slipperier than a silver caviar spoon from a platinum platter don't mean the rest of us who crack skulls for a Dixie cup of Cocoa Puffs are nutseekookoo.

A danger to myself. Well, that's a whole nutha slice of pie.

Principal LaChance is eyeballing me like a lion on a gazelle. I've been silent for seventeen and a half minutes. I wonder how long he can hold out before he pounces. Not long, I bet.

"I'm waiting, Cricket."

I know what you're waiting for, you fruity bastard.

Randall LaChance fancies himself proficient at the waiting game, but he's an amateur. I can sit here all day. He glowers at me. "And please remove your hood. It's discourteous."

I slip my hood off and instinctively raise my right hand to my right cheek. I imagine LaPoofta LaChance reaching forward and gently caressing my scar. The image makes me snicker.

He shakes his overstuffed teddy bear head and sighs. Randall has blazing orange hair that makes it look like his head's on fire. He parts his wavy locks in the center, which always makes me imagine a tribe of Judaic lice fleeing to the freedom of his forehead across his Red Sea scalp.

We sit for another eight minutes.

"You're not leaving my office, Cricket, until you tell me why you punched Mitchell Burke in the nose this morning and held his head underwater in the science lab fish tank."

I already told him, but I guess he didn't like the answer. "Remember? He stole Gregory Bullivant's lucky Popeye pen."

"Why did you immediately resort to violence? Why didn't you simply inform the teacher?"

I laugh. "Good one, Randy."

"I wasn't trying to be funny, Cricket. And please address me as Principal or Mr. LaChance."

You sure you don't mean "undress me," Lady LaChance?

"Well?"

"Well what? Why didn't I run to the teacher and tattle on Burke the Jerk? What, are you fuckin' shittin' me?"

Randy ManCandy scribbles in his notebook. Something else for my file. He speaks without looking up. "You know how I feel about your swearing, Cricket."

Fuck you, Froot Loops. I lean back in my chair and glance at my watch.

"Don't bother counting the minutes today, Cricket. You're here for as long as I want you."

"As long as I want you." Classic.

Cheesecake LaChance is a physiological dichotomy. He's *Beauty and the Beast* incarnate. From the neck up, he's as pretty as a transvestite prom queen. Ice-blue eyes, impeccably groomed butt-bandit beard, and perfect teeth like LEGO pieces. From the neck down, he's as pretty as an Amazon jungle queen. Tree-trunk thighs, an ass the size of Brazil, and a belly that looks like he swallowed a Galápagos sea turtle. It's hard to look at him without imagining his Grand Canyon ass-crack bent over a log-clogged toilet, a monkey wrench in his one hand and a plunger in the other.

"I'll refrain from giving you my Violence Isn't the Answer speech again, since I'm sure you know it by heart." Chubs LaChance licks his pudgy thumb with his slab-of-liver tongue and opens a manila folder. "We had this very same conversation on the last day of school in June, Cricket. If I remember correctly, we were discussing how you were going to turn things around senior year."

We weren't discussing shit, asshole. You were sermonizing and I was counting lint balls on the carpet.

"And here we are again, on the third day of senior year, and you're back to the same old shenanigans."

"Shenanigans"? A scene from *The Simpsons* flashes in my mind. *"Sorry, Mr. Burns, but I don't go in for these backdoor shenanigans. Sure, I'm flattered, maybe even a little curious, but the answer is no!"*

I chuckle and resume my lint ball count. I believe I left off at six thousand nine hundred and sixty-nine.

Principal LaChance pinches the bridge of his nose, which adults have been doing in my presence for as long as I can remember. Like I give them nasal congestion or something. "Frankly, Cricket, we're running out of options. If it weren't for Mother Mary intervening on your behalf with the school board so often, you would have been thrown out of here a long time ago."

La-di-dah LaChance gets up and sashays to the window the way he always does when he's searching for an in. Something I'll *respond* to.

I look at my mountainous file on his desk. It towers over the shiny mahogany like the landfill behind the church cemetery. Filled with as much garbage, too.

Randall speaks into the glass. "Someday, Cricket, you're going to have to start taking responsibility for your actions and stop blaming all the bad things in your life on other people and your past."

My chest tightens and my forehead warms. *Allthe-badthingsinyourlife. Otherpeopleandyourpast. All. Bad. Things. Your. Life.*

Principal LaChance turns from the window, drops one hip, and crosses his arms over his man boobs. "We all reach a point in our lives, Cricket, when we have to put the past behind us and live in the present."

Well, therein lies the problem, Cliché LaChance. My internal space-time continuum sank to the bottom of a bathtub when I was eight years old.

"It's high time you grow up, Cricket."

High time. You sure as shit got that right. I pull my hood on and take another gander at the lint balls rolling around on the fuchsia plush.

Another twelve minutes pass.

Chatterbox LaChance finally gives up. I got to hand it to him, though — he hung in there longer than usual.

Mother Mary squeezes her enormous frame out of a plastic chair when Dandy Randy escorts me to the front office to pick up my Get Out of School Free card. She doesn't look happy. In fact, she looks downright miffed. As soon as she sees me, she storms out of the office. I follow her at a safe distance to the white and rust Prison van in the parking lot. I don't really live in a prison, but I call it that on account of that's what the building used to be a hundred years ago, when respectable Maine men-folk dressed like beef thiefs in silky knee-highs and poofy pantaloonies. Now it's the Naskeag Home for Boys. It was a minimum-security facility, so the joint looks more like a mansion than a penitentiary, but you'll never catch me calling this jailhouse home. The state shut the prison down ten years ago and the Catholic Church converted the Naskeag House of Correction into the Naskeag House of Rejection.

Mother Mary Mammoth wrestles her bulk into the driver's seat and glares at me. She has a big, round face with rivers of veins and canyons of crevices. She has helter-skelter gray hair, a movie screen forehead, and Katharine Hepburn cheekbones. In fact, right now she reminds me of Queen Eleanor in *The Lion in Winter.* *"War agrees with you, Cricket. I keep informed; I follow all your slaughters from a distance."*

What can I say? I like old movies.

The only part about Mother Mary that doesn't look age appropriate is her eyes. They're glossy, bright, and young, like maybe she had an eye transplant. They grip you when she's mad, like monster fists. She never uses her bare hands to get your attention, which is good, 'cause she could choke an elk. Mother Mary Monument is six feet tall, and I'm guessing she's packing a good three hundred pounds under her grim frock. There's no ignoring her when she's in your vicinity. She's a presence. A planet. She has her own gravity. But in the end, it's her eyes that pull you in.

Mother Mary Mad-as-Hell slams the van door so hard, I expect the windows to shatter. She starts the van with several vigorous pedal pumps, then jackrabbits out of the parking lot. She doesn't speak until we're off school grounds. "I'm sick and tired of this, Cricket. It's the first week of school, for Pete's sake. The first week!" The wheels screech as she careens onto Main Street. "You're a senior now. I was hoping this year would be different. When is it going to end, Cricket? Please tell me: When is it going to end?"

"As soon as every asshole in that place sees himself for what he really is."

Mother Mary lunges her gorilla arm in front of my face and flings down the visor. There's a mirror on the other side. "Why don't you start working on that right now!"

Hey, good one, Mother Mary Mockery. I flip the visor up and chuckle.

"Not now, Cricket. Don't you dare push my buttons. I'm so mad, I could spit. And take off that blasted hood."

I slide my hood down. "Don't you want to hear my side of the story?"

"I've heard your side of the story. A thousand times. And it's always the same story." Mother Mary Mario is driving like an escaped convict. Pine trees zip past in a blur. She doesn't seem to notice the danger, or she doesn't care. She's taking turns so fast and furious, I'm nervous she's gonna flip the van and kill us both. I consider unbuckling my seat belt.

A few minutes later, she barrels up the gravel driveway to the Prison and jams on the brakes. The van skids to a dusty stop. I reach for the door handle.

"Don't you move your skinny ass from this van." She wriggles her prodigious mass out of the seat and slams her door. I see her kicking gravel and waving her arms around like a lunatic. She's yelling something fierce, but I can't make out the words. No matter. I know exactly what she's saying because it's always the same thing. Jeez Louise—Mother Mary Mushroom Cloud has finally detonated.

She waves me out of the van and I follow her to the barn. It's dark and shadowy inside. Holy cow—if I were a wiseguy, I'd think Mother Mary Mafia was gonna whack me. *I'm gonna make him an offer he can't refuse.*

She paces in front of the steel storage cages like a panther at the zoo. She massages her temples and sighs. "How long have you been here, Cricket?"

I consider making a joke, like *What do you mean? We just got here,* but decide against it since she's more pissed than usual. "I got here . . ."

"Shut your mouth, Cricket. I was being rhetorical.

I know when you got here, for crying out loud. I know darn well when you got here because I've been putting up with your nonsense every day since. Eight years, Cricket. Eight years." She paces some more.

I lean against a metal cage. I have a feeling I'm gonna be here awhile.

"It was one thing when you first arrived. You were just a little boy. A hurt, scared little boy. You fought then because it was all you knew. It's how you survived in Boston. But now, after so many years, so many lessons, so many . . ." She freezes like her brain's overheated. She rubs her huge, leathery hands together like a mad scientist. They remind me of boxing gloves. Maybe she's warming them up to use on me. "Well, guess what, Cricket? In case you haven't noticed, you're not nine years old anymore. You're eight months away from being a man."

Eight months. Tick-tock, tick-tock. My chest compresses like hourglass sand is piling up on it.

"And you don't live in the projects of Boston anymore. You live here. In Maine. In a small, civilized community among people who care about you. Have you learned nothing in eight years?"

I don't dare answer on account of that question might be rhetorical too.

Mother Mary's black-draped body is in the shadows, but her hands are glowing beneath a skinny beam of sunlight. She looks down at them and mumbles, "The voice is Jacob's voice, but the hands are the hands of Esau." She folds her arms and glares at me with an expression that's wavering between furious and confounded. "Perhaps this is partially my fault, Cricket. Perhaps I haven't kept you busy enough. 'Idle hands' and all that." She taps her forehead. "For starters, during your three-day suspension, you will write a five-hundred-word essay on some topic from the New Testament. You will deliver it to me no later than Thursday morning before you return to school." She sucks in several deep breaths and scratches her anvilithic chin. "You will also deliver a copy to Sister Elizabeth, the head of the CCD program, and one to Monsignor Dobry, the director of the Home. And you will write letters of apology to the three of us, as well as to Principal LaChance and the student you assaulted."

Yeah, right. Hallucinate much, Mother Mary Mushrooms?

"And you are grounded indefinitely. You will not step one foot off this property, except for school. Meanwhile, I will think of other ways to keep your troublesome hands occupied."

She walks along the storage cages, shaking each door to make sure it's locked. At the far end of the barn, she turns. Her long black habit melts into the background, and her fiery eyes ignite, making her head look like a floating jack-o'-lantern. "In any other community, Cricket, you would have been kicked out of school permanently a long time ago. But the residents of Naskeag have good hearts. They care about the boys here. They want to help them. They want to see them succeed. And this is how you repay their generosity. You ought to be ashamed of yourself. I know I am."

She turns and exits through the rear door.

A noise overhead startles me. I look up and see Caretaker climbing down the ladder from the loft with a coil of electrical wire looped over one arm. He's wearing denim overalls, and I can see his bulging biceps and jacked shoulders. He's in wicked good shape for an old dude.

Once his feet are on the floor, he wipes his brow with a hankie. A cobweb dangles from his frizzy gray hair. "Damn, it's hot up there."

"Serves you right for eavesdropping."

"I wasn't eavesdropping. I was getting some electrical supplies when Mother Mary stormed in here, so raving mad I didn't dare interrupt her."

"Sounds like you're scared of her."

Caretaker's eyes bulge wide like eggs. "Damn straight I'm scared of her. That ornery woman of God signs my paychecks." He stuffs the hankie into his pocket.

Caretaker takes care of the Prison. He does all the maintenance work that Mother Mary Miser can't pawn off on me. Plumbing, heating, carpentry, stuff like that. His real name is Mr. Cockburn, but that's just disrespectful.

"You need help with whatever you're doing?" I ask.

"That'd be great, if you got time."

"I'm in no hurry to go inside and face Mother Scary again."

"I don't blame you." He grabs his toolbox off the workbench and hands it to me. "Come on. I'm replacing the electrical service to the boathouse. You can climb onto the roof and pass me the new line."

"Gee, thanks."

"And when we're done, we'll have a training session. What do you say?"

"Sure. Anything to delay the inevitable."

He chuckles.

The boathouse is a cool place. Caretaker's been renovating it for as long as I can remember. It's got tons of tall, round-top windows and high vaulted ceilings like a chapel. The building's bigger than most of the houses in Naskeag. It's even got tracks in the floor so that boats can roll out the back door and right into the ocean. Caretaker told me that before the Prison was a prison, it was the private residence of some wicked rich lumber baron.

Caretaker set up a gym for me in the boathouse after he witnessed my first rough-and-tumble schoolyard brawl eight years ago. Unlike Mother Mary, he didn't have a problem with me fighting, but he did have a problem with me "fighting like a goddamn street urchin." I'm not sure which of my street-fighting tactics bothered him more — my bashing my opponent in the forehead with a brick or my biting my opponent on the ass when he tried to crawl away.

Caretaker's a purist. He boxed in the army. Everything I know about boxing I learned from him. He says he won a bunch of titles when he was younger, and I don't doubt him, 'cause he whips my ass every time we spar.

I remove my ring and rub the thick gold letters. BC. I stuff it in my pocket. Training's the only time I take it off.

"All right, let's go, Shirley."

Caretaker calls me girls' names when we train. I guess he figures it motivates me, but all it does is make me think of an interview I once saw on TV. A sportscaster asked George Foreman what he thought about all the trash-talking that goes on before a boxing match, and George said, "I don't care what you call me, just don't call me late for dinner." That cracked me up. I completely agree.

Caretaker waves his arms in the air like some mystical swami trying to hypnotize me. He's wearing training gloves that look like catcher's mitts. They're for taking hits, not doling them out, but that doesn't stop him from hitting me with them. And the edges are hard, so they hurt. Hell, Caretaker's shots would probably hurt even if he had stuffed animals strapped to his fists.

He starts jabbing half-speed shots at my head. It's fun to watch Caretaker shuffle and weave when we spar. He's smooth and graceful and powerful all at the same time. The way he wiggles and waggles makes me think he's got gummy-worm bones.

He pops me in the forehead with a jab. "Pay attention, Peggy Sue. Remember what we practiced all summer. Deflect my shots with shoulder rolls. Roll right when I throw right, left when I throw left. C'mon, Dorothy, roll. Buster Pitswaller is one big-ass son-of-a-bitch. You can't take his punches straight on. Make him miss, make him pay."

Buster "Pitbull" Pitswaller is a football jock who bullies my younger Prison roomies when we're all at school. I don't tolerate anyone picking on the Little Ones, so it's only a matter of time before we come to blows. His only redeeming quality is his angelic girlfriend, Wynona Bidaban. What she sees in him I'll never know. But she looked at me like I was a mass murderer when I dunked Burke the Jerk's head in the fish tank this morning, so she must be against his bullying.

Caretaker throws lefts and rights at my head. I twist left and right, trying to catch his punches on my shoulders instead of my chin.

"Pivot your whole body, not just your shoulders. Toes to nose. C'mon, shuffle your feet, Sheila."

I try to shuffle my feet, but I feel like a giraffe on roller skates compared to how Caretaker moves.

"Jesus, Cricket, you're so clumsy, you'd trip over a cordless phone."

I try not to laugh as his glove whizzes past my head.

"Bend from the knees, not the waist. You bend from the waist, what's gonna happen?" He pops me in the chin with an uppercut. "That's gonna happen. Slip back and right, then forward and left. Thatta girl. Up and down, not just side to side. You just go side to side, what's gonna happen?" He pops me in the forehead with a straight right. "That's gonna happen."

We spar for half an hour and Caretaker never shuts up. And he never stops throwing. Like I said, he's in wicked good shape for an old dude.

"All right, that's enough for today, Lucy." He smacks me on the side of the head. "Jesus, I'm sweating worse than a whore in church."

I take my gloves off and rinse my mouthpiece in the sink.

Caretaker unbuckles his overall straps and towels off his upper body. His stomach sticks out but not in a fat way. It looks like he's hiding a dozen cookie sheets under his chocolate skin.

He throws his stinky towel at me. "I'm going home.

See what the ol' lady whipped up for supper. I'm so hungry, I could eat the ass out of a rag doll." He pats his tin pan belly and laughs. Caretaker always laughs at his own jokes, even when they're not funny. He pulls his overall straps on and leaves.

I hang out in the boathouse to kill time until dark. I'm in no rush to see Mother Mary Malice.

I jump rope and imagine Wynona Bidaban sitting cross-legged on Caretaker's workbench, twisting her black hair around her finger like she does in math class. She's ogling me with a quizzical expression like I'm an unsolvable trigonometry equation. I drop the rope, pull her in to my sweaty body, and answer her question with a kiss.

CHAPTER 2

I wait until ten p.m. before sneaking down the fire escape. The nuns are always zonked by then. I pull my hood on and walk downtown to my friend Grubs's apartment. Grubs and I met at school three years ago when I was a freshman and he was a junior. He dropped out his senior year to work full-time as a mechanic. Well, that's what he told people. He actually dropped out to commit more time to his real career — dealing drugs. Grubs recruited me to help him collect money from his younger customers after he watched me pound the piss out of a football jock who had harassed one of the Little Ones. We've been hanging out ever since.

He lives in a one-room attic over the garage where he works. His front door is at the top of a rickety staircase attached to the side of the building. When I walk in (*sans* knock and *sans* lock), he's watching *The Three Stooges* on his tiny tabletop TV. He doesn't say anything, just nods.

The place smells like a potpourri of oil, exhaust, and dirty socks. I grab a lukewarm Budweiser from the mini-fridge and flop onto his grandma-print sofa.

He yanks his shirt sleeve up. "Check out my latest ink." On his upper bicep is a tattoo of an orange and black tiger. The tiger's head is surrounded by red and purple flames that spell the name *Toni*.

"That's awesome. She must be happy," I say.

"She ain't seen it yet. I was gonna show her tonight, but she's being a bitch, so I blew her off."

"What's her problem?"

"She's raggin' my ass about having dinner with her parents. She's pissed 'cause I ain't never met 'em and we've been dating for like a year."

"That bitch," I say, grinning.

"I know, right? And if it ain't that, she's naggin' me about buying her a fucking engagement ring. Like we're supposed to get married or something. You believe that shit?"

"So why'd you get a tat with her name on it?"

"I thought it'd shut her up about the ring."

We both laugh.

"I can't believe she wants you to meet her parents."

"Seriously. I'm the kind of guy you sneak out of the house to hook up with after your parents are asleep, for Christ's sake."

"I ain't even met Toni. You guys should buy me dinner before her parents."

"I hear ya, bro."

I grab a half-smoked doob from his ashtray and fire it up. I take a long hit and pass it to him.

"You should get a tat," Grubs says.

"Yeah, the nuns would love that."

"You could get a religious one, like boxers do. A giant cross on your back or a portrait of Jesus on your chest."

"Or an altar boy on my ass."

Grubs laughs. He takes a hit and points his beer bottle at my face. "You should have my man Angel ink up your scar. He could do each slice a different color — one red and one black, like two serpents battling it out for facial domination."

"You're fucked in the head, dude."

Grubs shrugs and chugs his beer.

I wonder what Wynona would think if I got a tattoo of her name. Would she be flattered or offended? Not like I'll ever know.

Grubs snags a paper bag from beside the couch and drops it onto my lap. Inside are a bunch of videotapes, some weed, and a bottle of vodka. It's my "paycheck" for helping him with collections.

Grubs could rough up his customers himself if he wanted to, 'cause he's a badass. But some of his clients are underage, and even though he has no beef about selling 'em stems and powder, he has this thing about roughing up a kid. Personally, I think he hauls me around more for show than dough. Makes him feel big-time in this small-time shithole.

"Thanks, man." I check out the most recent acquisitions from Naskeag Video courtesy of Grubs's five-finger discount. *Monty Python. Rebel Without a Cause. The Hustler. Easy Rider. The Public Enemy. Citizen Kane.* I watch movies on a contraband twelve-inch TV and 1980s yard-sale VCR I've got stashed in my closet at the Prison.

"Them crappy old ones are a cinch to pinch." Grubs drags his sleeve across his mouth. "There ain't nobody ever lurking around that dusty corner."

"Good for me."

"What the frig is Monty Python?"

"You ain't never seen it?"

"Nah," Grubs says, pushing himself off the couch. "Pop it in and I'll roll us a fresh one."

I eject the Stooges and slip in *Monty Python.*

Grubs hits Play on his stereo and "Smokin' in the Boys Room" by Brownsville Station starts up. He air-strums when the guitar riff twangs in. Grubs dresses like a seventies heavy metal rocker. He looks a little like Steven Tyler from Aerosmith, but maybe I just think that on account of his long stringy hair.

I plunk my boots on the shipping crate coffee table and look around while the video rewinds. The faint glow from a lamppost outside illuminates the shadowy space.

There are magazine photos of hot rods and hot babes taped to the plywood walls, and the particleboard ceiling has a giant stain in the center. The sofa smells mildewy, like the inside of a tent. The room reminds me of a place I have no interest in remembering.

I lean forward to click Play on the VCR and catch a glimpse of my face in Grubs's coke mirror. My scar looks flat and black. It changes color under different light, like it's alive. Like a chameleon. In direct sunlight, it's puffy and pink. Under the school fluorescents, it's deep and red. It's shaped like a tall, skinny X and runs down the right side of my face from my eyebrow to my chin. The crevices are deep and round, as if someone scooped out slivers of skin with a tiny spoon. Maybe Grubs is right and I should get it inked. At least that would disguise it.

Grubs plunks down on the sofa and fires up the joint he just rolled. It crackles and snaps and wafts wispy swirls of sweet escape in my direction.

He passes it to me and I take a long suck on the freedom stick.

"So what's this Mountain Python thing anyway?" he asks. "A fucking documentary or something?"

"*Monty* Python. It's a comedy group from the seventies. Right up your alley, era-wise." The skit starts and I parrot the lines word for word in my best British accent.

"Don't come here with that posh talk, you nasty, stuck-up twit."

"'Oh, thank you,' says the great queen like a la-di-dah poofta."

Grubs is laughing like crazy. Not at Monty Python—at me. "That's friggin' awesome, dude. Where'd you learn to talk that shit?"

"From dee telly, mate."

Grubs slaps his knee and chugs his beer.

"Me crack-whore mumsy plunked me young arse in front of dee telly fer hours and hours whiles she strutted 'er ax-wound up and down Keelumbus Avenue, looking to cream dudes' knickers for a block of rock."

Grubs stumbles to the refrigerator for another beer.

"Yuse sure gots dee wanky, wanky giggle fits, ya divvy dog," I say as he falls onto the sofa, laughing.

We watch some more skits, and Grubs cracks up at my Cockney gibberish.

After *Python,* I throw in *Rebel Without a Cause,* but Grubs falls asleep before James Dean is even arrested. I grab my bag and head for the door. As it squeaks open, Grubs wakes up.

"Don't forget, we've got collecting tomorrow night," he growls.

I nod and pull the door closed behind me.

• • •

I get home from Grubs's around one a.m. and sneak up the fire escape to my room. I'm the only kid at the Prison with his own room. Of course, I'm the only seventeen-year-old at the Prison too.

Two years ago, Mother Mary liberated the attic for me as my own personal nomad pad. It used to be packed to the rafters with a million cardboard boxes stuffed with tragic tales of the ugly and unwanted. But the newly appointed fire marshal — who looked about nineteen — was doing annual inspections and told her she had to clear out all the boxes on account of they were a fire hazard.

The timing was perfect, because Mother Mary Makeamends was in the middle of pumping her skull muscle for a primo punishment for my pummeling of a brown-toothed redneck who had pushed Bernie, a chubby Little One, down a flight of stairs. The tumble bruised Bernie's face up and busted his glasses. Seeing his busted eyeglasses bothered me more than seeing busted Bernie, though. Ain't that an itchy pair of husky irregulars? There was just something about Bernie's hand-me-down spectacles getting twisted and smashed that made me lose it. I popped the greasy douchebag in the head a few times and hurled his unshowered ass down the same staircase. Asked him if he still thought it was funny to push a helpless kid down a flight of stairs. He didn't answer.

Mother Mary made me empty the attic as penance.

After my millionth trip to the basement with my millionth box, I was staring at the old wood beams and tree-trunk columns and saying to Mother Mary how cool it must have been to be a builder back before there was electricity on account of how rewarding it must feel to look at something you built with nothing but muscle and mind. I guess something about me being enamored by the workmanship pinpricked in her the notion of letting me hang my hat up here. She was scratching her chin, going *Hmm-hmm-hmmmm,* and after about the hundredth *Hmmmm* she said I could move in once she got it renovated all modern and white and plasticized and *blaaaahhhh,* and I said *aaaahhhh* what a shame it would be to cover up all this nifty knobby craftsmanship, and so she let me move in as soon as I slaughtered all the dust bunnies that had taken up residence.

Man, I had a severe case of the Christmas jollies for I don't know how long after plunking my mattress down on this creaky floor. The coolest thing was that I was finally alone. After fifteen years of being held hostage in tiny rooms with screaming adults and screaming orphans, I finally had my own room.

I grab a pen and notebook and climb back out onto the fire escape. The view of the ocean is splendiferous. I spend more time out here than in the room. Sometimes I lie out here for hours, gazing at the stars and the moon and listening to the waves roll at me from God knows where, and sometimes being on this steel magic carpet makes it seem like things could be okay. But something always crashes the carpet—like a rainstorm or the sun rising or Mother Mary yelling, "Cricket, plunger!"—and I remember it's nothing more than a precarious fire escape attached to a precarious Prison attached to a precarious life.

I figure I might as well get started on my five-hundred-word essay for Mother Mary. Since it's also going to Sister Elizabeth and Monsignor Dobry, I intend to make it extra juicy. I tap my pen on my chin. I need an ultra-sacred topic to debase. *Ahh, I've got it.* The Virgin Mary. Nothing more sacred than that pristine hoo-ha. I fire up a joint, take a nice long toke, and start scribbling and sniggering.

The Inaccurate Deception
By Cricket Cherpin

There's more to the Virgin Mary story than meets the ~~vagina~~ eye. I mean, if there is a God, and He created LIFE, and He created PEOPLE, then He created SEX. Check it out — God was the first porn addict. He was peekabooing Adam and Eve snake charming each other's slippery figs. He gazed upon the sticky canoodle and said, It is GOOD!

So, if God created Paradise Spice, why'd the Bible scribblers flip it into Paradise Vice? How the hell else are these one—God wonders supposed to continue begetting rugrats onto God's List of Favorites? I mean, why'd the Bible writers say knocking sandals was bad when God said it was good? Why wouldn't God want His precious offspring squeezing through a contaminated wombikins when He was the One Who invented the modus contaminations in the first place? It doesn't make sense.

Personally, I think it all happened way different from what the Bible says. You can read all about it in Cricket's First Letter to the Cynicalians.

Here's a preview.

It ain't no secret that Roman soldiers shacked up with Jew broads all the time way back when. Heck, the Jews were hunkering on leased land with a temporary travel visa anyhow. The Romans let them slaughter up a kosher kebab now and then, but it wasn't like they were free or anything. And they sure as hell weren't the most popular chosen ones on the block.

Now, I don't know if these throwdowns were date rape or if the unsatisfied cream churners were taking donkey rides to the cheating side of town, but it doesn't really matter. It is what it is. All I'm saying is, it's pretty likely more than a few Jewish ladies filled their days polishing Roman swords, if you catch my meaning. But heck, can you blame them? Power's a horny-toading aphrodisiac. Always was and always will be.

Besides, compared to their yes-sirring, commandment-following, beanie-wearing boyfriends, those long-scabbarded warmongers had to be some smoking hot love-kebabs.

It's not that far-fetched when you think about it. Same crap goes on nowadays. The rich rulers screwing the poor servants. I mean, these soldier dudes could make your life a living hell or they could make things comfy-cozy. Why wouldn't a Jew chick chutzpah a soldier's knish?

The soldier would be like, Okay, Esther, here's the deal. I can whip you silly for half an hour or you can invite me in for a tasty bit of love-falafel.

Ummmm, the whip, please, sir.

Gimme a break.

So here's my angelic theory. Mary had a hot and heavy roll in the manger hay with the rough-and-tumble Roman warrior Stiffus Maximus while she was engaged to doughy Joey. No big thing, right? Joey was probably banging the daughter of some Saddjuicy he was building a DVD cabinet for anyway. But Mary was irresponsible. She didn't insist on Soldier Boy slipping on the ol' llama skin before they whoopsadaisied, and: Shazam! An unleavened bun in the oven.

So Mary finds herself in quite the kosher pickle. She can tell the truth and be outcast forever and maybe even stoned to death, or she can transmogrify her titillacious transgression into a God-injected miracle, and all it's gonna take is a little white lie.

Oh my goodness, Joey, this floaty, dreamboaty angelicious cherub slipped a magical roofie into my goat's milk and diddled me a ripe prophecy square in the burning bush.

And what could Joey say? He hadn't caught her in the act with her hand in the nookie jar. That would have been a little more difficult to explain.

That wasn't a Roman soldier, my love. I was milking our bull.

And Joey wasn't the only one who gobbled up that tasty Whopper with secret sauce. The whole damn world fell for it.

Imagine a dude trying that nowadays with his old lady.

No, sweetums, this ain't stripper glitter. It's angel dust.

Yeah, right.

CHAPTER 3

The following morning, I'm in the front seat of the Prison van again with Mother Mary. Groundings don't apply when there's God's work to do. My ears are still ringing from the thirty-minute tongue lashing she gave me on blasphemy and religious tolerance. I guess typing up and emailing her my Virgin Mary dissertation from the Prison computer in the middle of the night while still under the herbalicious influence of my spiritual mentor, Buddha Bambalacha, wasn't the smartest idea I've ever had. Wait till she finds out I also emailed copies to Sister Elizabeth and Monsignor Dobry. Mount St. Mary is gonna erupt big-time.

Mother Mary is driving rationally today due to delicate cargo. Eight Little Ones and one Big One (a fellow nun). The Little Ones are squawking like crows on a dumpster, and I can tell their giggling and jiggling is grinding on Mother Mary's last nerve. Her face is red like a stick of dynamite.

I flip around and jam my head between the seats. "Don't mess with Mother Mary, fellas! This ain't her first time at the rodeo."

They gawk at me and clam up pronto.

Mother Mary relaxes her death grip on the steering wheel and flashes me a sideways smirk. "You do a very good Faye Dunaway, Cricket."

"Thank you, Mother Mommie Dearest."

Mother Mary chuckles.

I'm embarrassed to admit where we're going, but I might as well on account of we'll be there in a few minutes. Prison kids get their clothes at the Salvation Army.

It ain't as bad as it sounds. The only time it really frosts my jewels is when the donation dumpster is overloaded, 'cause it reminds me that I'm stepping out in other people's garbage. This probably sounds whiny, but it kinda makes ya feel like a piece of trash when you see a pant leg from your future wardrobe dangling out of a Hefty Cinch Sak on the side of the road.

The worst part is that the store is conveniently located dead-ass in the middle of Main Street. I mean, why not string up a few Hollywood spotlights and blast some big band music from the rooftop while you're at it. And do you think Mother Mary Makeafoolofus would ever consider driving around back and using the rear entrance? Hell, no. Climbing out of that overloaded van with its giant Orphans-R-Us insignia on the side is a prime Saturday-morning fundraising photo op. Mother Mary Moolah intentionally sashays our Raggedy Andy asses up and down the concrete catwalk to drum up donations and bake sale volunteers. People gawk at us like we're wearing orange jumpsuits and might break free from our chains and pillage the village. Man, it sucks.

The enormous red and white sign comes into view. As do the bright orange cones reserving our parking spot. Jesus, you'd think we were escorting Madonna to a Rodeo Drive boutique. The Little Ones start bouncing and squealing and elbowing each other in the ribs. They don't realize this ain't Nordstrom for Orphans.

Mother Mary is greeted by a cheery woman in a bright red pantsuit. She looks like a mutant beefsteak tomato that just won first prize in the freaky fruit competition at the Fryeburg Fair.

I hop out and slide the side door open. Then I slip my hood off. As much as I'd like to hide my head in a trash can right about now, this sidewalk is the one place I never wear my hood. I know that probably sounds ass-backwards, but I ain't gonna give the glaring townie bastards the satisfaction. Fuck 'em. You wanna eyeball me, you're gonna have to do it straight into my eyeballs, asshole. Plus, this shitty feeling vise-grips my nuts when I think about hiding my face while I'm walking the Little Ones into the thrift store. There's something about the Little Ones being all antsy and chipper and not the least bit embarrassed about scoring new duds at the Salvation Army that wrenches my throat a guilt-choking mischief. I'm not sure why. Mother Mary Militant strutting her giant ass up that sidewalk with her chin so high, just begging someone to mess with her, might have something to do with it, though.

As soon as we pass through the double doors, the Little Ones scatter like it's a video arcade. Mother Mary and Sister Sarah pull out their shopping lists and start systematically scouring the aisles for utilitarian bargains. Practicality always triumphs over fashion, even when cool only costs fifty cents more than nerdy. I mean, I get where they're coming from. Maine winters are bitter and long, and skinny jeans and canvas high-tops don't cut it in a ten-foot snowbank. Not that it stops the outside kids from wearing them.

The Little Ones scurry back and forth from rack to nun, presenting their dudsy discoveries. They aren't allowed into the fitting room until their selections are inspected and approved by the Nuns of No Mercy. One good thing about fashion these days is that new clothes are supposed to look shitty and stitched-up, so you could do worse than getting your crap at Ragnation HarmMe.

Gregory Bullivant runs up to Sister Sarah wearing

a green windbreaker that's so thin, it wouldn't break the wind from a frog fart. She shakes her head. Charlie waves a pair of bloodstained army fatigues in the air. No dice. Andrew holds up a Black Sabbath T-shirt. That one warrants a finger jab.

If the Little Ones fail to locate acceptable apparel, Mother Mary will do the honors, and that is something to be avoided at all costs — unless you want to show up at school wearing wool hiker pants, grandpa suspenders, rubber trucker boots, and an orange XXL sweater that looks like it was knit by a blind Parkinson's granny at the senior center. Orange is great for alerting vehicular traffic in a snowstorm, but it's also highly effective at alerting ragtime traffic in a schoolyard shitstorm. *Nice highwaters, Salivating Arnie. Sexy flannel, Lumber Jack. Nice pants, SpongeSlob. Groovy red sweater, Santa Menopause.* Although I gotta admit, some of it's funny. I never get into fights over clothing. That's just regular schoolyard ribbing.

I stroll over to the Undies Emporium, where Charlie, Aaron, and Sam are rummaging through a mountain of tightie-whities beneath a huge blue sign that reads CHILDREN'S UNDERWHERE. The store's crack sales team has the entire underwear department color-coded. I'd love to meet the marketing guru who chose chocolate brown for XXL boxers.

I slip a pair of Batman briefs onto my head. "Hey, guys. Do these Underoos make my ass look fat?"

The Little Ones blow a laugh gasket.

Gregory sprints over holding up a sweatshirt with an enormous New England Patriots logo on the back. "Check this out."

"Mother Mary will never let you get that, stupid," Sam says. "The sleeves are chopped off."

"I know. Just like how Coach Belichick wears his," Gregory says.

"There's no way," Charlie says.

"Hey, Greg, maybe Sister Cricket can sew some sleeves on for you," Sam says.

They all crack up.

"Very funny, Sammy." I yank the underwear off my head and throw them at him.

One of my chores at the Prison is sewing up tears and snares in the Little Ones' hand-me-downs. The nuns taught me how, and it ain't as fruity as it sounds. It's cool, actually. Relaxing. Taking something that would have been tossed in the trash and zipzapping it right as rain. Most of the time I fix it so you can't even see where the tear was. The trick is to work the needle from the inside so the scar's on the flipside of what everyone sees. Like in life.

I wander around, killing time until my fitting room

duty starts. That's why I'm here — to monitor the changing rooms. Nuns ain't keen on I-Spying XS dingles swaying in the breeze like picnic frankfurters, so I'm a permanent participant in the Saturday shopping extravaganzas. There's forty-seven Little Ones at the Prison, and the van only carries eight at a time, so we come here a lot.

I wonder what Wynona would think if she knew I got my clothes at the Salvation Army. I wonder if stuff like that matters to her.

Charlie Brittlebones runs up to me with an armful of attire. Brittlebones ain't his real name, but that's what it feels like when he bumps into you.

"Sister Sarah okayed me to try on all these, but I can't go in unless you're with me."

I slap Charlie on the back. "Let's do it, dude."

Charlie reminds me of me when I was little. Well, one tiny sliver of me. The sliver who pretended to be happy to keep the peace. He's got the same nervous smile. Like his teeth are made of glass and his lips are laminate.

"Look what she's letting me try on." He yanks out a pair of green painter pants. "They look like army pants."

"Cool."

"And check out this sweater. It ain't got no rabbits or ducks or snowflakes or nothing on it. It's like the ones you wear, Cricket."

"I like it. I should see if they got one in my size."

Charlie smiles wide and glassy.

I grab his shoulders and steer him toward the changing rooms so he doesn't see my eyes getting damp. I must be allergic to wool or something.

CHAPTER 4

I only got a three-day suspension for my Football Bully Fish Tank Fiasco, so I'm in English class bright and early Thursday morning. Moxie Lord — mole-nosed, broom-humping Good Witch wannabe — is dishing out a humdinger of a writing assignment. The *ASS*ignment is to draft a letter to someone we have a beef with but ain't never had the nads to tell.

"The letters are not going to be delivered, so you can write whatever you want." Moxie whisper-growls the word *whatever* like she's some highfalutin' street corner candy bar. Oh Henry! Sounds like she wants to Butterfinger my Thingamajig. I wouldn't have believed it myself if her titillating tone hadn't tickled me a mischievous fancy in the you-know-what.

"Your letter can be to anyone," Moxie says. "A parent, friend, relative. Even the president of the United States."

I raise my hand from the back row.

Moxie flips me her usual *Drop your hood if you expect to be called on* finger twirl.

I flick my hood off. "What about teachers?"

Mademoiselle Moxie peers over her granny glasses and squirts me a slippery hiss. "Even teachers." Actually, it's more like *Eeehhven teeecherrrrsssss, Hangzlow Studmuffin*. It's possible I imagined the *Hangzlow Studmuffin* part, but not the slurpy mattress-tumbling tone. Lambikins Lord wants me *baaaad*. She strolls to the front of the class and starts writing on the blackboard. "These are just ideas to help you get started. *Dear Aunt Beatrice: About you chaperoning the school dance . . . Dear Uncle Garlic: About your breath . . .*" Some of the girls giggle.

Foxy Moxie is sexy in a hippie fruitcake way. I've imagined myself getting high with her on more than one occasion, and I've imagined other things, too. She has kinda big boobs, but it's hard to tell for sure because they're *beaucoup* saggy. She wears droopy tops and lacy bras, and she leans over a lot when she makes corrections. She's got a Milky Way of freckles on her happytime tatas, and, I tell ya, freckles on boobs are freaky — like maybe she should go to the doctor and get a bazongagram.

Sometimes in the winter when the heaters aren't working good, Moxie's funbag bulbs poke through her flowery tops right in the bud of a daisy or the eye of a black-eyed Susan. That cracks me up. Like she's springtime blooming just for me. I haven't had sex yet, but somehow I know Foxy Moxie screams a lot during sex, and she definitely prefers the top. Well, at least with me she does.

Moxie taps the blackboard with the tip of her chalk. *"Dear Dad: About me getting my own car . . . Dear Coach Martin: About me starting in the game on Saturday . . . Dear Little Brother: About you reading my diary . . ."*

I start thinking about who to address my letter to. It's obvious this stupid assignment is nothing more than a trap to lure kids into skinny-dipping personal feelings they wouldn't otherwise flash, so I'm pounding my mind muscle for something that will knock her lamebrained, acid-induced subterfuge off her medulla hippopotamus. I start scribbling possibilities.

Heil Hitler,

You rock! I wish you hadn't checked out early so we could hang out and rap about old times. Stay up way past our bedtime eating buttered schnitzel-corn, drinking Manischewitz, and watching old movies like Ben-Hur and Fiddler on the Roof. I miss you.

Azzfartz,
Cricket

No, too political.
And revealing.

Dear Principal LaChance,

If you went missing, would they put your picture on fruitcake cartons?

Curiously,
Cricket

No, too sexual.
And revealing.

Dear Attorney General Lynchmynuts,

My baby brother was killed when I was eight. And it's all my fault.

Sorry,
Cricket

No, too personal.
And revealing.
Aha. I've got it. If this don't scrunch her tie-dyed Depends into a knot, nothing will.

Dear Life,

You SUCK!
I want out.
See you on the flipside.

Sincerely,
Cricket

On my way out of class, I stealthily slide my letter onto Moxie's desk like it's a ticking time bomb, which in a way it is. Should make for some interesting fireworks tomorrow.

CHAPTER 5

That evening, I head to the Prison kitchen for cooking duty. A bunch of Little Ones are already there, chopping, peeling, mixing, and measuring. A few are pummeling lumps of dough like miniature punching bags. The place always makes me think of Santa's workshop, except Mother Mary Merriment wears black.

I do a lot of cooking at the Prison. That probably sounds faggy, but it's actually okay. We make everything from scratch and I've cooked with the nuns almost every day since I was nine, so I know how to make tons of different dishes. Caretaker teases me, saying I'll make a good wife someday.

Tonight we're making lasagna, mashed potatoes, sourdough bread, and spaghetti sauce. The spaghetti sauce is dual purpose since it also goes in the lasagna. We're *killing two birds with one stone,* as Sister Sarah likes to say. We kill a lot of birds with very few stones here at the Naskeag Home for the Criminally Stingy.

We do what I call *hibernation cooking*. That's when you prepare huge quantities of food and freeze it for later. Probably like they do in the army or in real prisons, except the food we make here tastes good. I read a book about World War II where they referred to their eats as "shit on a shingle." I don't think I'd survive very long in the army if that's what I had to eat every day. I like to eat. It's one of my favorite things to do.

Feeding forty-seven Little Mouths (plus my Big Mouth) three squares a day is a lot of work, so no one's excused from kitchen duty. Age doesn't matter. I'm seventeen and the youngest kid is five, but everyone pitches in. The nuns have a simple rule when it comes to kitchen duty: *You eat, you cook.*

Sister Gwendolyn spots me when I enter the kitchen and claps her hands to get my attention. "Cricket, we need you on cooktop right away. The lasagna noodles are ready, so I need you to brown the beef while the boys chop the rest of the ingredients for the sauce. I'm going to the basement for more tomato paste."

I salute Sister G and head to the sink to wash my hands. Behind me, Sam and Archie are peeling potatoes and arguing.

"I do not."

"You do so."

"No I don't."

"Do so, you stupid liar."

"You're the stupid liar."

I dry my hands and turn around. "What's the problem, boys?"

"Sam told this girl I like that I talk in my sleep," Archie barks.

"Well, you do!" Sam yells.

"I do not, ass-breath!" Archie yells back.

I laugh. *"Ass-breath?"*

All the boys laugh, except Sam. Archie's laughing the hardest.

"Yeah, ass-breath," Archie says loudly. "'Cause his breath smells like fat, stinky nun ass."

The Little Ones howl.

Sam grabs an enormous half-peeled spud and slams Archie in the forehead, sending him flying backwards off his stool.

Archie jumps up and grabs the closest cooking utensil, a huge wooden spoon, then smacks Sam on the back of the head.

Sam screams and charges Archie.

They wrestle to the ground like a pair of wild hyenas.

I grip their shirts and pull them apart. They keep swinging, so I use my pissed-off voice to get their attention. "Knock it off!"

They both stop wriggling immediately. I shove them

onto stools on opposite sides of the table. "Now get back to your potato peeling while I get the meat going."

The melee's over by the time Sister Sarah runs into the room. "What the devil is going on in here?" she yelps like a Chihuahua.

"No problem, Sister Sarah," I say, dumping a bucket of ground meat into a sauté pan the size of a saucer sled. "A runaway spud caught Archie in the forehead."

The Little Ones bury their giggling faces in their shirts.

"Well, try to be more careful, Archie," she says.

"Yeah, Archie, potatoes don't grow on trees, you know." I turn to Sister Sarah. "Musta been an Irish potato, Sister. Mean-spirited little spuds. And even meaner after they've tossed back a pint."

Sister Sarah stares at me like I just spoke Swahili, shakes her head, and leaves the kitchen.

Once the meat's sizzling hot and greasy, I grab a stool between Sam and Archie. "Listen up, ladies. I'm gonna edumacate you on the intricacies of the finer sex."

"Huh?" Sam says, rubbing the back of his head.

"Tits and ass, Einstein," I say.

The Little Ones laugh.

"Girls are tough to meet, right? Like, it's tough to just walk up to a girl and start talking to her."

"It's 'cause they're never alone," Justin says. "There's

always like fifty million of them clumped together in a circle."

"That's true. And you know what all fifty million of them are talking about?" The boys all shake their heads. "You! They're talking about boys. That's all girls ever talk about. Now think about it. If you trash-talk one of your pals, how many other girls are gonna hear what you said?"

"Fifty million," Archie grumbles, glaring at Sam.

"Exactly. Fifty million girls are gonna hear that shit in five minutes flat, 'cause girl gossip travels at the speed of light."

"So what are we supposed to do?" Justin asks from behind his flour-dusted spectacles.

"You gotta tag-team girls like in professional wrestling. You talk to a girl for your buddy, and then he'll do the same for you. Get them alone in class or study hall and tell them something cool or smart or brave your buddy did. You know, talk your pal up, make him look good. 'Cause even if that particular chick don't go for you, news of that cool thing you did will travel at the speed of gossip, and fifty million girls will know about it by the end of the day."

"Is that what you do, Cricket?" Bernie asks. "To get girls. Have your friends talk to them for you?"

Andrew speaks without looking up from the garlic clove he's peeling. "Cricket don't got no friends."

The table goes dead silent. Andrew looks up and his face goes white. "I mean . . ."

"Don't worry about it, Andrew. For me, not having friends is a choice. Besides, I got friends. But we ain't talking about me—we're talking about you, you little shitstains."

The Little Ones choke out half-laughs.

"Now, as I was saying . . ."

"Cricket!" Andrew yells, pointing at the cooktop.

Smoke's billowing out of my beef pan. I run over, turn the heat down, and stir like crazy. When it's done, I dump it into a large mixing bowl. "No worries, just a little well done." I slide the bowl onto the worktable. "Now, where was I?"

"You were teaching us how to tag-team girls," Sam blurts just as Sister Gwendolyn returns from the basement.

Sister G blushes and scurries into a walk-in freezer. I pick up a spud and start peeling. "The other thing you can do is talk to a girl about something she and your buddy have in common. Like if a girl's really into kickball, tell her how your buddy kicked a grand slam in the last game you played."

"What if you stink at kickball?" Aaron asks.

"I'm just using kickball as an example, Wienerschnitzel. It don't matter what you talk about, so long as it's something she's into. It could be friggin' astrophysics."

"What if you like a girl that you don't have anything in common with?" Gregory asks.

I toss the peeled spud onto the pile. "In that case, you resort to the more traditional method of scoring chicks. You lie your ass off."

The Little Ones crack up.

"But the main reason you never trash-talk your pals is 'cause any chick with half a brain knows real friends don't trash-talk their friends behind their backs. So never do it. All it does is make you look like a first-class dickhead."

Just as I say "dickhead," the boys' eyes rise to something behind me, and their faces go white as flour. *Shit.* I turn and Mother Mary's standing right behind me with her enormous arms crossed over her enormous chest.

"I'm sorry, Cricket," she says calmly. "I didn't mean to interrupt. Please continue. You were saying?"

The Little Ones drop their heads and return to their work.

Sister G walks over, clapping her hands. "Come on, boys, let's get the lasagna finished so we can get everything in the freezer. While you're layering the ingredients, I'll tell you a nice Bible story."

The Little Ones groan, and Sister G pounds the table with a wooden mallet to shut them up.

I wrap a dishtowel around my neck and mime a lynching behind Sister G's back.

While we layer and ladle, she tells the Parable of the Lost Son. It's this long-ass tale about a father who gives his two sons their inheritance, and one of them stays home and works for his dad while the other one heads for the hills and blows all his cash on booze and hookers. The party kid finally returns home, and his father throws a big bash for him because he thinks his son has had some grand spiritual awakening, when really the kid just came home 'cause he ran out of dough. Jesus should have named the story the Parable of the Gullible Father.

I nudge Gregory Bullivant, flash him a wink, and raise my hand. "Sister Gwendolyn, may I ask a question about the story?"

"Certainly, Cricket—what is it?"

I speak in my best phony-baloney little kid voice. "What's a harlot?"

The Little Ones look from me to Sister Gwendolyn. A few of the older ones bite their lips and look at the floor.

She glares at me through crinkled eyes. "A harlot is a woman who has strayed from God, Cricket. Now let's get the lasagna finished and the potatoes in the pots."

"Strayed how?" I ask innocently. "What do harlots do?"

Sister G's face tightens. "There are many ways people stray from God, Cricket."

I keep going. I want to see how much hot air I can pump into Sister G's already overinflated patience balloon. "Would a man kill his best calf and throw a big party if his long-lost harlot came home?"

Sister G clears her throat and wipes her forehead with the back of her hand. "I'll be happy to talk to you privately after dinner, Cricket. Now let's get the lids on the sauce tins so we can get things cleaned up."

I raise my hand again. "Sister Gwendolyn?"

Sister Gwendolyn's face is as red as the lasagna sauce, and her lips are tight and white. "No more questions, Cricket. It's time to clean up."

"But I'm confused. When I was living in Boston, daddies didn't welcome their harlots home with open arms and throw big parties for them after they ran away with their money. They mostly just beat them silly and put them back to work on the streets. Are city harlots different from Bible harlots, Sister Gwendolyn?"

Sister Gwendolyn grabs me by the bicep and leads me out of the kitchen.

After the Ragamuffin Resort goes silent for the night, I pull on the most ridiculous recycled rags I own, fill my thermos with lodka and venomade, roll a pregnant Tijuana bush baby, and sneak down the fire escape to spend some quality time in the great outdoors with my good pal Ignatius Podiddle. Mr. P is my iPod, a birthday gift from Grubs, courtesy of his five-finger discount. He showed me how to download free tunage on the Prison computer. I hope the FBI doesn't show up and arrest Mother Mary Misappropriation.

I race across the moonlit lawn toward the giant wooden staircase that scales the treacherous cliff to my Silky Jets. No, my Silky Jets isn't some Civil War–era Studio 1854 discotheque. My Silky Jets is just a jetty. A giant heap of granite boulders that at night feels like a mile-long balance beam suspended between here and hereafter.

No one ever comes to my jetty. It's on private property owned by the servants of God, and you have to walk down a ten-thousand-step staircase to get to it. Even the Little Ones avoid my peacetime peninsula. They're afraid to walk it during the day, let alone in the almighty black.

The jetty's awesome at night. It makes you feel like you're on the tip of a forever-long catwalk with the moon moonbeaming your thoughts to every living soul in the universe. Of course, the crackling cannabis and gloss sauce might have something to do with my star-studded perspective. Okay, that's a lie. Not a lie. More like an *imagination fabrication*. The only reason I can perform my crazy, freestyle, bootilicious rumpus ruckus is 'cause I know there ain't a soul on the planet peering at my primordial tangotations. Maybe that's why I like it here so much. The blackness. I ain't never been anywhere with so much black. Except maybe Boston. The only other way to bury yourself in this much darkness stretching into this much forever is to close your eyes, but that emptiness doesn't come with hurricane gusts, salt spray, and surf sighs. I love my jetty. I'd live out here if I could.

I always chill at the last rock on the left 'cause it's got the biggest dance floor and the best view. I jam my earbuds in and start with Eminem. Then some Linkin Park and Everclear. You may have surmised by my carefree lifestyle and happy-go-lucky attitude that I am a student of the dance and the earthly rhythms that birthed her. No? *Beaucoup de strange.*

If this was all there was, things might be okay. This and my fire escape. Fluid and fog to raise me up, Matisyahu. Ultimate darkness to make me invisible. Kick-ass tunage to drown out ancient sounds.

Before long, I'm down to my boxers and boots, spinning and spinning and spinning, and I swear, one of these nights the spinning's gonna rocketship my ass into outer space by the centrifugal force of my own insanity.

I'll tell you one thing, though. If there is a God, He dances. He dances His omniscient ass off! I guaranfuckintee it. That Son-of-a-Biscuit can cut a serious rug.

After a while, I crash on a boulder and dangle my

goosebumpy legs over the bellicose brine. My head's swaying more than the sea on account of I guzzled too much whoop soup.

I pull out my earbuds and close my eyes. The only sound is the waves on the rocks. It's a great sound. Deep, heavy monster sighs. It's funny to think that the same waves will be rolling over the same rocks long after I'm gone. The ocean snores my gray matter to sleep and awakens some silver. I imagine the rock breaking off and drifting away with me on it, like the iceberg does for Hermey the Dentist and the gang in *Rudolph the Red-Nosed Reindeer*.

Of course, my iceberg doesn't find a distant shore. My iceberg finds the black unknown. That darkness in the middle of nowhere, where things are calm. Calm and final. It could work. Me and Hermey ain't that different. A couple of goofy cartoon characters. Scribbled ideas on scraps of paper. Except my comic strip doesn't have a happy ending. My story got torn out of its notebook, crumpled up, and three-pointed into the nearest trash bin.

A wave splashes over my boots, and I open my eyes. The water's almost to the surface of the dance floor. Almost high enough to swoop in and carry me off like I'm a happy-go-lucky dwarf dentist. Maybe it'd be for the best.

Of course, there's a flipside to that cliffhanging coin. Death might be like in horror movies. Which is why

I'm still here. Ain't that a heart-ripping, brain-twisting, pickle-poking puzzle? Fear of staying makes you wanna go, but fear of going makes you wanna stay. Well, shiver me timbers, Captain Complexity.

Ah, fuck it. I don't need to decide anything tonight. D-Day's still eight months away. I grab my stuff and head home.

CHAPTER 6

The following day, Foxy Moxie shocks the shiitake mushrooms out of me with her response to my Dear Life letter. I expected to be confronted at the entrance by a flapping gaggle of school officials, police, paramedics, and psychologists waving straitjackets and testicular jumper cables. Instead, mild-mannered Moxie simply slips the marked-up letter onto my desk with a smile, then pirouettes away in footwear that could easily be mistaken for two of Janitor Menken's mop heads.

She does corrections with an old-fashioned fountain pen that dispenses way more ink than necessary. Her swirly penmanship reminds me of the Declaration of Independence. Her comments blow the wax out of my ears. She's all patronizing and inquisitive like I wrote a letter to the lunch lady complaining about the size of the toenail clippings in the chicken gumbo.

Dear Life,

You SUCK!
I want out.
See you on the flipside.

Sincerely,
Cricket

Wonderful choice of recipient!!!
Excellent start but needs more detail.
Specificity!
What in particular sucks?
Why do you want out?
What do you imagine awaits you on the flipside?

Regards,
M. Lord

What the hell's she playing at? How come she didn't psychoanalyze my letter like a typical tight-ass adult and have a mental conniption? She's a teacher, for Christ's sake. She's at least supposed to pretend to care. If not about me, then about herself. Isn't she worried about the backlash from one of her students telling her he's gonna push the F THIS CRAP button on the Afterworld Elevator? She'd get canned for sure if someone found this bloody letter pinned to my stiff corpse.

I should do it. Tonight. Show her who's boss. That would teach her cheeky ass a lesson. Suicide-bomb my abdullah oblongata right off this axis of evil. *Boom! Dead. Aha! What do you have to say for yourself now, Miss Smug-a-Dub-Dub-My-Bloody-Balls-in-a-Tub?*

Moxie's throaty bedroom growl interrupts my muddled musings. "As you can see, I've written comments on your letters. Today in class, I want you to rewrite your letters, incorporating responses to my remarks. You may start now."

I read her comments over and over, hoping her hidden meaning will crack me in the forehead like a stiff jab, but nothing. Her words just shuffle around my head like Muhammad Ali in his prime.

The voice of an angel startles me. "Mind if I sit here?"

I look to my left. Wynona Bidaban slides into the seat beside me. I scratch my right cheek.

"It's hard to concentrate next to the Distraction Twins," she says.

I sneak a peek at her boobs. *Tell me about it.* Then I glance up the aisle. Two cheerleader bimbettes are waving cherry-red fingernails in the air and hooting like horny barn owls.

Wynona flashes me a cute smile. "What'd you write about?"

I'm so shocked Wynona Bidaban is speaking to me, my mind flushes all rational thought. I flip my letter over. "Nothing."

Wynona turns back to her paper.

Shit! Why'd I say that? But what am I gonna say? I can't tell her what I wrote.

Wynona tosses me a lifeline. "I wrote about my dad." Her voice is chirpy, but sadness seeps under the frothy bubbles. "Dear Dad: Why did you marry Roxanne?" She jerks a glimpse at me, then stares at her sneakers like she's as surprised as I am that she's talking to me. "I mean, why didn't he at least ask my opinion about something so major? I wasn't a kid when he did it. I was fifteen." Her straight black hair is draped over her face like a veil.

I wonder why she's telling me this. Not that I mind, but Wynona Bidaban has never said one word to me. No, I take that back. She did speak to me once. Last year, in detention. She asked me what time the late bus arrived, and I shrugged because I didn't know, and she shook her head and sighed like I was a retard. That was our first and last encounter.

"Like, didn't he care what I thought? Didn't my opinion matter at all?"

No, Wynona, it didn't. And I'll tell you why. Because parents are all the same. They're selfish, soulless slugs. They only care about one person. THEMSELVES!

"I would never do something like that without asking my daughter first," she says. "I just don't get it."

I don't get it either, Wynona. Why you're talking to me, I mean. She probably figures since I'm such a screwed-up social outcast, I'll be able to relate to her family troubles. She's not far off.

"I'm sorry," she says quietly. "I don't mean to unload this stupid stuff on you." She turns back to her paper and starts taking out her rage on her notebook.

I spend the rest of the class trying to think of something clever or funny to say. A few things come to mind, but I pussy out and the bell rings. Wynona flashes me an uncomfortable smile and leaves. I stuff my letter in my pocket.

Goddamn it! Why didn't I say something? Anything. I'm such a loser.

I ditch History and spend the period chillaxing with Professor Panama.

The lunch lady glares at me when I pile two cheeseburgers, two slices of pizza, two helpings of Tater Tots, two brownies, and two milks on my tray. She knows I don't have a girlfriend. She's probably wondering how a hat rack like me can pack away so much grub. I don't know where it all goes, 'cause it sure as hell ain't sticking to my bones. Good thing the Mainiacs feed their orphans for free.

K–12 share the cafeteria and gymnasium on account of the small student population. The high school building is on one side and the little kids' building is on the other, like wings on a pigeon. I sit with my roomies from the Prison. It's worse than sitting alone, but I can't sit alone because that would hurt their feelings. Plus, the Little Ones catch less abuse when I'm with them. Well, usually. Right now, Buster Pitswaller is harassing Charlie Brittlebones at the dessert counter. Pitbull's dangling a slice of pie over Charlie's head, and Charlie's doing the worst thing possible, which is reaching for it. His undersize sweater is hiking up, and his oversize boxers are hanging out. Charlie isn't aware he's center stage at the Laugh Factory. He just wants pie.

Goddamn it. I haven't had a single bite of burger. I tell the Little Ones to watch my eats.

Heads turn like paparazzi to a coked-up starlet as I walk over. My stomach knots like someone's wringing out my intestines. I hate doing this when there's a crowd. The lunch lady scurries into the kitchen. Probably to dial 911. Where are the lunch monitors when you need them?

Then I see her. At the table next to Pitbull. She's the only one not watching the show. She's picking at her salad like this is brunch at the Ritz. *What the hell? How come she doesn't do anything? He's her boyfriend.* Suddenly, she does something. She looks up. But not at him. At me. With an expression of . . . what? Contempt? Fear? Pity?

Fuck you, Wynona. Pity yourself. You're the one sitting on your hands.

My thoughts must be seeping through my pores because her expression crinkles into pissed off, and she storms out of the cafeteria. Pitbull calls after her, but she ignores him.

I tap Brittlebones on the shoulder. "You need something, Charlie?"

"My pie."

Laughter erupts.

"Why don't you grab another slice?"

"'Cause this was the last slice of blueberry."

More laughter.

I push my hood off and turn to Pitbull. He's clenching the pie in one hand and a fist in the other. I never remember how massive he is until I'm right beside him. I'm five-eleven, and he towers over me. This gigantic dolt has the facial hair of a thirty-year-old and could play professional football. How many times has he been held back? "Why don't you give him his pie," I say.

"Sure, hero." Pitbull flicks the slice at Charlie. It bounces off his chest and lands on the floor.

Louder laughter.

My first thought is *Shit, I just washed that shirt. And blueberry stains are a bitch to get out.*

Charlie sniffles. I can tell he's about to burst into tears.

Pitbull squares off and stares me down.

"I got an extra brownie on my tray, Charlie," I say, without taking my eyes off Pitbull.

"But I w-want pie," he stutters.

Kids start mimicking his high-pitched squeal. *I want pie. Gimme pie. Oh no, my blueberries.*

"Well, eat it off the floor then."

No laughter.

Charlie looks at the pile of pie, slumps his shoulders, and walks off.

Pitbull kicks the heap of blue mush at me. "You gonna do something 'bout it, Scarface?"

A cacophony of *oooooh*s.

Just to set the record straight, I never start fights. Never. It's a rule I live by. And I never fight for no reason. That's another rule. There has to be a reason. A big reason. Like Pitbull. Truth is, if there wasn't a reason, I'd probably get my ass whupped every time, so I reckon my fisticuffin' commandments are more self-preservational than moralistical.

I consider breaking my fighting rule and hurling a right hook at Pitbull's left temple. I could land it before the *oooooh*s end. But, we're in the cafeteria. And I'm hungry. And it's just pie.

I turn.

I hear scuffles and whispers behind me as I walk away.

"Didn't think so, faggot."

I don't turn.

Something slams me hard in the back of the head. A bolt of pain slices my temples and my vision blurs. I drop to one knee. I think baseball bat, but that theory is debunked when I'm doused.

Laughter erupts like in a stadium.

It's a Mountain Dew cocktail. A high school variation of the Molotov cocktail, except you get engulfed in soda instead of flames. It's done by opening the can, covering the top with duct tape, shaking it like crazy, and throwing it.

I'm drenched and sticky, and my head is throbbing.

I stand and turn.

Pitbull lifts his arms to say *Bring it on*.

Teachers swarm. Nice of them to show up.

Mrs. Hershberger scurries to my side and touches my shoulder.

I shrug her off and walk away.

The Little Ones are terrified.

I plaster a smile over the pain. "Anyone want some Mountain Dew?"

They don't laugh.

"No worries, guys. Just high school hijinks. Go on, get to class."

They clean up and leave. Charlie Brittlebones is crying. He hasn't taken one bite of brownie.

I kneel beside him. "Charlie, this ain't your fault. Pitbull's an asshole. You know that. If it wasn't you, it'd be someone else. Now eat your brownie and get to class."

He sniffles and takes a mousy nibble.

I wrap my food in a napkin and head to my Subterranean Day Spa and Smoke Shop.

My underground grotto is an abandoned locker room adjacent to an abandoned gymnasium in the basement. It was boarded up a few years back when the new physical fitness emporium was built, but I have my ways in.

The sink in my day spa has one of those faucets that runs for five seconds and then shuts off automatically, so I have to press it a thousand times to rinse my hair. A lump is already forming on the back of my head. I scarf down my cold lunch while I sit under the hand dryer.

Part of me wants to ditch for the rest of the day. My clothes are sticky and my head's pounding. I can't deal with teachers today. Or students. Or Little Ones. Or walking. Or talking. Or thinking. Or breathing. Maybe I should stay underground for the duration and chill with my good pal Podiddle. But our dickhead science teacher, Professor Pitstains, has already assigned a big-ass research project, and my partner, Green Day, is expecting me in study hall. I don't wanna dump the entire assignment in his lap. Not that he'd mind.

I enter study hall through the back door and spot Wynona. She's sitting front row center. I can only see the back of her head, but I'd recognize Wynona from any angle. Green Day's sitting rear row right. The farthest seat from the preaching podium. The exact spot I would have chosen. It's one of those lecture rooms where the rows are tiered so everyone has an unobstructed view of the performing monkey on stage.

Green Day's real name is Reggie Tibbler, but I call him Green Day because he wears T-shirts with environmental messages and puts Save the Planet stickers all over his books and locker. He's wicked smart and he reads like crazy. He's a total geek, but I like him. He's the only kid in school who's ever asked me about my scar, and he's the only person on the planet I've ever told how I got it. The football assholes used to bully him, and that's why I partnered with him in science last year. They saw me hanging out with him and haven't bothered him since.

"Hey, Green Day." I slide into the chair next to his.

He blinks his big brown eyes from behind his goofy Buddy Holly glasses. "Good afternoon, Cricket." He stares me up and down like he's surprised I'd been walking. "I wasn't expecting to see you here."

"How come?"

"The cafeteria ruckus, of course."

Green Day uses fancy, old-fashioned words when he talks, which cracks me up 'cause he's being totally serious. Unlike me.

"Yes, it was one humdinger of a hootenanny," I say, grinning.

He pushes his glasses up the bridge of his nose. "To be sure. How's your head?"

"Sticky."

We've been assigned the Yellowstone Caldera, a very inspiring topic, and Green Day is sketching the internal components of a volcano, which look disgustingly similar to the female reproductive organs. *Holy cow, I wouldn't want to stick any part of me inside that molten mess.* There's a giant poster in health class of Olivia Organs, so I know what those hazardous internals look like.

"Yes, Mountain Dew can be extremely difficult to extricate from hair follicles," Green Day says as he shades a periwinkle fallopian tube. "Trust me, I know. But not as troublesome as bubblegum." Green Day draws as he talks, which makes it seem like he's talking to himself. "The cheerleaders gave me a baseball cap last year as I was entering the homecoming rally. They asked me to wear it to show my support for the football team. As you know, I'm not a hat person, but I complied, as I felt it a worthy display of school spirit. It turned out the interior of the cap had been laced with numerous pieces of already-chewed bubblegum. My mother had a frighteningly difficult time remedying that clotted conundrum." His expression is flat, like he's telling me how fertilized eggs attach to the uterine wall. "She had to cut the gum out with scissors, which, needless to say, resulted in numerous unsightly bald spots."

"You wore a lot of hats last fall."

"A season steeped in irony, to be sure."

I look up and Wynona is suddenly standing above me. She's biting her lower lip and tugging an earlobe. "I'm sorry about what happened in the lunchroom," she says.

"You have nothing to be sorry about," I say flatly.

"Yes, I do. I don't know why I just sat there. I wanted to say something, but then you started walking over, and I couldn't say anything then because it would look like, well, you know, like I was taking your side or something. I am sorry. I hope your head's okay. Maybe, I don't know, maybe sometime . . ."

The double doors to the study hall crash open and

Pitbull barrels in like a running back through two defensive tackles. His nickname is mostly on account of the way he plays football. Like a rabid dog. Turns out Buster's a nickname too. His real name is Bartholomew. A sophomore called him Bartholomew once, and the kid missed a week of school, Pitbull pounded him so ugly. *Bartholomew*. What a joke. Like calling Freddy Krueger *Frederick*. Wishful thinking, Mom and Dad. Northern Maine's butt-plugged to the borders with wishful thinking.

I turn to Wynona, but she's already talking to a girl a few seats over.

Pitbull's entourage marches in behind him. Pitbull peruses the room; when he sees me, he smiles big and wide, then flips me the bird. He sees Reggie and converts it to a double bird. Fortunately, Green Day doesn't notice because he's busy sketching a bloody discharge erupting out of the top of a volcano.

My throwdown with Pitbull is getting closer by the minute. He's been hassling me like a warthog in heat since last spring, saying I have a horseshoe stuffed up my ass and that's the only reason I managed to kick the snot out of two of his football buddies who were bullying some Little Ones. He's been promoting this fight like he's Don King or something.

Wynona returns to her seat. She ignores Pitbull, who's directly in front of her, faux-boxing with one of his football pals. They're both wearing varsity jackets with enormous drooling wolverines embroidered on the back. If our school were located in a more civilized part of the world, they'd be throwing their fists into a nice game of rock, paper, scissors instead of at each other's heads. Fighting ain't a big deal here in Lumberjack Land. It's like a hockey game brawl. Everyone pretends to be against it, but it's what they root for. Which is messed up when you think about it.

I wonder what Wynona was going to say to me. *"Maybe sometime . . ."* Maybe sometime what, Wynona?

"Cricket, did you know there were volcanoes near Lake Winnipesaukee in New Hampshire approximately one hundred and twenty-five million years ago?" Green Day asks.

I don't answer him. I'm pretty sure he's speaking rhetorically anyway.

Wynona looks at her watch, shakes her head, and picks up a book.

Pitbull's noticed me again. He's flicking his chin in my direction and whispering to his teammates. One of his pals is holding him back by the bicep. He yanks his arm away and steps toward me. "You wanna go right now, Scarface? Finish what you started, asshole."

Everyone in the room looks at me.

I stare at Pitbull without flinching.

I see Green Day shift in his seat out of the corner of my eye.

"Cricket?" His voice is low and jittery.

"Don't worry, Reg. He won't do nothing in school."

Wynona sets her book down. "Buster, please."

He ignores her.

The door swings open and Mrs. Emory rushes in even later than usual. She breaks up the football huddle and they take their seats in the second and third rows. Pitbull starts fiddling with Wynona's night-black hair. He looks like a toddler poking a kitten.

Mrs. Emory walks the aisles as everyone settles in. She's a spindly brainiac. Tall and gangly with long limbs and a puny head. Kinda like me.

Green Day passes me a sheet of paper. It's labeled *Yellowstone Caldera Project Outline and Research Strategy*. Jeez Louise, it's typed and everything. And we just got the assignment last week. Green Day's a schoolaholic.

The word *Strategy* makes me think about my boathouse boxing workouts with Caretaker. Caretaker and I have been working on a Pitbull fight strategy since the beginning of the summer. You need a strategy when you fight a dude that's got a hundred pounds on you and is gonna charge you angry and wired like a pit bull. Brawling's more about mind than size. A lot more. Most people don't understand that. Don't get me wrong. Some swizzle stick, chess champion, asthma dork ain't gonna mindify his way out of a down-home ass-whupping. But a small fighter with skill and brains can stomp an ignoramus no matter how much poundage the dunderhead's got on him.

One thing Caretaker said stuck in my head like peanut butter to the roof of my mouth. He wasn't exactly talking about fighting, but I knew he meant it about fighting—one of those metafornical-type tales where the teller aims the words at your ears while he's poking you elsewhere. He said if a killer dog ever charges you with the aim of chomping you a chew toy destruction, grab him by the front legs and yank them apart like you would an oversize turkey wishbone. You'll rip the dog's heart in half. I think about that heart-ripping story a lot when I'm training for my Pitbull fight.

Wynona spins around and swats Pitbull's hand away from her head. She's got a fake smile plastered on. Pitbull keeps poking her like he's checking the firmness of a bundt cake.

Saying I have a crush on Wynona is an understatement. She's been global warming my southern hemisphere ever since she moved here. She's only lived in Naskeag for three years, and that length of time don't count for nothing in Maine. Maine's glacial. She's lived in Maine all her life, but if your house isn't inside the county lines and wasn't built by the bare hands of a blood relative, you're from *away*. Mainers are wicked particular about geographical origins. *Hatchin' chickens in the stove don't make 'em muffins*. Whatever the hell that means. To make matters worse, Wynona's from Portland, so she's also a *suthunah*.

I look at a rendering of a volcano in Green Day's textbook. *Lava*. I gaze at Wynona's coal-colored mane, and another four-letter L-word comes to mind. I wasn't going to admit this but here goes. The old L-word has tickled the lining of my cranial squeezebox during various Wynona ruminations. I don't know, though. Tough to affix a word to something when you don't know its meaning. And even if I did, how can you *L* someone you don't know? You can *F* people you don't know, but you can't *L* them.

But if I'm not prepared to use the L-word, what word should I use? *Attraction*? Lame. *Caring*? Super lame. *Fondness*? Oh, sweet Jesus, just bedazzle my ass in leather chaps and ship me off to Big Gay Al's. *Lust*? Disrespectful. Don't get me wrong. I get plenty knotted south of the equator when Wynona's nearby, but it's the good kind of knots, not the knotty kind. Not like the raunchy naughtytime hankerings I have when I reminisce about the working girls I knew when I lived in Boston with my foster whore. Yeah, I had friends who were pros. No big deal. I ain't whore-aphobic.

Wynona's dating Pitbull is an enema I'd like to get

to the bottom of. My guess is she's ice-screwed herself to Pitbull since he's the quickest route to Popularity Peak. I can't imagine she'll care much for the view once she's up there, though.

I look at the back of Wynona's head. Pitbull's still fiddling with her long black hair.

I imagine her spinning around and screaming like Bette Davis in *Of Human Bondage*. "*It made me sick when I had to let ya kiss me. I only did it because ya begged me, ya hounded me, you drove me crazy! And after you kissed me, I always used to wipe my mouth! Wipe my mouth!*"

The vision makes me chuckle.

CHAPTER 7

When the final bell rings, I grab my books from my locker and head to the courtyard to meet the Little Ones. As soon as I step outside, I know I'm gonna be in a fight. Every eye is on me. Hundreds of them. It's a familiar glower. Like I'm some friggin' horror movie villain.

Andrew Pendleton, one of my roomies at the Prison, is sprawled on the ground, sobbing next to his knapsack. Pitbull's hovering over him, flipping though Andrew's Spider-Man comic book. He looks like Godzilla in his army fatigues and green T-shirt.

Tiny bubbles tingle in my calves, float to my thighs, stomach, chest, throat, head. The pressure builds.

So, today's the day. I guess this afternoon's cafeteria incident motivated him.

I push my hood off, drop my books, and start toward Pitbull.

I know what the landscapers were thinking when they decided on cobblestone, but I'm thinking something totally different. Wobbly and uneven. Tricky to keep your footing. And damn hard on the noggin when you go down. Not like dirt or grass. I stuff my iPod in my pocket next to my letter and wonder if what's about to happen should be listed as a reason on my response to Foxy Moxie. Reckon this could be diddled on either side of the page.

The sun's bright, so I squint, which the rabble probably figure I'm doing to look angry and badass, but I'm not. I'm just trying to see. I'm not badass. Angry, yes, but not badass.

I smirk. Pitbull gawks at me with the same confused expression he gets in class. He can't figure out how a skinstick like me comatosed his linebacker buddies. His teeth are brown, and he drools when he barks. "Well, looky here. Asshole season opened early this year. You ready to eat some dirt, hand-me-downs?"

I stare at him with a blank face. No words. Never words. Just the stare. Part of Caretaker's strategy.

I zoom out my view. *Damn, he's big*. Bigger than Caretaker's heavy bag. Concrete-statue big. My gut fizzles like there's a wrestling match going on in there between two cobras whose tubey shoots are full of shaken-up Mountain Dew. I sure as hell hope Caretaker's strategy works, 'cause if phase one fails, there ain't gonna be a phase two.

Unless collapsing to the ground in a puddle of my own blood can be considered a phase.

The crowd's huge. All swarming around Pitbull like he's Rocky friggin' Balboa. Never ceases to amaze me how many people will watch a fight but how few will participate. I mean, here's this helpless little fifth-grader who can't be more than three feet tall sprawled on the ground, and there's not a single person stepping forward to help. And you wonder why I ain't all sappy-happy to hang around this asshole-infested ball of gall.

In fact, this scene proves my point perfectly. No one gives a damn about anything but themselves. These pocketed hands are proof of that. Bunch of no-good wastes of space. Makes me want to skull-pop every jostling puss here. Gotta remember to include this reason in my Moxie letter. *People suck.*

"I'm gonna wipe my ass with your face, orphan," Pitbull growls.

I rivet a deep stare at Andrew. His face is so pale, it looks like some brownnose clapped the blackboard erasers clean on it. I focus on his tears. Stare until reality morphs into memory, memory into fear, fear into pain, pain into rage, and rage into energy. Another part of the strategy. It usually doesn't take long. There it is.

"Teach you to mind your own friggin' business, flatlander. You think you're some fuckin' hero or something?"

Out of the corner of my eye, I see Wynona running

toward Pitbull. The sea of students parts. I'm glad she's here, but it raises the stakes. I have to win now. Her black hair is bouncing wildly, like she's filming a shampoo commercial. Other things are bouncing too, but it wouldn't be gentlemanly of me to elucidate those jiggling profuntitties. Her face is the color of sunset. I bet her skin's as soft as the inside of a rose petal. Like velvet. *Damn, she's pretty.* As pretty as Pitbull is mean.

Pitbull takes a step toward me. "I'm talking to you, faggot!" I glimpse a twinge of fear in his face. *Good.* Every twinge in him releases one in me. He's got reason to be scared. Not about whipping me, 'cause he's got a better-than-average chance of doing that. But about the price. Anyone who's ever fought me knows the price. Even those who've won. You may win, but you'll feel like you lost. I don't go down easy. You'll limp away with painful mementos: split lip, bruised ribs, black eye, smashed nuts, a busted nose. That's why I've never had a rematch. Not one.

I twirl my ring and it jars a memory. *They're only fists. All he has are fists.*

Some would say the honorable thing would be to twist that hunk of metal so the jagged letters aren't pointing forward with the intent of slicing my opponent a back alley mischief. If Pitbull weren't twice my size, I'd concur. But fightin' and politin' ain't compatible roomies.

I learned that lesson the hard way. The bigger the dog, the dirtier the brawl. That's a life truism for sure. *Truism.* Sweet word. Sounds like one of my made-up ones, but it ain't.

There's a story behind my ring, but Pitbull's close now, and I don't want to think about it.

Wynona's almost to him, but he's not gonna wait.

I breathe and balance. I'll only have one chance to get this right. Caretaker's words echo in my head. *Wait, wait, till he takes the bait. Make him commit before you duck and hit.* Everything around me fades. The only sounds are his footsteps and my breathing. *Wait, wait, bait. Commit, duck, hit.*

Pitbull charges me with his fists high. "Say hello to my little friend, you scar-faced fucking freak." He pulls his right hand back toward his shoulder and twists his body.

I drop my chin, tense my legs, clench my fists.

He launches his right fist at my head with all his weight behind it.

In one smooth motion, I do the move I've been practicing for months. I dive under his punch and hurl a straight right into his solar plexus. I connect hard just under his ribs. His fat swallows my fist. I yank it out and spin.

Pitbull groans and buckles. It's knocked the wind

out of him. He wheezes for air and drops to one knee. He's trying to cuss me out something fierce, but words aren't coming. Just growls and drool. Suddenly, I don't see Pitbull. I see a Doberman pinscher.

The crowd reappears, and I hear them mumbling. Some of them turn away. They think the fight's over. *Think again, dipshits.* The only way I'll keep this dog from coming after me for revenge is by ripping his heart in half here and now.

I charge Pitbull and bash him in the side of the head with my boot heel.

He topples over.

Pitbull still has his fight face on, which surprises me. He's got one hand on his head and the other on his gut, but he's far from giving up. His expression is an amalgam of fear, rage, and embarrassment. He tries to push himself to his feet, but stumbles. A tinge of admiration drips down my throat.

I can hear Wynona screaming something from somewhere, but I can't make out her words. I'm glad she's still here. Teach her what a bigmouth, all-talk asshole her boyfriend is. I want to look for her, gaze into her emerald eyes, but I don't dare turn my back on Godzilla. If I give him more than a few seconds, he'll be on his feet, and that's the last thing I want. Rage makes people monster-strong. I know that firsthand.

I don't want to get too close yet, so I go to work on his midsection with the steel toe of my boot. After a few vicious kicks to his gut, he rolls onto his back.

More kids leave. Others cover their eyes. *Yeah, a tough show to stay tuned into when it's on the Real Life channel, eh, pussies?*

Pitbull's blubbering like a baby. I can tell that he's done fighting. Too bad I ain't. His moans jam more rage into me than pity.

I drop to one knee and start bashing him in the face with my ring fist. His head thuds against the cobblestones.

Spectators shriek and scatter.

Bam, mouth.

Bam, cheek.

Bam, forehead.

Bam, nose.

Bam, eye.

Each time I cock my arm for the next strike, I see the cut my ring has made. It's strange to see up close. Each bloody slice unleashes a desire to rip open a new one. As his face blurs, reality fades, so I keep hitting. I hit and hit and hit.

I don't know how many punches I land before I'm yanked off Pitbull, but it's plenty because his face looks like a slab of raw roast beef in a deli case. But before I can stare too long it dawns on me that the dudes tugging at me might be Pitbull's football pals carrying me into round two, so I flail my arms wildly to break free. My elbow strikes something solid and the hands gripping me go limp. I jump back and square off.

I realize it's not his football buddies, because they're all the way by the flagpole cowering. Two of them are dudes I pounded the piss out of last year, so it doesn't surprise me that they never had any intention of jumping in to help their friend.

I turn and see Mr. Tupelo, the social studies teacher, with his hand over his nose and blood gushing through his fingers. *Uh-oh, not good.* But sorta funny. That musta been my elbow shot. *Good.* Serves the caddywhompus prick right for sticking his pompous snoot where it don't belong. My body warms and tingles.

Golly gee, Trots McGee, reckons yee shouldn't-ah jammed yer bulbous beak far and yon where it don't belong, ya scrumpy smeghead. Now ponce off 'fore I squiff ya a fer-ther comeuppance, ya toffee-nosed twit.

Principal LaChance's shrill voice interrupts my miffy musings. "Cricket, I am not going to say this again. Either drop your fists right now and come with me, or I will have no choice but to call the police."

I don't realize I'm still holding my fists up until I hear LaChance. They don't look attached. They look like someone else's fists, floating in front of me like a video game. My left hand's pristine, and my right's a bloody mess. Heaven and Hell. Glorytown and Mischiefville.

"I'm not going to say it again, Cricket."

I glance at LaChance. He looks like a cartoon character with his blazing orange hair and beanbag belly. I sure as hell wouldn't mind popping him one. Hell, I'm already all bloodied up.

He reads my mind and raises his hands like I just drew a nine on his convenience store ass. *What a pussy.*

"Now, Cricket, calm down and try to think clearly, son. This has gone far enough."

A warm, tingly fluid floods my veins. Like that feeling when blood returns to your limbs after they've been asleep. *Yeah, this has gone far enough, Chicken LaChance.* Still, his fear amuses me, so I take a step toward him just to freak him out.

He jumps back and almost tumbles over a bicycle rack.

I lower my hands and laugh. My cackling emboldens him, and he prances toward me.

The voices around me are loud now. A vision of Caretaker floats into my mind, and an anxious exuberance floods my chest. I look back at the swollen, purple lump I've just pummeled. He's rolling around on the cobblestones like a beached walrus on hard sand.

Principal Pisshimself boldly poses beside me like a

mutant Munchkin Land mayor. He points his pudgy finger at the school. I follow the cobble-brick road toward the entrance doors.

Two lady teachers are dabbing Tupelo's nose with paper towels.

The warm something in my veins is gushing furious now, like I'm full of hot tea. My right hand's stinging. The back's a sticky mess, but the inside's sparkling clean like I just washed it.

Lily Liver LaChance shoves me toward the school.

I pull my hood on.

Just before we enter, I turn for one last look at my crumpled adversary. Pitbull's on his back with his hands crossed over his chest like a corpse in a casket.

Wynona's on her knees beside him, but she's not looking at him. She's looking at me. I can't read her face. It's blank but strained, like she's trying to ESP me a message. *Damn, she's beautiful.* She was invisible until she started dating Pitbull. I liked her better when she was invisible. I liked feeling like I was the only one at school who could see her. Stupid, heart-thumping bullshit. She's far from invisible now.

The urge to run to her bubbles inside me. I imagine myself grabbing her by the arms and pulling her in to me. All I need is a trench coat and a fedora. *"Wynona, I'm no good at being noble, but it doesn't take much to see that*

the problems of three little people don't amount to a hill of
beans in this crazy world. Someday you'll understand that.
Here's looking at you, kid." A grin slices my face.

Her expression twists from fear to anger.

My throat tightens, and my mind clogs.

CHAPTER 8

Nurse Aubrey's dangling my hand over her stainless-steel sink and dousing it with hydrogen peroxide. Her sleeves are rolled up and she's holding my arm away from her body so she doesn't get any blood on her marshmallow-white uniform. She looks like a nun wannabe in her refrigerator-box dress, white Frankenstein shoes, and goofy hat. You'd think a nurse would want to get blood on her uniform to show people she did something useful with her day instead of just saving schoolboys from paper cuts.

"I don't know why you boys insist on fighting to solve your petty differences." She dabs my cuts with a cotton ball. "When I was your age, my brothers were in the army fighting to protect this great nation of ours. They fought for a reason."

"Which side, North or South?"

Nurse Aubrey scrunches her wrinkly puss. "Very

funny, Cricket." She dries my hand and starts bandaging my finger with so much gauze you'd think it'd been chopped off.

"Jeez Louise, a Band-Aid would be sufficient."

"Thank you for telling me how to do my job, Cricket. With just a Band-Aid, you risk infection."

My finger's wrapped thicker than an Egyptian mummy, but it still stings like a son-of-a-biscuit.

My ring's in my pocket. There's blood on it so now there's probably blood on my letter to Moxie. Like it battled alongside me. *Cool.* If it weren't for my ring cutting into me, I wouldn't have a scratch on me.

"Who was it this time, Cricket?" Nurse Aubrey asks.

"Buster Pitswaller."

"Oh, dear Lord. You're lucky I'm only bandaging your finger."

"Yeah, lucky me."

"Where's Buster? Did he get hurt as well?"

"His face got a little banged up when he used it to cut open my finger."

"Oh my. Are they bringing him here?"

The butterflies in my gut start flapping. "I don't know."

"Stay here while I get you some antiseptic and bandages to take home." Nurse Aubrey disappears into a walk-in closet and returns with a small paper bag. "Be sure to change the dressing tonight before you go to bed and then twice a day, morning and evening, or that finger may get infected. Now go sit in Principal LaChance's waiting room while I go see what's happening with Buster."

I take my usual seat in LaChance's waiting area. The school's hauntingly quiet. Probably on account of everyone's in the courtyard.

I'm feeling amped and tingly, but palpitations about Pitbull's condition are poking holes in my fuzzy inflation. Like I said before, getting into a good game of Fist Scrabble ain't a big deal Down East. But a hospital trip crosses a line that even the animals inhabiting this missing-teeth menagerie can't ignore. If Pitbull has to leave school grounds to get patched up, I'm toast. *Ass toast,* if you get my meaning. With a side of grape jelly. And extra *margareeeeeeeeen.*

Not that I would have done anything differently.

I need to pull it together. Stop letting these whirlpooling worries suck me inside out. It's completely ruining my post-whup-ass fuzzies. I need to mind-munch something commensurate with my infernal combustications. Something the exact opposite of Pitbull. Something silky smooth and sweet-smelling. Something caramel creamy and rose-petal soft. Something Wynonatatious.

I wonder which side she'll fall on. I wonder if she'll hate me for what I did, or be impressed. I wonder if she'll love Pitbull more or despise him for his flabby failure. If she decides to despise him, she'll need a replacement. This could be my chance. *Yeah, my fat chance.* A beauty like her would never be drawn to a hooded, fisticuffin', Prison-dwelling, scar-faced beast like me.

My fuzzies fizzle.

Either way, I won't need to percolate my ruminations much longer, because here she comes. She's marching straight at me like a prison warden delivering a nightstick enema, and I can practically hear her growls from here. Two football coaches are behind her, dragging Pitbull by the armpits. *Jesus, his face is trashed.* Nurse Aubrey looks whiter than her uniform.

Wynona's got Pitbull's varsity jacket draped over her arm, which is funny, like she's his mother or something. I must be smirking, because her snarl sharpens and she bites her lower lip.

There are two kinds of lower lip bites. There's the wide-eyed *Golly gee, you're cute, and I sure as heckfire would like to squeeze you tight into my love melons,* and then there's the *Holy hell, you're an asshole, and I sure as shit would like to squeeze your nuts in a vise.* Guess which one Wynona's wielding? Suffice it to say, I'm glad we're not in shop class.

Wynona freezes at Nurse Aubrey's door while the coaches drag Pitbull inside. She's glaring at me with gonad-slicing lasers. It's hard to take her anger seriously because she's so adorable. Even her bubblicious hatred is inflating me with ooey-gooey lovey-doveys. Her face is smooth like beach sand after a storm. *Damn, she's fine.* She's wearing blue jeans that look two sizes too big on account of they're cinched tight around her petite waist like on a scarecrow. She's short, about five feet, but right now she's looming like a skyscraper. Her lips are twitching, which is confounding my efforts to imagine planting a tender wet one on her. She looks like she'd bite me if I tried. That'd be okay. Any Wynona contact would be fine with me. I should ask her out before she says a word. Toss her a psychological stumper before she gets too deeply entrenched in hatred.

She appears to be contemplating her next move. She tosses Pitbull's jacket on a chair and stomps toward me. *Oh, shit, she's decided.* She takes one step onto the carpet in LaChance's waiting area and stalls like she's stuck in tar. Wynona and I are alone. I imagine drawling a classic John Wayner from *The Man Who Shot Liberty Valance.* *"You're awful pretty when you get mad."*

I try to calm myself the way I do before a fight, but Caretaker's strategy isn't working as good on girly anxiety as it does on squirrelly anxiety. My brain's whirring like a ceiling fan on max speed, trying to think of something clever to say. I wonder if she can read my mind, and that's why she hasn't spoken yet. Maybe she's mad at Pitbull for picking on poor, defenseless Andrew. Maybe she came to apologize.

"I hope you're proud of yourself," Wynona blasts.

Oh, well. I guess not.

She has her arms crossed over her chest, which is unfortunate because she has awesome nubbies that I wouldn't mind canoodling a gander at since this will probably be my last day in this fine Institute of Dire Yearning. They're perfectly sized and shaped for her petite frame. Not boyishly small or whorishly large. What I wouldn't give to be one of her forearms right now.

"Well?" she barks.

I'm sorry, my cantankerous love muffin, but I interpreted your question as rhetorical in nature. I assumed you were simply preaching and not actually expecting a response. That's what I should say. But I don't because I'm distracted by the tug-o'-war going on between her expression and her words. An opposing enemy is skulking behind her bulwark of rage. An undercover operative. A traitor. What is it? What is she squinting at that she won't leak out in a million years?

"I asked you a question," she says through quivering lips. "Are you proud of yourself or what?" Her eyes are intense but not angry intense.

A response pureeing in my blender bubbles out.

"Yes, I am." *Shit, who said that? That's not what I wanted to say. Comments like that won't woo her. They'll just chafe her ass into an itchier rash.*

She uncrosses her arms and plants her hands on her hips. "Oh, really? You're proud of yourself for being a complete brute?" Her body jiggles as she speaks, which spikes my already dangerously high distraction fever. The tears she's fighting back make her eyes look greener than usual, like acid-melting emeralds. She looks scared and uncertain. More real than I've ever seen her, which makes me realize I've been seeing her through a make-believe veil all the time I've been stalking her.

Wynona stomps her foot to get my attention. "Are you going to answer me or not?"

Man, she's adorable. She's sulking like a cranky Little One demanding a sugary treat before dinner. Which, truth be told, is tearing me in half. She may be adorable, but she's also being an asshole. I won't kiss her ass just because she has a perfect one. "Sure, if you ask me a question that's not retarded." *Whoopsy.*

Her face explodes. Holy Moses, smell the roses, she's plenty riled now. "Oh, so you don't think you're a . . . total . . . brute? You think what you did is okay? You think viciously attacking a . . . helpless . . . person . . . is okay?" There's that tone again. Her voice is stuttery, like she's auditioning for a role in the remake of *Network*. *"I'm as mad as hell, and I'm not gonna take this anymore."*

My forehead's sizzling a bacony mischief, and that ain't the only pork oinking a stand-at-attention tumult. "I'm sorry—what was the question?" I consider ending my question with "Professor Pantywad," but my cooler head prevails.

Apparently, she hasn't been paying attention either, because my question flusters her. "What? I mean . . . which one?"

I gawk into her pretty eyes.

Her cheeks twitch as she glowers. She scrunches her mouth. "What the hell is wrong with you?"

How much time you got, sweet cheeks? Sometimes I wish I could open my mouth and free the untamed swarm of thoughts buzzing around in my head. Oh, shit, I just thought of something. Perhaps she's not interpreting my reticence as confidence and charm. Maybe she thinks I'm retarded. "I simply asked if you could repeat your question."

"Well, the first thing I said . . . about an hour ago was, I hope you're proud of yourself."

"Proud of myself for what, Wynona?"

She blinks as if she's shocked I know her name. "Proud of yourself . . . for . . . almost killing Buster." Her volume decreases with each syllable, so by the time she gets to -*ster*, she's practically whispering.

Wynona, my love. I sincerely apologize for pummeling your genteel and kindhearted beau. But you must admit, he started it. He was physically abusing a defenseless young boy. And he stole his favorite comic book. That is fairly brutish behavior, wouldn't you say? Certainly worthy of a stern physical reprimand. That's what I want to say, but it's not what comes out. "What, are you fucking kiddin' me? It would take a hell of a lot more than a few pops to the noggin to kill that Neanderthal." *Shit, I did it again. Jesus H. Christ on a stripper pole! Why can't I shut, shut, shut my stupid cock-blocking mouth?*

Wynona's jaw drops. "Well, you didn't just punch him. You kicked him too. Like a little girl."

I chuckle as I realize Wynona has no problem with the fact that I called her boyfriend a Neanderthal. Perhaps she concurs with my assessment. I should club her on the head and drag her back to my cave.

"What's so funny?" she barks. "Only girls kick when they fight."

"Are you suggesting the only reason I defeated your asshole boyfriend is because I utilized the fighting techniques of a girl? Because if you are, I'm not sure who you're offending more, me or the entire female population."

Her face drains. "Well . . . you don't . . . kick someone when they're down."

Her words are a punch to the gut. "Wynona, I'm not sure what time you arrived at the melee, but did you happen to notice the scrawny fifth-grader on the ground in tears?"

"Well, I didn't say he didn't start it. I just said you don't, you know, kick a man when he's down."

"But it's okay to kick a little boy when he's down?"

"No, I didn't say that. I just said you . . ." Her mind melts midsentence. Jesus, maybe she's the mentally unstable one. *Holy mad cow, I've fallen for a dunderhead. I'm trapped inside a comic book. It's Malice in Dunderland!* A chuckle slips out.

She stomps her foot. "Stop laughing at me!"

"I'm not laughing at you, Wynona. I'm laughing at me. And to finish your sentence, you said I fight like a girl."

"I didn't mean it like that, and you know it. All I meant was, he was lying down defenseless, and you kicked him like an animal."

"That is true. I did kick him like an animal. Because he is an animal."

Wynona scrunches her face and I can see her mind sparking. Her thick black hair looks like a silk frame around a Fourth of July fireworks display. "You're the one . . . who's the . . . animal."

I lean back, stretch out my lanky legs, and cross them at the ankles. "Well, I won't argue with you there, Wynona."

She drops her arms and clenches her fists.

I'm struggling to keep my eyes off her chest. It's like there's an enormous gorilla manhandling my skull in inappropriate directions. *Whoopsadaisy, too low. Not okay to stare at the ol' hooty-hooty-ha-ha this early in the relationship.* My crotch tingles. I force my gaze back to her eyes.

"Stop staring at me like that, you weirdo."

Oh, shit, apparently I'm staring. I should tell her why. Drop the hammer. Reveal my love. Take her in my arms like I'm Humphrey Bogart. *Of all the principal's offices in all the towns in all the world, she walks into mine.* "Yeah, you're dating Bartholomew Pitswaller, and I'm the weirdo." *Uh-oh.*

Her mouth drops open like I just kicked her square between the candy canes. Then it closes. Then it opens again. Then it closes. What's this crazy bitch doing, catching flies? Her mouth starts to twist, and, for a nanosecond, I think I glimpse a smirk, but then it boards the Angrytown Express.

"My life is none of your business. Besides, who the hell are you to judge me, you freak? Maybe you should spend your time straightening out your own life instead of judging other people. Maybe if you weren't such a psycho loser, you wouldn't get in fights with, like, every boy in school. Nobody gets in as many fights as you. Nobody. You're like a fight magnet or something. Have you ever stopped to think why that is? It's not a coincidence, you know. It's just not. Why do you hate everybody so much? What's so bad about everybody that you have to go around beating them up? What has everybody done to you to make you hate them so much?"

Pheeewwwy-klabeeewwy, that was a mouthful. *Beaucoup des questions difficile, mon cheery.*

"The thing is, you don't know Buster. You don't know the real him." Her voice is softer. Maybe she realizes she's poked a tiny hole in my armor. She sounds more understanding. More genteel. More annoying. "He bullies people because he's insecure. His father's a bully, so it's all he knows. I'm just saying you could have handled it differently. You could have talked to him. You could have stood up for that little kid without getting in a fight."

Oh, Wynona. Dear, sweet, naïve Wynona. My ripe kumquat. My delicate dandelion. My innocent ignoramus. I did consider other options before stepping into the ring with Sugar Ray Pitswaller. But just as I was about to suggest to tender Bartholomew that we adjourn to a quiet spot under a cherry tree for a nice spot of chamomile tea and a friendly chat, he charged me with fists the size of Volkswagens. So with all due respect, sweet sweety sweetykins, fuck you. "Jesus, you two belong together. You're as thick-headed as he is." *Uh-oh. See you on the flipside, Cupid.*

Wynona takes a step toward me and stops like she's afraid of what she might do if she gets too close. Her mouth opens wide, her forehead wrinkles, and she screams. "Fuck you, asshole!"

I smile.

Principal LaChance's office door swings open. "What the devil's going on out here?"

Andrew Pendleton squeezes through the crack between LaChance and the door frame. His face is wet. He sees me and charges. He grabs me around the chest and buries his face in my sweatshirt.

Wynona glares at Andrew, and her scowl drips from rage to confusion. She's squinting like she can't believe he didn't burst into flames the moment he touched me.

I rub Andrew's head. His body's quivering, the poor little dude.

Wynona redirects her gaze to me, and her scowl returns. But it's a phony scowl. Pasted on. Like a mask.

LaChance points at Wynona. "Either go into the nurse's office or go home, Wynona."

I wave goodbye with a discreet finger jiggle.

Wynona mouths *asshole* and grabs Pitbull's coat off the chair. She disappears through the nurse's door.

Wynona, I think this is the beginning of a beautiful friendship.

CHAPTER 9

Nancy LaChancey paces when he preaches. "Andrew told me what happened. That you were defending him from Buster. That this whole thing was over a comic book."

A comic book? Jesus, how brain-dead do you have to be to become a high school principal?

He leans against the desk, crosses his arms on his chest, and puckers his lips. It's what authority figures like principals and nuns do right before they word-wrangle your ass into a corral of punishment. Pace and pucker. "I've spoken to the teachers and coaches who arrived toward the end. They confirmed Andrew's version from talking to witnesses. That Buster started it. That he threw the first punch."

He scratches his orange whiskers intently in one spot like he's located a plump scab. "Still, that doesn't excuse you for taking it as far as you did. The general consensus is that you took Buster out with one blow but proceeded to kick and punch him after he was down."

Layaway LaChance grabs his belt and yanks up his Wal-Mart corduroys, but there's nowhere for them to go because they slam into his fat barricade. "You're going to be in serious trouble if the police get involved or his parents press charges."

Yeah, right. Pitbull's parents pressing charges. That's a laugh. The only thing Pitbull's dad's gonna press is his drunk-ass fists against his dumb-ass son's face. The pounding his pops will lay on him for losing a fight will make the beating I laid on him look like a bitch slap from a quadriplegic monk.

Chunky LaChance is staring out the window into the parking lot. His breath is fogging the glass, which makes it look like steam is puffing out of his jackass ears. He's probably wishing he was out there. I wonder if he's remembered that he has to drive me home after he's done yelling and expelling. That's another funny thing about living in East Fumbuck, Maine. Teachers have to think twice about doling out a detention because the late bus doesn't run most days, so they gotta taxi your ass home after they dish out the discipline. That cracks me up. Makes getting in trouble totally worthwhile. Watching a teacher wince when they realize they just lashed their own ass. Principal LaChance bawling me out after a fisticuffin' brouhaha and then saying, "All right, come on, I'll drive you home." The ride home always sucks the sting out of the cuss session because for some reason adults don't get as angry in cars. Or maybe they just don't like yelling at a kid right before saying good night and booting them out of their El Camino. Or maybe it has something to do with being off school grounds that transmogrifies a kid into a human being from whatever the hell teachers think he is inside these icy walls of enlightenment.

"Or if Nurse Aubrey determines he has to go to the hospital, which is a distinct possibility."

Wrong again, Captain Oblivion. The only way Pitbull's gonna approve a field trip to the hospital is if he's nighty-night unconscious, and I don't think that's the case on account of his face was wincing up painful sensibilities when they dragged him into Aubrey's office.

"I am curious to hear your side of the story, Cricket, but if he's taken to the hospital or the police get involved, it will be out of my hands."

I feel like Andy Dufresne in *The Shawshank Redemption.* An innocent man wrongly accused. A ward of the state. A dangerous troublemaker LaChançe would sure as shit love to toss into solitary confinement for the rest of the year. *"I believe in two things. Discipline and the Bible. Here you'll receive both. Put your trust in the Lord. Your ass belongs to me."*

"After Buster went down, you should have walked

away, Cricket. You'd made your point." Warden Jellybelly orbits and leans his hefty frame against the windowpane.

I imagine the glass shattering and Lumpy LaChance tumbling out ass-over-teakettle. The last thing I see before he's gone forever is an *F* painted on the bottom of one shoe and a *U* painted on the other.

He shakes his head. "Keep it up, Cricket. You'll be smirking all the way to a jail cell."

This is effed. I didn't do nothing wrong. Why am I the friggin' villain instead of Pitbull? I hate this world. And every hypocritical lump of shit running it.

LaChance drops his Frankensteinian frame into his chair. He folds his pig-knuckle paws in front of his pink slug lips and scans the plastic award certificates on the wall like it's his first time being here. His face sags. Something about the blend of remorse and shame in his expression tells me he doesn't want to be here. And not just on account of me. His glassy blue eyes reveal this wasn't his choice. This wasn't the plan. This just happened. Like all things that just happen to losers. I mean, principal of a high school? What could be worse than that? A nun, I guess.

He drums his fingers on the desk. "After one pop to the nose, Pitbull very well may have learned his lesson and dropped the whole thing."

This is LaChance's biggest lie so far. My ass is starting to itch like I'm sitting in seawater. I glare into his eyes so he knows I know he's lying.

"You never know," he says.

I lean back and pull my hood on.

LaChance's lips tighten, and he slams his fist on the desk. "The bottom line is you incapacitated Buster with one punch, and for the rest of the fight he was on the ground completely helpless." LaChance quotation-marks the air when he says *fight,* which I find thoroughly offensive. Especially from a seven-foot monster who wouldn't step into the ring with Pitbull for all the Astroglide in Provincetown. "What's wrong with you? Do you take pleasure in hurting people? Do you enjoy inflicting pain on completely defenseless victims?"

LaChance's cheeks are glowing like targets under his orange eyebrows. The urge to jump on his desk and hurl a bull's-eye is making my hands quiver.

"Answer me, Cricket!"

I grip the arms of my chair. Rage bubbles float from my gut to my throat. Each one carries a message. But unlike LaChance's hot air, my bubbles are inflated with truth.

Buster Pitswaller is the biggest bully and meanest asshole in the school.

Pop.

He abuses everyone, including teachers.

Pop. Pop.

There isn't a person in this school who wouldn't love to kick the ever-lovin shit out of him, including teachers.

Pop. Pop. Pop.

But no one does because they're either too scared, too weak, or too shackled-up by rules.

Pop. Pop. Pop. Pop.

But not me 'cause I ain't scared (well, a little), I fight back, and fuck rules.

Pop. Pop. Pop. Pop. Pop.

He started it and I'm the one getting booted square in the blame sack.

Pop. Pop. Pop. Pop. Pop. Pop.

LaChance knows goddamn well what woulda happened tomorrow if I had stopped at one punch.

Pop. Pop. Pop. Pop. Pop. Pop. Pop.

How the hell can he leave the whole shithole world flipped upside down with all them truth bubbles trapped inside?

Pop. Pop. Pop. Pop. Pop. Pop. Pop. Pop.

While Pitbull strolls off into the sunset with his tasty squeeze.

Pop. Pop. Pop. Pop. Pop. Pop. Pop. Pop. Pop.

Fuck that! I ain't living in that world. Screw Pitbull. Screw LaChance. And screw this whole friggin' school. Go ahead, kick me out. See if I care.

Pop. Pop. Pop. Pop. Pop. Pop. Pop. Pop. Pop. Pop.

"I'm telling you right now, Cricket. You're not leaving this office until I get an explanation. We can sit here all night for all I care. I want to know what this fight was about, why you didn't walk away, and why you attacked Buster so viciously after he was down. I want some answers right NOW, mister!"

POP. POP. POP. POP. POP. POP. POP. POP. POP. POP.
SNAP.

I jump out of my seat and push my hood off. I step forward until my thighs are against LaChance's faux-wood desk. I stare into his fat, hairy face. It's a hard stare. The kind of stare that tells him what I'm thinking without words. His bulging blue eyes tell me he gets my meaning. I turn and head out the door.

In the hallway, an old framed photograph on the wall catches my attention. I lean in. It's LaChance standing beside two rows of smiling kids. Well, they're not all smiling. A dirty runt at the far end of the front row is scrunching a tough-guy scowl under the hood of his oversize Salvation Army sweatshirt.

My chest tightens and my forehead warms. Memories of drop-off day eight years ago flood my brain. The wrought-iron gate under the giant Naskeag Home for Boys sign. The granite gargoyles guarding the foyer. The rows of metal prison beds. The stainless-steel bathtub that looked like a giant mixing bowl. The click-click-click of the body snatcher's heels marching past my bed in the middle of the night.

My heart starts thumping like it's being pumped with too much blood. It feels like it might explode. I run down the hall, kick open the exit door, and run, run, run. I don't stop running until I reach the driveway to the Prison three miles away.

Just before I reach the wide granite steps, an invisible broadsword hara-kiris my gut, so I bang a sharp left down the rhododendron trail to the cliffs. I'm not ready to face Mother Mary Mortified. She's bound to know about the fight by now.

I drop my body onto the last boulder at the edge of a hundred-foot cliff and suck in the salty air. After catching my breath, I slip out my wallet and dig into the secret compartment for a flattened funk stick. I pinch it good with the tiny pliers on my Priss Army Knife that the generous Sisters of Mercy gave me last year for Christmas. If they only knew. *Have mercy. Classic.*

I fire it up and recline on the comfy boulder. No better pollution on the planet than the commingling fumes of ocean and herb.

I movie-reel the fight in my mind. The first punch. The first kick. The thud, thud, thud of Pitbull's head against the cobblestones.

Wynona's hair. Wynona's glare. Wynona's scream. *Fuck you, asshole.*

I suck another toke and close my eyes.

Pitbull's not the only one I obliterated today.

CHAPTER 1Ø

I feel a hard shove on my back, and I start slipping down the boulder over the edge of the cliff. I lunge my hands out to grab something, but the rock is smooth, and there's nothing to hold on to. Black terror explodes inside me. My mind goes blank. I scream.

A hand grabs my sweatshirt and yanks me back up the boulder. I roll away from the edge and scramble to my feet.

Grubs is laughing like crazy, pointing at me. "Oh my God, I got you so fucking good, dude."

I charge him and swing a wild right hook at his head. It connects on his chin and he drops like a sack of rice.

My entire body's trembling. "That ain't fucking funny, you fucking fuck!"

Grubs is on his back, holding his chin, still laughing. "Are you shitting me? That was the funniest damn thing

I've ever seen." He mimics my high-pitched scream. "Ahhhhhhhhh!"

"Fuck you, asshole." I grab one of his feet and drag him toward the cliff. He starts laughing louder.

I throw his foot to the ground. "You really wouldn't care, would you?"

He stands up and wiggles his chin with his hand. "What do I care? We all gotta die someday." He punches me on the shoulder. "Nice shot. I didn't even see it coming."

I try to light the joint with my shaking hands. "You scared the shit out of me, man." I finally get it lit, suck a giant toke, and pass it to Grubs.

He takes a hit and coughs a laugh. "Man, that was friggin' funny."

"Fuck you. I thought it was Buster Pitswaller come to settle the score."

"Yeah, I heard you pummeled that big idiot today. Good job. Should make collecting easier. No one will dare mess with you now."

I look away. I can feel Grubs staring at me.

"You need help with this dude?" he asks. "You think he'll come after you with the whole football team or something?"

That's exactly what I'm thinking. "Nah, I got it under control."

"Well, let me know. Hey, can you get out tonight?"

The herb's starting to mellow me out, and my body's not shaking as bad. "Is there ever a night I can't get out?"

Grubs smiles. "Good, 'cause I'm tapped, and I need to collect some dough. A bunch of idiots ain't paid up." He walks to the edge of the boulder. "Damn, it's beautiful out here."

The sea's dappled black and sparkly under the late-day sun. There's no horizon. No end to it all. I can relate.

I walk to the edge of the cliff.

I call this God Art. Not that I believe in the Dude. Frankly, I'm a Skepticalian. Still, it's a good name on account of no one knows shit about Him, and that's how I feel gazing at this supernatural scene. God Art. As opposed to Man Art, which is the copycat shit hanging in big city museums and rich folk's foyers. It's funny to think about. Poor-ass schleps like me get to view God Art every day, while rich-ass hoity-toits dangle million-dollar replicas over their bidets. *A Girl with a Watering Can.*

Grubs pulls a bottle of Southern Comfort from his pocket and takes a swig. "Damn, I guess if you gotta be incarcerated somewhere, you could do a hell of a lot worse than this." He hands me the bottle. "Just looking at it makes you think about shit. Like about doing shit. You know what I'm saying, Cricks?"

I chug some Comfort. "Yeah, sorta. It's the paradox of it that fucks me up, though."

"Speak English, dickhead."

I hand Grubs the bottle. "Beauty like this ain't right. It ain't supposed to be here."

"What the hell are you talking about?"

"When I see a scene like this, all I can think is, how can something like *that* have anything to do with something like *this*."

Grubs chugs a gulp and crinkles his face. "Something like what?"

I try to think of how to say what I'm thinking without sounding like a total dweeb, but I can't. "Nothing."

Grubs passes me the bottle. "You're high, dude."

What I want to tell him is that me and Art have a problem. The same way me and God have a problem. I mean, this scene is so *out* of this world, so inhuman and infinite, so boundless, so worthy and eternal. And human life is just so *not*. Yet I can't deny a connection. An intermingling. A gravity. A pull. I mean, it sucks at my soul. Probably so it can digest me and shit me out when it's done. That's how the infinite makes me feel. Like a hunk of beef it's gonna process and return to the dirt as fertilizer.

Art is supposed to engage and uplift, not enrage and set adrift. It's supposed to peekaboo a glimpse of the possible, not flaunt a mural of the enormous chasm between me and it. But that's what it does, so it's wicked depressing. Scenes like this bum me out 'cause the boundless makes me think of the bounded.

"Hey, I've been meaning to ask you something," Grubs says.

"What?"

"You got plans for next year?"

I imagine myself scraping skidmarks off the porcelain thrones at the Prison. "Yeah, I start pre-med at Harvard next fall."

Grubs smiles. "Seriously though."

"I'm weighing my options."

"Weighing your options. That's a good one. Naskeag ain't got a scale small enough."

I shrug. "No, I ain't doing nothing. I asked Mother Mary if I could keep living at the Prison and work off my eats and sheets, but she hasn't given me an answer yet. She has to clear it with the higher-ups. Why?"

"I'm thinking of expanding. Maybe start selling up in Bangor and Bar Harbor. They're big-ass towns, so I could make a shit-ton of bread. But I can't do it alone. I'd cut you in on the action. Then you wouldn't have to stay at Nun Central. You could get your own place."

Shit. Dealing. I never thought about that. I would hate to get busted, though, and end up in a real prison. *Squeeeeaaaal.* But Grubs is pretty well connected with the local cops on account of he rats out the competition, so I'd probably be okay. My own place. That would be friggin' awesome. "Sounds good."

"Cool." Grubs hands me the joint. "I gotta roll. Pick you up at ten fifteen?"

"Yeah, sure," I say, but he's already walking away.

I fire up what's left of the blunt and think about Wynona. Talk about God Art. So infinitely unattainable.

I suck the last toke of the dead soldier and consign his ashy corpse to the briny deep. I can't get Wynona's words out of my head. They're bouncing off my eardrums like a lame-ass rock ballad.

You're a fight magnet, you know it's true
You fight with every boy in school, get a clue
No one gets in as many fights as you
That's why you have no girlfriend
And your balls are blue

Don't judge me, you psychotic geek
And stop staring at my tits, you ugly freak
Take a high dive into Fisticuffin' Creek
While I scale to the top of Popularity Peak

Why do you hate everyone so much?
Your maniacal detachment is nothing but a crutch
You're a psycho loser

A drunk-ass boozer
A fucking stoner
A pathetic loner
Nothing but a fight magnet, yeah
A freaky loser fight magnet, yeah

I'm not mad at Wynona. I'm not even offended. What she said is true. In an outside-looking-in sort of way. Besides, a lot of what she said was probably in response to my remark about her dating Pitbull. Deep down, she has to know he's an asshole. That she's lying to herself. I called her on it, so of course she's gonna attack me.

It's not like I haven't thought about the stuff she said. I've thought about trying to be more social, more outgoing, to make more of an effort. But I can't. And it's not because I don't want to. It's really not. Some of the kids here are okay. Most of them are dickheads, but some are okay. There's a handful I could hang with. Maybe even be friends with.

But here's the thing. I have a wall. It's not an ordinary wall. Everyone has ordinary walls. My wall's the friggin' Great Wall of China.

I inch my feet closer to the edge. A gentle breeze pushes me back. The ocean swells rolling over the rocks remind me of my favorite God Art. Hurricanes. I don't feel disconnected from them. I feel close. At home. Alive. As alive as a dead person can feel.

Okay, enough talk of God and Art. As Sean Connery would say, *"Here endeth the lesson."*

I spot her shadow but don't turn. The endless desert of sea grants me permission to pretend she's not there. To imagine her voice. To detach from the g-force of guilt that's kept my feet planted here all these years. To imagine my responses. To pretend none of it's real. None of it.

"Come in for dinner, Cricket," Mother Mary says.

My stomach backflips. I dig in my pocket and twirl my ring, bracing for her hurricane of words.

"Andrew has a seat saved for you next to him."

What the hell's she playing at? How come she ain't screaming? I picture Andrew trembling against my chest in LaChance's waiting room. I slip my ring onto a finger of my non-punching hand.

"I must admit, Cricket, I'm at a complete loss. I simply don't know what to say. It's all been said so many times. Too many times. Just come inside. We'll deal with this tomorrow."

I step to the edge of the cliff. Closer than usual. Too close. The thought of jumping squeezes my skull. I twist my ring.

I feel her massive blackness beside me. "Kinda late in the season for cliff diving. Water's pretty nippy this time of year."

I speak to an emptiness that makes infinity look like a pail of piss. "Water temperature wouldn't matter. Full moon. Tide's way out."

She glances over the edge. "Oh my goodness. I guess you're right. That's one thing you can always count on in this place. High highs and low lows. No way around that."

Clouds drift overhead and the sky darkens. "There's one way."

A starched rustle like wind over dead leaves. "That's not a way."

"How would you know?"

"I wasn't born this old, Crick. I was seventeen once." Fabric flaps like a flag in a storm. "Teenage years are like the full moon. They push and pull much more powerfully than at other times."

"Don't matter one way or the other. Tide's out, you smash on the rocks. Tide's in, you drown."

Her voice is dark and heavy, like the sea. "It matters to me."

The density crushes my chest. *Why?*

Cloud soft. "It matters."

Waves crash far, far away. So far away I feel them inside.

"I know what a struggle it can be, Crick. I know it feels like this darkness will last forever, but it won't. You have to trust me on that. I know it's a lot to ask, but you have to trust me on that one point."

"No offense, but it's your job to say that. That don't necessarily make it true."

"It's more than a job, Cricket. You're more than a job. You've been here a long time. Longer than anyone. Like me. You know I don't lie to you. Good or bad, I'm always straight with you. You know that. True, I can't predict the future. But I can speak from experience."

The pressure in my head builds. I take a deep breath to keep from choking on my words. "I'll be there in a minute. Tell Andrew to keep saving my seat."

"He's quite the celebrity tonight. Not that I can say I'm happy about the reason, but he's enjoying the spotlight."

Mother Mary's shadow fades with the afternoon light.

"Don't be long." It's weird how many shades of dark there are. "It's pasta night. Sister Gwendolyn made her famous garlic bread."

I listen as her footsteps disappear.

I want to say thank you to Mother Mary. Thank you for letting me live here all these years. Thank you for the warm, dry room. The bed, blankets, hot showers, and free eats. The soap and towels. The toothpaste and toothbrushes. The clothes, even though they're hand-me-downs. The library card. The notebooks and pencils at Christmas. The trips to Principal LaChance's office after the fights. The yelling. The punishing. The grounding.

No, I don't want to say thank you for any of that stuff. I was just trying to sound normal. If I was gonna say thank you to Mother Mary for anything, which, of course, I'm not, it'd be for not locking me in the basement when I cried too loud. For not making me walk to the store to buy Lucky Strikes in bare feet in January when I complained about the holes in my sneakers. For not tying me to the bed when I wet it. For not piercing my ear with a drug needle. For not pushing me into street fights with crackhead culls twice my size and betting against me. For not beating the back of my legs with a ********. For not Scotch-taping matches to my **** and ************. For not ****************************
****
****
****
****************.

But like I said, thank-yous ain't gonna cross these chapped lips anytime soon. 'Cause in the end, adults are all the same. Ain't no difference in the what. Only in the when.

I pull the letter from my pocket and read Moxie's

words under the last glow of daylight. I could have read them just as well from inside my pocket. *Why do you want out?*

When I turn, Mother Mary is a distant apparition.

I follow my ghostly shadow toward the darkening Prison walls.

CHAPTER 11

I get a standing ovation when I enter the dining room. Don't that beat off? Smash the bloody crap out of a mutant arse mole, and the Little Orphan Andys who've been raised their entire lives by Sister Turntheothercheek and Padre Peacebewithyou stand and applaud the evil marauder. Holy reality-flippin' cartwheels, Batman. Pass me another slice of upside-down cake.

Sister Gwendolyn is doling out smellorific slabs of garlic bread when the ruckus erupts, so she drops the basket and claps her hands, but not for the same reason as the Little Ones. She's trying to hunker control of the underdog ovation, but the jittery animals keep barking. The Little Dudes' claps must be connected to some invisible, anti-gravity heart-pumping dingus in Sister Gwendolyn's chest, because her plump cheeks are redder than a tampon dumpster at a that-time-of-the-month convention.

The crazy chimps finally stop tossing their feces around and sit down. I take my seat next to Andrew, who's glowing like a little hunk of God Art that fell from the sky. Funny how life waddles and swaddles this way and that.

The Little Ones start firing questions at me about the Pitbull beatdown like I'm Muhammad Ali, but a funny thing happens: All of a sudden, I'm flooded with the nut-strangling realization of how easily the fight could have done a tumultuous backflip. One little slip, and the Little Ones would be pressing their palms together outside a hospital emergency room instead of inside this free-eats pavilion. Damn, life sure is carving crop circles in my ass tonight.

I wait until there are no nuns around and clink the congregation to order on my Mayor McCheese milk glass. "Dudes, listen up. You gotta hear me and hear me good on something. If I'd missed that first punch on Pitbull, he woulda pummeled me into mincemeat pie. Fightin' ain't all roses and fairy tales. Remember that if you ever decide to swing. It's a two-way street, monkeys. Don't go cracking open that giant pumpkin if you ain't willing to swallow a few slimy seeds." Yeah, I'm deep, I admit it.

Some of the Little Ones dribble out nervous giggles. Others cock their heads. I survey the rows of faces. Most of them realize they're celebrating something they want no part of. Like how rugby's fun to watch on the boob tube but being at the bottom of that pile would suck balls.

"And remember. I prepared long and hard for that throwdown by pounding heavy in the boathouse for two hours every morning while you ladies were cuddled in your beddy-byes, dreaming of sugarplums and peeing your panties."

Their prepubescent screeches scale the mahogany walls. If you're wondering what the Prison dining room looks like, think Newport mansion. I ain't kidding. This place makes the high school cafeteria look like a kebab cart in Sarajevo. The walls are dark wood like in the chapel, and the dangling chandeliers are so giant that if one of them slinky links snaps, it's mashed brains for dessert. There are four long wood tables like from a King Arthur movie, and stained-glass windows that make you feel like you're eating your Last Supper. There's twelve kids at each table, which is kinda funny, right, like it's nosh time at Jesus' crib. I wonder if the nuns planned it that way. We have forty-eight disciples here, not twelve.

The Little Ones deliver their dishes to the kitchen and follow me to the story room.

I get excused from cleanup on account of I'm an extra-fabulous fabulist. (It means phantasmagorical fable fabricator, Billy Shakemyspear.) Yeah, I'm a regular Brothers Dimm.

The storytime room used to be an open-air guard tower, but the charitable contractors who renovated the Prison decided it should be fancified for the homeless lads, so they removed the machine-gun turrets, added a roof, and wrapped the sides with floor-to-ceiling windows. The nuns plunked down a few stubby bookshelves, tossed in a couple of tons of previously-drooled-on pillows and previously-farted-on beanbag chairs, and voilà, the Poor Boys Fifty-Book Readatorium in the Clouds was born. It's actually a pretty cool place. I sneak up here when there's a thick fog on the bay, and it's eerie, like you're in a spaceship.

The best part is that to get here you have to pass through an ancient steel door with a menacing Do Not Enter sign bolted to it. Creeping in through that dungeon doorway gives my stories goosebumps they'd never have down in the game room.

Storytime's popular with the Little Ones, so I always get a good crowd, like twenty or twenty-five. I do a separate storytime for the littler Little Ones on Sundays.

I motion to Charlie Brittlebones to close the door.

"Settle down, munchkins. And move in closer. I don't want no outside ears eavesdropping on my testes-frying tribulations."

Grins flash, whispers hiss, and scraggly-haired heads rubberneck. The Little Ones are used to my worditatious confabulations. Half the time they don't get the crooked configurations, but they giggle anyway on account of the words sound silly.

"Can it, animals. I have some news." I raise my arms like a modern-day Moses hushing the multitude.

Eyes bulge into perfect silence.

"It is time you heard the truth about this place we call home, this Orphan Island." I say "Orphan Island" all deep and creepy to tingle the peach fuzz on their berry sacks into a bedwetting frenzy. I dim the lights and extricate a purple velvet bag from my knapsack. Necks crane to piddle a gander. They figure I'm gonna yank out an invisibility potion or dead bat or rattlesnake. Little Dudes are so goofy. I empty the contents onto the rickety, low-tide-smelling coffee table built from an old wooden lobster pot and a scratchy square of Plexiglas and step back so they can see.

The Little Ones gawk at the oddly shaped seashells.

"Any of you chowdaheads know the reality of how this palace sprouted from perdition to fruition?"

Freckle-faced Justin Bellamy raises a curled hand to his chin like he's imitating a retarded meerkat.

I nod.

"Mr. Cherpin, Sister Sarah said Jesus changed the

prison into our house the same way he changed five loaves of bread and two fishes into enough food to feed five thousand people."

I imitate the gymnasium buzzer. "*Ahhhnnnttt.* And you believe that cow plop, Justin FellOnMe?" The Little Ones giggle. "No, Jesus had nothing to do with busting this prison into a playpen. He was too busy remodeling souls to be bothered with earthly renovation projects. But it was someone just as mystical and mythical."

I pause to make sure they're all paying attention.

"Now, before I commiserate this secret tale, I need every one of you snot-nosed ankle-biters to promise you won't breathe a single word of it to a single soul outside this room. You got that?"

Heads bob.

"I need to hear it, jellysticks."

Promises puke at my feet like the last gasp of froth at the end of a dead wave.

I punch my fist into my palm. "You rugrats know the punishment for breaking a promise."

Mouths stretch and eyes stare.

"All right then."

I pace in front of the black glass and glance around the room all CIAish. "Now, some of you are gonna think this story is a bunch of Harry Potter hogwash, but it ain't. If you numbskulls spent the kinda time I do in the library instead of mining green gems out of your nose caves, you'd appreciate the geomorphic science behind it."

I sit on the edge of the coffee table, corral the shells into the bag, and pass it to Sherman Tewksbury with a finger twirl. He removes a shell and passes it to the next kid.

"This is the story of the founder of Orphan Island—Apollo Zipper."

Laughter erupts.

I jump to my feet. "You think making fun of a dude's name is cool?"

Scary silence. The little nuggets catch on to their faux pas lickety-split.

"You think a dude ain't got enough to deal with in life without you little scabs picking at his given name? That's better."

I settle back down and tell the Little Ones a goofy story I made up about this sixteen-year-old British kid who took a trip to Paris with his parents but never made it on account of his ferry was sunk by a rogue wave in the English Channel during the crossing.

"You're probably wondering what this sad aquatic tragedy has to do with our silly little lives here on Orphan Island. Well, I'll explain what it has to do with us, and I'll edify you on how I know all these historical gee-whizzes."

I fraudulate a tale about hearing Apollo's story from an old-timer I met at the Naskeag Public Library a few years back who told me his name was Zachary Zipper and claimed to be Apollo's great-great-great-great-grandson.

A little hand way in the back of the room goes up.

"Who's that?" I ask.

Gregory Bullivant's pudgy towhead floats above the sea of hair. He's a brainy little sixth grade butterball who helps me tutor some of the other Little Ones.

"Yo, Bull."

"Excuse me, Mr. Cherpin, but how could Zachary Zipper be a direct descendant of Apollo Zipper if Apollo died in the ferry accident?"

Faces scrunch, eyes squint, noses crinkle, and asses are diligently scratched.

I rattle my fist in the air like I'm clanging a front porch dinner bell. "Ding, ding, ding, ding, ding. Well, I'm glad every pumpkin head in here ain't mashed summer squash. How could this old dude be Apollo Zipper's great-great-whatever-grandkid if Apollo died when he was only sixteen?"

Archie Dalper raises his hand. "Maybe his kids were orphans like us."

I glare at Archie. "Archibald, if I had a stun gun, I'd zippity-zap your minuscule testicles." The Little Ones giggle. "How can a dead kid adopt kids?"

"Oh yeah, right."

Another sky-hunkering hand. "Maybe he had kids before he got on the ferry."

"Well, slightly less retarded, but remember, this dude was only sixteen, and he didn't have a permanent squeeze he was canoodling back home."

Hands wave and mouths bullhorn.

"Maybe he had clone babies, like in a test tube."

"Maybe he had brothers and sisters who had babies, so they was kinda like his kids."

"Maybe God sent him kids like the Virgin Mary."

"Maybe he didn't die."

I jump up and scan the ragged heads. "Who said that?"

"Me, Mr. Cherpin."

"Who's me, nub-ass? Stand up."

Aaron Weidlemeyer slowly stands.

"What'd you say, Wienerschnitzel?"

Schnitzel is scared schnitzel-less, so he freezes.

"Come on, Wienerschnitzel, what'd you say?"

"I said, maybe he didn't die, sir."

"Wasn't you paying attention, Schnitzelgruben? I said he was never seen again after the ferry tanked."

"I know, sir, but you didn't say he died. Maybe he banged his head and got amnesty or something and didn't remember who he was, and some French people took care of him and raised him, like wolves do."

"Well, well, well, Whineyschnitzel. You ain't half as stupid as you look, you little frankfurter. Your story's only half right, but it's a hell of a lot righter than the mental macaroni these Chef Boyardees been dishing up."

Aaron smiles big and wide, then sits.

"Ladies and ladies, Aaron is correctamoondo. Apollo Zipper did not drown on that fateful day. His ship sank, but he did not drown."

The room fills with hushed *ooooooohhhh*s.

The door swings open and Mother Mary Makemyday enters. You woulda thought she was wielding a .44 Magnum the way the Little Dudes jump into a single-file line.

I cross my arms over my chest and rumple an intimidating stare. "Excuse me, Mother Superior, but I'm not done with my story." I'm thinking Mother *Posterior* but don't say it.

"You're done for tonight, Cricket."

She snaps her fingers and the room empties.

"I was just getting warmed up."

"Cricket, you were born warmed up."

I grab my knapsack and head for the door.

"Cricket."

I stop.

"Tomorrow morning. My office. Ten a.m. We need to talk."

"There's nothing to talk about."

"I believe there is."

"Same old story, same old song and dance."

"You can reserve the ambiguous song references for the musically oblivious, Cricket. I was rocking out to Aerosmith before you were born."

Mother Mary Metallica rocking out. A creepy consideration. Her shoes are big and square like Frankenstein's. Tough to dance in.

"You've been suspended from school again. This time for a week."

"Right is right."

"I assume you're speaking to the suspension."

"No."

"Fighting isn't the answer, Crick."

"Maybe not in your world."

"We live in the same world."

I turn and glare at Mother Mary to see if she's gonna keep a straight face after that lie. Her face is granite. "We ain't even in neighboring galaxies." I turn to leave.

"Oh, and by the way . . ."

I stop.

"Storytime for the big kids is now twice a week."

I spin around. "Are you shittin' me?"

She jabs a finger at me. "Twice a week. No exceptions."

"What?! I couldn't rattle tales to these midget twits twice a week if I wanted to."

"I don't care if you want to or don't want to. Storytime is twice a week from now on, so you'll just have to do whatever *the hell* it is you do in that Tasmanian devil mind of yours to come up with more stories. Discussion closed."

"Request to reopen."

"Request denied."

"What the hell?"

Mother Mary pinches the bridge of her nose and sucks in a few deep breaths. "I was listening at the door, Cricket. The good Lord has blessed you with an imaginative mind and an energetic spirit. It's high time you put them to better use."

"This is bull . . ."

"Pardon? Something to add?"

"Bull . . . oney."

"Look at it this way, Crick. You have a whole week off from school to get a head start on lots of interesting adventures. You can work on them in between the mountain of extra chores I'll be assigning you tomorrow."

I glare at Mother Mary knowing it's a wasted glare. She knows me too well. I turn.

"Good night, Cricket. Sleep well."

"Yeah, right."

CHAPTER 12

*O*n the way to my room, I peer into the chapel to see if any of the nuns are begging God's forgiveness for pushing us meek little orphans around. You know, on account of us inheriting the earth and all that. I've been waiting on my deed for seventeen years, but nothing yet.

The chapel's empty. They musta all got their pardons already. I tiptoe inside. There's a candle burning on the altar. A hundred years ago, this was the men's shower room. Caretaker told me. That's probably why the air feels so thick and steamy. He says converting a prison bathhouse into a Christian chapel is one of God's all-time best practical jokes. I'm not sure what he means, but I'm guessing it has something to do with bathing and baptism or the dirty getting clean, or something like that. Whatever it is, I know Caretaker doesn't mean any disrespect because he believes in God and loves Him a wicked lot and would never do anything to offend Him on purpose. Unlike me.

I slide into the back pew. I don't like being too close to God's workbench on account of a stray thorn might catch me in the eye. I always feel shifty and slippery in here, like some dirty old man trying to sneak a peek at a little girl taking a tinkle.

Like I said before, I don't believe in God. Well, I don't believe in God the way the nuns and priests want me to. I don't believe some white-haired old dude is sitting in a Barcalounger on a cloud, doling out good and bad and happy and sad with an almighty Xbox controller. That's just stupid.

I've read most of the Bible. Talk about nutseefuckingkookoo. God punishing people for being good. God loving some people more than others. God asking fathers to kill their kids as proof of their faith. God giving kings special powers so they can slaughter entire nations. God not jumping in when His own kid gets murdered. That's some crazy shit. If that's the God they want me to believe in, no thank you. Ship me off to Hell right now so I can toss back a cold one with the zillion other people God never tortured with His infinite kindness. If you ask me, the existence of the Bible is the strongest argument against the existence of God.

I believe in something. I'm just not sure what. I think

the way life started, that Big Bang thing, is a clue. Like maybe God's the explosion, and we're the particles, and the purpose of it all is to get back together. Hey, I know I ain't no Plato or anything, but it makes more sense than believing some old fart is standing beside a pearly gate in a velvet bathrobe with a Naughty and Nice clipboard like Santa Claus.

I hear a sniffle up near the altar, so I stand to see who it is. If I'm wrong and God's been eavesdropping, I could be in deep shit. I peek over the back of the second pew and see a curly brown mop nestled in two tiny hands. It's Charlie Brittlebones.

I slide into the pew next to him and kneel. The kneeler creaks, and Charlie jumps. His eyes are red, and his cheeks are wet.

"Sorry, Charlie. Didn't mean to disturb you. Just wanted to send up a few prayers before bedtime."

Charlie cracks a smile under the tears. "Yeah, sure. I ain't never seen you pray, Cricket. Even when the nuns are watching."

I was eight the last time I prayed. It was in my mom's bathroom. I begged God to bring my baby brother, Eli, back to life. God ignored me and I never prayed again.

"Yeah, I ain't big on prayer, Charlie."

"How come? Don't you believe in God?"

I look at Charlie's big brown eyes bulging out of his

pale, skinny face. "I don't know, Charlie. God kinda confuses me."

He wipes his face with his sleeve. "Me, too."

"What are you praying for?"

"Lots of stuff."

"Like what?"

"I don't wanna say. You'll goof on me."

"No, I won't. I promise."

Charlie glances at the crucifix behind the altar, then at the floor. "It's stupid."

"Tell me."

He speaks without looking up. "I pray that some long-lost relative, like an aunt from Australia or something, will find out about my parents dying and take me to live with her in her ten-bedroom mansion."

My head gets hot and fuzzy.

"Stupid, huh?" Charlie mumbles.

"No. That's a good prayer."

"It's stupid 'cause it'll never happen."

"You never know. Stranger stuff has happened."

Charlie rubs his eyes. "You can say that again."

I get off my knees and sit in the pew. I pat Charlie on the back.

His lips tighten, and he grips the seatback like he's gonna rip it out of the floor. "You know what else I pray for?"

"What?"

He faces me. "To be like you. To not be scared of bullies."

I think about the snake party in my gut this afternoon right before the Pitbull fight. "I'll let you in on a secret if you promise not to tell anyone."

He nods. "I promise."

"I get plenty scared before fights."

"Yeah, right."

"I ain't lying. My gut knots up, and my arms and legs go all wobbly and numb."

Charlie pushes himself off the kneeler and climbs onto the bench. "The same thing happens to me when I get shoved around."

I scan his spindly neck, scrawny arms, and cardboard chest. "You want me to teach you how to fight, Charlie?"

He looks away. "Nah. I don't want to be a fighter. I just wanna stop being scared."

"I don't see how you can be one without the other."

"Huh?"

"Not being scared and not being a fighter. Fear and fighting are intertwined. If you don't know how to fight, you'll be afraid to fight. If you're afraid to fight, you'll get pushed around all the time. If you get pushed around all the time, you'll always be afraid."

Charlie slumps his shoulders. "Guess I'll always be afraid."

"Unless you learn how to fight."

Charlie extends his arms toward me. "Look at me. Penelope Lintmeyer can whup me."

I smile and extend my arms toward Charlie. "Look at *me*. You ever figure these string bean arms could pummel Pitbull Pitswaller?"

Charlie picks up a Bible off the seat and smoothes the cover like he's dusting it. "I just figure there's gotta be another way."

"Another way what?"

"Another way to be brave without fighting."

"Well, let me know when you find it."

Charlie opens the Bible and rubs a random page with his fingertips. "Jesus got picked on all the time, and he never fought. And he wasn't a coward."

"Yeah, but Jesus . . ." I run out of words. I don't have an answer for that one.

Charlie closes the Bible and slides it into the rack on the seatback. "Maybe I'm asking for too much, and that's why God doesn't give me nothing."

"I don't know, Charlie. I ain't never been able to figure out how He decides who gets what."

"Me neither. Sister Elizabeth says we're supposed to be grateful for what we got 'cause plenty of kids around the world got it a lot worse."

I look at the giant wooden Jesus on the cross. The red velvet curtain hanging behind his crucified carcass looks like some religious fanatic doused it with a hundred gallons of holy blood. The carving on the bony savior is intricate. You can see every rib, muscle, vein, and strain in the poor dude's bashed body. Talk about having it a lot worse.

That's the thing that's always crimped my cojones about his limp-wristed turn-the-other-cheek philosophy. What omnipotent moron would let a herd of hornswoggled hypocrites whip the holy ghost out of him when he could walk on water and then abracadabra that salty sea into a nice glass of Cabernet? Why'd this all-powerful dude let those evil bastards kick his peace-lovin' ass up and down the dusty Jerusalem donkey trails?

And what about his pops? I mean, this dude was the *son* of God, which means he had a *dad*. Now, I can see a human dad standing on the sidelines while his kid sizzles in the hot sun, 'cause I know how evil human dads can be. But a God dad doing that? A God dad chillaxing on a poofy cloud with a bowl of popcorn and a brewsky, watching *Desperate Prophets of Jerusalem County* while His kid gets tortured to death—when He could save him with a wink? He flooded the friggin' earth on account of a bunch of coattail relatives being dickheads, but He ain't willing to sneeze up a simple Dead Sea tsunami for His own son? At least give His kid the thumbs-up to fight back. That's some backward-ass shit.

That's where my faith gets completely dingleberried.

Jesus' dad is way too human to be the real enchilada. Makes an orphan wanna stay an orphan. Who the fuck would want a dad like that?

Charlie scooches past me. "I gotta go. They're gonna do lights out soon, and I don't wanna spend another weekend scrubbing toilets."

"Okay, see ya. Let me know if you change your mind."

"About what?"

"About me teaching you how to fight. After a few weeks in the gym, you'll be able to whup Penelope Lintmeyer's scrawny ass."

He grins and scurries out the side door.

I lie on the bench and stare at the ceiling. The glow from the candle dances on the knotty pine. I pull my letter from my pocket. The bloodstains are smeared. Like the words have been bleeding.

What in particular sucks? Why do you want out?

I read the questions over and over. I don't know what it is about Moxie's comments that freak me out so much. Is she serious? Does she really expect me to answer her questions?

Excellent start but needs more detail.

Excellent start? My letter was supposed to be *The End.*

Why do you want out?

I sit up and take another gander at the shadowy

Jesus. His chiseled face looks peaceful. Happy, almost. Imagine that. Being all calm and content while assholes are nailing you to a tree. Must be on account of he understood. Understood the *why*.

It suddenly dawns on me why Moxie's comments are shriveling my nutsack. It's not that she's asking the questions. It's that I can't answer them. I don't understand the *why*. My *why*. Not with any *specificity*. I didn't compose my Dear Life letter. I puked it. Truth is, I haven't given my *why* much thought. *Why do I want out?*

I look up at Jesus' pained, peaceful face. He's at peace because he understood his *why*.

I look down at my letter. I suddenly know what I need to do. What I need to accomplish.

Back in my room, I grab a pen and notebook, climb onto the fire escape, and recline in my lawn chair.

Dear Life, You Suck
Reason Number One
By Cricket Cherpin

ADULTS SUCK AND I DON'T WANT TO BE ONE.

My parents are adults. Where the fuck are they? Splitsville, North Crackalina, that's where. They know they have a kid. I ain't no Homeland Security secret. What the fuck? How can you make a kid and then punt him over the backyard fence and be like, I'm bored, game over, let's go grab a beer. It doesn't make sense.

Not that I'd want those deadbeat crackheads for parents anyway. I read my file. My biological whore was worse than my foster floozy. All she ever did was drugs, crime, and time. Went to prison twice. Probably isn't even out. Huh, wouldn't that be a stitch in the ass seam? We both end up in the same crimeatorium. The file didn't say nothing about her tricking, but I wouldn't be surprised. She had a serious love affair with Captain Crack and Major Meth and had to support those bloodsuckers somehow.

My biological sperm worm wasn't any better. Didn't just do drugs. Sold 'em too. The bad ones. He's still on the inside too if he hasn't made parole. I hope he's getting beat to a pulp every day so the asshole knows what it feels like.

I've thought about looking them up through one of them Find Your Lost Parents websites. Not for a teary-eyed hugfest. More like a cheery-bye plugfest. Yeah, I've considered tracking them down for the sole purpose of planting lead slugs in their soulless hearts. See what color their blood is. Black, probably. Black heart, black blood.

You probably think I'm kidding, but I ain't. Grubs can get me an untraceable hunting rifle. I've already asked him. I'd do it, too. Walk right up to them and blow their fugly heads off. I wouldn't even ask for an explanation. They'd just lie anyway. I bet I'd get away with it too. Who's gonna waste their time tracking down the killer of those two wastoids? I'd be doing society a favor. Plus, even if I got caught, all I'd have to do is weep up an Academy Award—winning sob story for the jury. They'd eat it up like soap opera spongecake.

I mean, if you hate kids, don't have 'em. That's all I'm saying. I ain't saying kids are anything great, and I can see how they can be a royal pain in the ass and the wallet. But shit, don't have 'em then. Ruin your own life if you want. Who gives a shit? But why drag down some helpless little son-of-a-biscuit with you?

I finish scribbling Reason Number One at ten o'clock. Just in time to sneak down the fire escape and rendezvous with Grubs.

CHAPTER 13

Grubs musta dumped me on my fire escape sometime during the night, because I wake up to Mother Mary Megamiffed walloping me in the head with a broom like I'm a rascally raccoon. I don't realize what she's so pissed about until I sit up and see the dozen empty beer cans on the fire escape. *Good one, Grubs.* He likes to pull pranks like that. One morning, Mother Mary found me in boxer shorts, a bra, high heels, and a priest collar. An instant Grubs Dillar classic.

Mother Mary climbs onto her broom and flies away, so I head inside.

I can't remember how last night ended. After collecting, we went to this dive bar in Penobscot called Duckies where the bartenders don't check IDs, and the rest of the night's a blur.

I change into my workout duds and check out the inspirational literature Mother Mary Micromanage has left on my pillow. She's like Felix Ungar in *The Odd Couple*. "*I told you a hundred and fifty-eight times, I cannot stand little notes on my pillow. 'We are all out of Corn Flakes. F.U.' It took me three hours to figure out that 'F.U.' was Felix Ungar.*"

She's always leaving crap in my room about college or technical schools or job opportunities in the local area. Today it's a brochure for Saint Alban's Seminary on Grand Manan Island. *Holy cow!* Sister Sarah must have slipped some LSD into Mother Mary's BLT.

Mother Mary Missionary likes to torture me on a regular basis with discussions about my future. Adults call it "career," but nuns call it "calling." The only difference is that normal blokes with parenting folks pick their own careers, whereas God picks paths for Prison inmates. I can see Him now, skull-thumping futuristic follies for my dirtbag ass. His long white beard and squinty eyes poking through a poofy cloud with a Burger King hair net in one hand and a greasy spatula in the other, belting out a hymnalicious *yodleaaayheehooooo*.

After stealing a few aspirin from Sister Sarah's private stash in the kitchen pantry, I head to the boathouse. I usually work out at six a.m., but I wristed too much silly cider last night. No regrets. I'll sweat the booze out in no time. I start on the heavy bag.

Caretaker shows up at his usual time, 6:55 a.m. Sometimes he's early, like 6:45. Sometimes he's late, like

6:58. Never later than 6:59, though. His hours are seven to three, six days a week, and he's never late. And he never misses a day. Flu, blizzards, holidays, nothing. Caretaker's a worker. He's wicked responsible.

Work is like religion to Caretaker. He worships it and fears it and all that other voodoo bullshit. I know it's not about money, even though he talks like it is. *No bacon from the man means no bacon in the pan.* That's one of his favorites. He's proud of what he does. Talks about it like he's a hunk of clay and work is the hand that molded him into the crooked flowerpot he is today. Like he wouldn't exist without it, or he'd exist but not in the same way. Not as a man. A real man. Instead, he'd be like one of those dried-out hunks of clay we see standing in line at the welfare office when we drive to the hardware store. Caretaker shakes his head and *tssssk*s every time we pass the place, like the folks are standing in line to purchase one-way tickets to Hell. He talks like he'd die without work, and I know he ain't talking about body dying. Work is deep in him like blood.

"Drop your chin, slackass." Caretaker's raspy growl interrupts my proletaratious musings.

I glance at him through stinging sweat beads. As usual, he's not looking at me. *Can't interrupt work for a damn fool kid like you.* He's wiping tools and hanging them on the wall. He must have borrowed them to fix something at the shithole shack he lives in down on the

Papadingo River. I've been there a bunch of times. Just him and his old lady. He has a bunch of kids, but they're grown and scattered all over the country.

He turns halfway to me. He can hear my hangover. "Damn it, Sally, snap the jab. You leave it hangin' out like that, you're gonna get your head squashed like a melon." He punches his fist into his palm. "Snap. Snap. Snap." He shakes his head and waves his hand at me like I'm an annoying housefly. "You think you ain't gonna be brain-dead and sore in the tenth round, you drunk slacker?"

I grit my teeth and slam the bag with all my might, but my balance is off and the bag spins.

"Holy Moses, look at you. Put your body into it, Nancy. Shoulder, hip, heel, all together. Step, spin, throw."

I'm so tired, I can barely lift my arms.

"For the love of Pete, my momma hits harder than you, and she's been dead twenty years." Caretaker buckles over and slaps his thighs.

I try to throw my body into my punches, but it's not cooperating.

"Good Lord, Lucy, I know you weigh less than my left nut, but power that shot, you lazy bastard."

I fall into an old lawn chair and pull my gloves off. The gauze on my finger is red and sticky.

"Finished so soon, Mabel?" Caretaker's tinkering with something at the bench.

"I've been awake and here since six thirty, asshole."

"Yeah, sure. You probably ain't even been to bed yet." He snuffles at his joke.

"Yeah, I have. With your wife."

Caretaker turns and raises his left eyebrow, which he always does right before saying something he thinks is clever. "Yeah, the missus did mention a nightmare she had 'bout a visit from a pale, dickless alien." He cackles and turns back to his work. "You should probably drink less during the week, Crick. You wouldn't have such crazy hallucinations."

I hop onto the bench next to Caretaker. He's wire-brushing some rusty mooring bolts. "Whatcha cleaning them for? Nuns ain't had boats out in years."

He answers without looking up. "Well, they was rusty, and you never know. Maybe Mother Superior's thinking 'bout taking up water skiing."

I grab one of the bolts. "Imagine her in a bikini?"

"No, thank you." He takes the bolt back and sprays it with WD-40. It gets all over his hand, but he doesn't care. His hands are like beat-up leather gloves. "I heard you laid out Pitbull pretty solid yesterday."

"Yup."

"So the strategy worked."

"Like a charm."

"I knew it would." He bangs the U-joint on the bench, and rust and oil fly everywhere.

I don't say anything.

"No need to thank me."

"Okay."

"Asshole."

I skip breakfast and go to Home Depot with Caretaker as a way of saying thanks, and he knows it, but he's cool enough not to say anything or rub it in my face. He got permission for me to go by calling Mother Mary and saying he needed help loading the van. We shoot the bull about a bunch of stupid stuff. I like talking to Caretaker 'cause he talks to me like I'm a real person. He never preaches, either. He's got opinions, and he'll bullhorn me a righteous keister-kicking when he thinks I'm being an idiot, but it's never preachy. Imagine a real preacher trying that. *Stop sinning, ya stupid asshole!* Hell, it'd probably work, but the congregation wouldn't stick around long enough to hear it. Churchies don't like getting bogged down with spiritual trifles like truth. They just wanna pop in for a quick fix of holy-ass wafer and blood-curdled wine. Rip off a quick forgiveness certificate like they're snagging a number at the deli. Something to give them the strength to asshole their way through the upcoming week with a clear conscience.

"How many days you get?" Caretaker hands me a bundle of roofing shingles.

"What makes you think I got any?"

"Don't gotta be no fortuneteller to know you're gonna get days for putting a kid in the hospital with your fists."

"Pitbull never went to the hospital."

"Yeah he did. Last night. My niece seen him. Said that fat head of his wouldn't stop gushing, so they had to stitch it up with 'bout a hundred stitches."

Shit. The cobblestones. My gut spasms like Caretaker's dropped a ten-pound box of roofing nails on it. A week suspension might be the least of my worries.

"So how many did you get?"

"Five."

"Shit, that ain't nothing. You can help me while you're off."

"I think Mother Scary's booking me solid with Prison chores."

"Well, you can work for me when you ain't working for her. Idle hands is the devil's playground."

"Principal LaChance thinks *my* hands are the devil's playground."

Caretaker chuckles and hands me another bundle. "Did you start it?"

"What the fuck kinda question is that?"

"Just making sure. If you didn't start it, then as far as I'm concerned every son-of-a-bitch in that backward-ass school can pucker up and smooch my hairy black ass."

"I'll tell them you said so when I return."

"I don't give a damn. Tell 'em what you want. Ignorant sons-of-bitches think they're doing you slack-ass Willies favors by teaching you how it ain't. The spoiled giveme-somes they graduate from that baloney factory ain't got a goddamn clue how to get along in the real world. Gimme, gimme, gimme, that's all them lazy corndogs know."

Caretaker's fun to listen to when he's on a roll. You don't need to wind him up or spur him on or nothing. Once he gets going, he's like a boulder tumbling down a mountainside. He just gets louder and faster.

"What the hot damn kinda example are they teaching them kids when they punish the only one in the whole flippin' place that got the sack to do right by them kiddlins who can't defend themselves and teach that gorilla son-of-a-bitch a lesson 'bout bullying? They shoulda dragged your skinny ass onto that leaky gymnasium floor and jammed a ten-foot trophy in your bruised-up hands for laying that fat SOB out. That place is upside down and inside out, if you ask me."

Caretaker shifts into mumbling mode, so I can't make head or tail of what he's saying, but it doesn't matter 'cause it's always the same thing.

On the way home we take a detour and Caretaker pulls down a skinny side street, parking beside an overloaded dumpster.

"What are we doing here?"

"C'mon, I wanna show you something."

I follow Caretaker through a dinged-up steel door into a brick building that smells musty, like the laundry room at the Prison. As we walk toward a set of red swinging doors, I hear men yelling and rap music blaring. Caretaker pushes the doors open.

It's a boxing gym. There's a bunch of guys slamming heavy bags, jumping rope, and shadowboxing in front of a long wall of mirrors. There's two rings with guys boxing in them and trainers hanging on the ropes shouting instructions.

Caretaker ambles up to one of the trainers and smacks him on the shin. The guy's old, pale, and wrinkly like a bleached raisin. He nods at Caretaker, scowls at me, and turns back to the fighters. He yells nonstop until the bell dings. He reminds me of Mickey from *Rocky*. *"Get out of here! Don't ya ever interrupt me while I'm conductin' business. Move your little chicken asses out."*

After the boxers finish their fight, the trainer climbs down from the ring and shakes Caretaker's hand with two hands, like a politician. He smiles, big and toothless.

Caretaker turns and points at me. "Bolo, this is Cricket."

Bolo crinkles his already crinkled face. "Cricket? What the fuck kinda nickname is Cricket? That ain't gonna scare no one. Only gonna make guys wanna squish him under their boot."

Caretaker laughs. "It ain't a nickname, Bolo. That's his real name. Cricket Cherpin."

Bolo lifts his rumpled eyelids. "What's the deal, kid? Folks didn't like ya?"

I stare into his gray pebble eyes. "Guess not, *Bolo*."

Bolo snaps a slap to my cheek so fast, I don't see it coming. "Watch your mouth, son. I'm King Kickass around here."

I don't say nothing, but I don't move. I don't want him to know I'm scared he'll throw something more powerful that I don't see coming.

Caretaker puts his arm around Bolo's shoulder. "Bolo, this is the kid I was telling you 'bout."

Bolo glares at Caretaker like he just blew in his ear. "This beanpole is the powerhouse? Bullshit."

"I'm telling you. I trained him myself."

"Well, let's see what he's got."

Caretaker steers Bolo away and whispers in his ear so I can't hear. He comes back alone a few minutes later. "You wouldn't think it looking at him now, but Bolo was a champion featherweight when he was younger. Guy's got lightning hands."

No shit, Sherlock. "So what's the deal? How come you're talking to this guy about me?"

"Well, I thought you might wanna get trained in a

real gym by a real trainer. Maybe set yourself up for making some dough with your fists once you turn eighteen."

What the fuck? Why would Caretaker think I'd be interested in bashing skulls for a living? "No, thanks." I walk to the water fountain.

I hear his footsteps behind me. "There's good money in fighting, Cricks."

Why's Caretaker suddenly pushing boxing on me? I got no interest in fighting for money. Why the hell would I bash the nuts of someone who ain't never done anything against me and who I don't even know? So I can live in a mansion and wear a shiny-ass clown belt that would make me look like some Special Olympics Ronald McDonald goofball?

"Hell, I bought my house with prize money," he says, like he can read my mind. "There's an annual competition just up in Bangor with a five-thousand-dollar purse, Cricket."

Now, maybe if they had a competition where you could line up to bash the skull of some scumbag son-of-a-bitch who smacks his boy around or sexes up his little girl or fisties his wife to the emergency room, then fuckadoodledoo, I'd catch the first train to Justiceville faster than a Catholic priest on a mute altar boy. But to throw fists for a tuna on rye? What the frig?

Caretaker slaps me on the shoulder. "Nothing to snub your nose at. And you got skills, son."

Then it hits me. Like a straight right to the forehead. Caretaker thinks that's all I'm good for. Fighting. I take a long drink of ice-cold water from the fountain. "I ain't snubbing nothing. I just don't want to."

"How come?"

I shrug.

"Cricket, there ain't nothing to be scared of. I've seen you fight. You'd whup every country bumpkin in here."

"I ain't scared."

"Then what's the problem, son? You gotta have some way to make a living once you're out on your own. And you never talk about what you're doing after high school, so I figured maybe you need a plan."

"I got a plan."

"Oh you do, do you? What's your plan?"

I imagine myself sweeping palm fronds off the chapel carpet.

Caretaker crosses his arms over his chest. "I hope to hell your plan don't involve that dingleberry Greg Dillar you're always hanging around with. That kid ain't nothing but trouble, Cricket. All he'll do is drag your ass down into the mud right alongside him."

Bolo bangs the bell beside one of the rings with a tiny metal hammer and yells to Caretaker. "We doing this or what?"

Caretaker waves a finger at him.

There's a guy in the ring wearing headgear and banging his gloves together.

"I ain't fighting."

"Why not?"

"I don't fight for no reason."

"I sure as shit know that, Cricket. Hell, you forget who you're talking to, son. I've looked in your eyes when we spar. I *damn* sure know you got some big-ass reason for fighting."

"Exactly, and it ain't money."

"Course, I also know the reason ain't the one you pawn off on the nuns and them other gullible galoots, so you can cut the crap. Don't blow smoke up my ass and say you fight to protect the Little Ones. *Puuh.* How fuckin' stupid do you think I am? I know better, Cricks. I know you're fighting something a damn sight scarier than them little kiddlins getting picked on."

My scar itches, so I scratch it.

"All I'm saying is, why not fight them demons in the ring and get paid for it? 'Cause they sure as shit ain't gonna go away on their own. You gotta beat those fuckers outta ya, Cricks. Demons got staying power."

I look into Caretaker's face. I can tell he's pleading for me, not him. Not like the other adults in my life. "I appreciate what you're trying to do, and I don't mean no disrespect, but I ain't interested."

The guy in the ring dangles his arms over the ropes and hollers at me. "Come on, Tony Montana. Show me what you got."

A bunch of boxers standing around look at me and laugh.

"Come on, Cricket. Show this loudmouth what's what." Caretaker jabs me on the shoulder.

I look at the boxer in the ring. He's bouncing up and down on his toes and smiling at me from behind his big red mouthpiece. "No. I ain't got no beef with him."

"It ain't got nothing to do with having a beef, son. It's about using your God-given talents to earn yourself a living. Boxing sure as shit beats working sixty hours a week in some shit-ass factory."

My God-given talents. All my life, adults have been tanning my hide for tanning kids' hides, and now all of a sudden ass-kicking is life affirming. Typical adult about-face crapola. What's good for the goose I'm gonna cram up your gander. "No, thanks." I start walking to the door.

"You're being a damn fool, Crick."

As I push the door open, the guy inside the ring hollers at me. "Running away, pussy?"

I stop mid-push and look at my hand. The dark red on the door matches the dark red on the gauze. *Caretaker doesn't know what he's talking about. I fight to protect the Little Ones.*

"C'mon, Mary," the boxer yells. "What you 'fraid of? I'll be gentle, cherry."

I turn. The guy inside the ring straightens up and puffs out his scrawny chest. Rage bubbles explode inside me. I should do it. Jump into the ring without headgear or gloves and shut the jerk up. Beat the living fuck out of the bigmouth asshole.

Everyone in the place is staring at me. They remind me of the kids in the courtyard standing around Pitbull yesterday. An image of Andrew crying on the ground next to his Spider-Man comic book flashes in my mind. *I fought Pitbull to protect little Andrew.* A memory of lying in a Boston alley with a busted-up face while kids pull the sneakers off my feet flashes in my mind. I shake my head to chase it away. *No, I fought for Andrew. He was on the ground. Pitbull shoved him there. God only knows what Pitbull might have done if I hadn't stepped in and stopped him. I fight to protect the Little Ones.*

I continue walking, and the blood-red door swings shut behind me.

Chants of *pussy* and *faggot* chase me down the hallway.

I fight to protect the Little Ones.

CHAPTER 14

I get to the chapel seven minutes early for my ten a.m. tongue-lashing with Mother Mary Mywayorthehighway, so I lie down in the guilt-enshrouded rear pew.

My morning with Caretaker is still sitting heavy in my gut, like I chowed a dozen of Sister Eliza's bran muffins. Should I consider fighting for money? Would bashing a kid's brains in with my fists be any different from bashing them in with drugs? Fists or drugs. Are those really my only two options? Grubs's words play in my mind. *Naskeag ain't got a scale small enough.*

Maybe I could come up with my own option, like getting a shit-ass minimum-wage job pumping gas or mowing lawns. But that would just prolong the inevitable. *Demons got staying power.* And I don't think I'd last very long being ordered around by two-faced, skinflint adults.

Option number three plays in my mind. A shiver

scrubwiggles the back of my neck. I sit up and shake it off.

Mother Mary Mothballs taps me on the shoulder and I follow her into her hallowed sanctuary of disciplinary inquisitions and monetary requisitions. A print of the Ten Commandments hangs on one wall, and a chalkboard of the Ten Budget Deficits hangs on another. You'd think an organization that owned so much valuable real estate and priceless art wouldn't be so friggin' cheap. Mother Mary grows gray hairs and gets years sliced off her life every September during budget negotiations with the Diocese. At least, that's what she says.

She plunks her enormous black-draped frame into her enormous brown leather chair behind her enormous black walnut desk and crosses her enormous white fingers in front of her enormous white face. Did I mention Mother Mary is enormous?

She stares at me blankly. If I didn't know her so well, I'd think she was waiting for me to speak, but she knows better.

We sit like this for a while. How long exactly I don't know, because if I break away to look at the clock, I lose.

Eventually, she opens a drawer and places a legal-size notepad on the desk. She pulls a pencil from above her ear and starts scratching on the yellow paper. "The rosa rugosa along the stone wall near the west cliff need to be cut back. Weed the rock garden while you're at it. We don't have funds for a fall remulching, so just scratch up what's there and make it look fresh."

"What's wrong? Sales of Pope Soap on a Rope been down?"

She sighs, scratches her cheek with the pencil eraser, and scribbles a number two. "Prune the rhodies along the east trail."

"Maybe the pope should sell a few of them nudie statues he's got in his master bedroom. He could buy enough bark mulch to landscape the planet."

"Don't start, Cricket. I'm in no mood. Three, there are several large tree limbs scattered about as a result of the recent storm. Haul them into the woods behind the barn. Don't push them over the cliff like you did last time. I don't want another call from the harbormaster."

"I don't know what you're talking about. The wind must have blown them there."

"Please." Mother Mary digs a number four into the paper and sets the pencil down. She closes her eyes and massages her temples. "You're almost eighteen, Cricket. You're practically a man. This has to stop."

"All right, I'll drag the tree limbs into the woods."

"That's not what I'm talking about, and you know it." She hasn't opened her eyes yet. "If you keep this up after you turn eighteen, I won't be able to bail you out by having a heart-to-heart with the principal."

"How can you have a heart-to-heart with someone who doesn't have a heart?"

Mother Mary opens her eyes and glares at me with a granite expression. "This isn't a joke, Cricket. Principal LaChance has talked to Buster's parents, and they're not going to press charges. But he will be discussing yesterday's incident with the school board. He's going to recommend that you be expelled permanently if you are involved in one more fight in school. And if you're expelled from school, the Diocese will recommend to Social Services that you be transferred to a more appropriate facility."

My gut leaps into my throat. I don't want her to know that, so I speak slow and calm. "It was self-defense."

She glares. "Bullspit. It was assault and battery, and it's a crime."

"Ask anyone there. I didn't start it."

"It's not about starting it. It's about ending it."

"I did end it."

"Ending it before it starts, Cricket."

"I can't control what other people do."

"You can control yourself."

"If controlling myself means being a coward, then I'd rather be out of control, thank you very much."

"Well, prison will control you lickety-split."

"I can't get in trouble for defending myself."

"You have all the answers, don't you, Cricket?"

"I know my rights."

"And I know you're wrong," Mother Mary Mastiff barks. "What you did to Buster went way beyond self-defense, and you know it. You're lucky you weren't arrested."

Here we go again. Fucking grownups. "The only thing a fighter understands is being put down. It's the only thing he respects."

"Then fighters have a lot to learn."

"Easy for you to say from inside these fairy-tale walls."

Mother Mary looks down at her hands like she's thinking about balling them into fists and punching me in the face. Her eyes drift slightly, and I realize she's not looking at her hands so much as through them. I get that weird mouth-watering, forehead-warming feeling.

She lifts her head and looks at my face like she's reading off a teleprompter. "You should have walked away, Cricket. Andrew would have survived." I don't respond. "Well, what do you have to say for yourself?"

"I don't have anything to say for myself. You've said enough for both of us."

"Don't be a wiseass, Cricket. I know that's like asking a fish not to swim, but try to indulge me."

A thick brass crucifix hangs on the wall behind her. It's tilted slightly, like Jesus is leaning over to catch a glimpse of all the people who betrayed him so he can kick their asses when he returns. I hate Jesus right now. He fucked up a lot of shit for those of us who have to live in the real world. "I ain't gonna turn the other cheek if a dude attacks me, if that's what you're wondering. I'd rather go to prison than be a coward. I ain't Jesus."

She slips out a crooked smile. "Thank you for clearing that up, Cricket."

Mother Mary can be tough to read. Sometimes she doesn't look so menacing. Right now she reminds me of one of those giant teddy bears that dangle from cables in toy stores, so expensive they don't have price tags.

"We learn more from example than from anything else. Especially when we're young and impressionable."

"I agree. That's why I made them impressions on Pitbull's face."

Mother Mary doesn't laugh. She doesn't even crack a smile. Bye-bye, teddy bear. Hello, fire-breathing dragon.

"The only thing people learn at the hands of violence is more violence. Someday even Buster Pitswaller will learn that. Who knows — perhaps you'll be the one to teach him."

"I seriously doubt it."

"You never know. The Lord works in mysterious ways. Everyone deserves the benefit of the doubt. Everyone deserves a second chance."

"Everyone except me."

"Oh, Cricket, I think we both know you're way beyond second chances."

"So I'm not supposed to defend the Little Ones? That doesn't sound very Christian to me."

"First of all, let's not pretend we both don't know what your fighting is about. Secondly, there are ways of defending the meek without jeopardizing your future."

"Wow. If Jesus had followed your advice, we'd all be wearing beanies at prayer time."

Mother Mary's face hardens. "Jesus never used violence to get his point across."

"Yeah, I know. How's he doing?"

Now her fists harden. "Don't you dare compare the life-and-death struggle of our Lord and Savior to a playground scuffle."

Playground scuffle? "And don't *you* dare pretend Jesus wasn't pissed off at his friends for not sticking up for him when he got hauled off to the cross. They were no better than every one of them assholes who stood around the courtyard while Andrew got whaled on. Turning the other cheek is bullshit!"

Mother Mary's face is expressionless, but I can tell she wants to pick up her desk and smash it over my head. "I told you to watch your language, Cricket. I won't stand for it."

"Well, you're acting like dudes who lived two

thousand years ago are more important than Andrew Pendleton."

"I'm not saying they're more important than Andrew. I'm just saying Jesus didn't go around beating people up to get them to accept his beliefs. And neither did his disciples."

"Well, maybe they should have. I mean, they got stoned and burned to death and crucified. You saying you'd let someone burn up little Andrew if you saw it happening?"

"No, I'm not saying that, and you know it."

"So you'd defend Andrew if someone tried to hurt him?"

"Of course I would. Just not with violence."

"With what, then? A fucking prayer?"

"Watch your mouth, Cricket!"

"Well, you're being a hypocrite. You're saying you'd help Andrew, but not if you had to use violence. What if violence was the only way?"

"Violence is never the only way. Jesus was very clear about that! He never laid a hand on a living soul! Not even his worst enemies!"

"Yeah, and they nailed him to a fucking tree on account of it!"

Mother Mary's face is beet red. "Jesus' death was ordained by his Father. Jesus said so himself."

"Then Jesus' father was an asshole!"

Mother Mary pushes herself to her feet and slaps me across the face. Hard.

I stare at her. My cheek stings.

She's huffing like a bull.

"What the fuck you do that for?"

"You want me to do it again?"

"I don't give a fuck."

"Leave my office right now, Cricket!"

I overturn my chair and head for the door. "I thought violence was never the way."

I hear her fist slam the desk. "Sit down, Cricket."

"Screw this. I'm outta here."

"Sit down right now!" she screams.

I pick up my chair and sit.

She pushes the pad of paper aside and rubs her forehead for about a month. "Cricket, you have to understand something. You are the only male role model these kids have. What you do and what you say resonates with them. They look up to you. They learn more from you by example than they will ever learn from books and speeches."

"Good. Then they can learn that you don't mess with other people just because you're older or stronger."

"Cricket, violence is a temporary solution."

"Oh, really? You think Pitbull will ever come after me again?"

"No, I don't think Pitbull will ever come after you again."

"See?"

"But he will come after someone. Someone weaker than you. He will exact his revenge on someone."

"He knows what he'll get if he does."

"You won't be around forever, Cricket."

A knot clenches my gut.

"You'd be helping the Little Ones a lot more if you tried to teach them real-life solutions to real-life problems."

A few years back, I took a baseball bat to the vegetable garden one night. I'll never forget the looks on the Little Ones' faces when they saw the plants all busted up the next morning. Turns out they helped plant them. Made me wanna puke. "The Little Ones ain't my problem."

"I know that, Cricket."

Jesus, she has a way of saying shit that twists my insides.

She rips the yellow sheet off the pad and slides it to me. "By the way . . ." She pauses.

Oh Christ, what now?

"I spoke with the Diocese. They have denied your request to remain living here after you turn eighteen."

My chest tightens. I twist my ring. Guess I'll have to deal for Grubs. Or fight for Caretaker. Or grow a set of nads and take the not-so-easy way out.

"Perhaps if you had taken my essay assignment a little more seriously instead of choosing to be a smartass, Monsignor Dobry would have been more open to the idea. Your Virgin Mary hypothesis did not go over well with him."

My face must be movie-reeling my thoughts.

"Don't worry, Cricket. We'll cross that bridge when we come to it."

Don't you mean jump off that bridge when we come to it? An image of Colonel Saito from *Bridge on the River Kwai* flashes in my mind. *"A word to you about escape. There is no barbed wire. No stockade. No watchtower. They are not necessary. We are an island in the jungle. Escape is impossible. You would die."*

I pick up my to-do list and leave.

CHAPTER 15

I don't have much time to mull over the historically bad news I just received, because when I walk out the front door, something stabs me in the eyes sharper than Mother Mary's dagger in my back. It's Wynona Bidaban. Gliding up the driveway like a daydream come to life. So much for getting any chores done.

She stops when she sees me. Just like in Principal LaChance's waiting area. Except today she's *sans* scowl. She isn't smiling, but she isn't snarling either. She looks nervous. Like she's worried I might hurl a Japanese fighting star at her forehead. She's got her bike with her and she's wearing tight denim cutoffs that remind me of a *Dukes of Hazzard* poster Grubs has hanging in his apartment. Her white cotton tank top has trouble written all over it. Trouble with a capital T. Two capital Ts, actually. How the hell am I gonna keep my eyes off those puffy marshmallow delights?

I stroll toward her like a suave, no-cares movie star. I have no idea what's propelling my legs. I must have a goofy expression on my face, because she giggles and shakes her head.

Once I'm beside her bike, my suava guava melts to grape jam, so I swipe some dead bugs off her reflector. She's staring at me with her mouth open like I just pole-vaulted over the Prison.

"What?" I ask.

She wrinkles her bunny nose and squints. "You look different. Way different from at school."

I am different. Way different. It's about time you noticed.

She looks down at the gravel between us like she's reading a message.

I'm glad to see you. I'm glad you came. "What are you doing here?" *Shit, that came out wrong. Cold and rude.*

"Well, I just, uh . . . I was riding around and I . . ."

"I mean, it's cool. People come here all the time. To tour the gardens and stuff." *Shit, now I sound like a friggin' tour guide. The Prison was built in 1854 to house retarded, never-gonna-get-laid high school vampires.*

"Oh, that's cool. I didn't know." She erases the message with the tip of her pink sneaker.

Come on, Crick, pull it together. "You want me to show you around or something?"

"Oh, sure. That'd be nice."

I start walking toward the trail between the giant rhododendrons. *Shit, maybe I should have let her go first. Now she definitely thinks I'm a dickhead. No, she can't go first. She doesn't know the way.* I wish she did. I wouldn't mind hankering a hypnaughtyc stare at the back of those huggy Daisy Duke shorts. That'd be one hell of a sweet view. Sweeter than anything I'm gonna show her on this pussytoe trek. (It's a plant, dirty birds.)

Her footsteps sound tentative, like she's tiptoeing on Cheerios.

When we get to the end of the trail it opens onto a flat boulder at the edge of the cliffs and she gasps like she's stepped on a nail. "Oh my God, what a gorgeous view."

I gawk into her happy face. It's glowing like there's a five-hundred-watt light bulb inside her head. *This one's pretty spectacular too.*

She steps to the edge.

"Don't jump. The nuns will think I pushed you."

She giggles.

As she gazes at the awe-inspiring panorama, I ogle her erection-inspiring assorama. It's breathtaking. Stimulating. Surreal. The most uplifting God Art I've ever seen. I don't get to enjoy the view for long because I notice a trickle of blood on her calf.

"You have a cut on your leg. Want me to run to the house and get some hydrogen peroxide and a Band-Aid?"

She turns and smirks like I asked her if she wants a lollipop. "No, that's nothing. Happens all the time. Just a flesh wound."

I raise my eyebrows. "You are indeed brave, Sir Knight."

"Oh my God, you got that? No one ever gets my Python references."

I try to think of another funny Python line, but her big smile and happy eyes have me tongue-tied.

She turns and steps closer to the edge. My stomach tingles. No one ever stands that close. No one except me.

She sits and dangles her legs. I sit on her right, not too close, my chest buzzing like there's a swarm of bees in my lungs.

She's not talking, which is cool. Most girls would be jabbering a mile a minute. I can't hear her breathing over the crash of the waves, but I can see her chest rising and falling out of the corner of my eye. Like the sea's tugging at her, and she's tugging back.

She's breathing deep and smooth like she's doing yoga or preparing for one final high dive into the great unknown. *What the hell? That's my gig.*

"I didn't come here to tour the gardens." She hurls the statement at the waves like she's trying to lasso something.

My heart dangles from her words like a chimp on a tire swing.

She looks at my face. "I came here to see you. To apologize for yesterday."

I raise my right hand and pretend to scratch an itch on my cheek.

She looks down at her hands, so I stare at her face. She looks different today. Like maybe she cut her hair or isn't wearing makeup or something.

"I feel terrible about the things I said to you. How I called you those names and stuff. I didn't mean any of it. And then that little kid came running out and started hugging you and I . . ." She turns her head, like something in the ocean has caught her attention. She pulls on her ponytail and sniffs. "Well, it just made me realize I don't know you. *Know you* know you, I mean. I don't know anything about you. I feel so bad about what I said. The mean stuff. That's not me, I swear. I don't know what came over me. Well, I sorta do, but still that's no excuse. I think it was just the whole fight thing, and I was looking for someone to blame, so I didn't have to face . . . some stuff . . . I've been avoiding. Boyfriend stuff. Buster stuff. I mean, you said it, but I wasn't going to listen to you, the guy who just bashed up my boyfriend." She freezes like there's an interruption in her Internet connection. "Why do I keep saying that? *Boyfriend. Paaahh.* I think I was madder at myself than you, but I wasn't ready to admit it. This is stupid. I'm sure you don't even care about this, and why would you, but I'm usually pretty good at being straight with myself and not playing games and not caring about popularity and what people think and stuff, but recently I . . ." She sucks in a bunch of air and holds her hands up in front of her like she's ordering the ocean to stay back.

All I can think about is the *paaahh*. She *paaahh*ed Pitbull.

"I swore I wasn't going to do this. I swore I wasn't going to get emotional."

Chicks are funny. They're always saying stuff out loud that they're supposed to keep inside. It makes me feel like I should say something out loud. Something I'm supposed to keep inside. "It's no big deal. I wasn't mad or anything. Everything you said is true."

She looks at me and grabs my arm. "No, it wasn't. It wasn't true at all. It was stupid and mean. You're not a freak or any of that stuff I said." Suddenly she sounds like Mother Mary.

Her hand is warm on my goosebumpy skin. "How can you be so sure? Like you said, you don't know me. Maybe I am a freak." Her gaze warms my cheek. I wonder how she'll respond. Honest or nice.

She lets go of my arm and turns her head away. My cheek cools.

"I guess you're right. I don't know you." She lowers

her voice to a goofy, guttural growl. "Maybe you're like some psychotic murderer."

My throat constricts. *Maybe is right, babycakes.*

She snaps back to perky and pleasant. "But I think I'm right. Seeing you yesterday with that little kid and seeing you here today, in your own element. I don't know, call it a woman's intuition."

A tingle tickles the back of my neck.

"It must be cool to live here. To have all this in your backyard," she says.

Wynona is like a tiny door in my Great Wall of China. "Yeah, it's pretty sweet. I come out here a lot. Especially at night."

"That must be awesome. And the wildlife must be killer."

"A lot of African swallows," I say, quoting Monty Python.

"Oh, really? Carrying coconuts, I presume." Cool. She gets it.

"Migratory coconuts."

"A swallow carrying a coconut?"

"It could grip it by the husk."

We both laugh.

She tilts her head and stares at me with a different kind of stare. Maybe I look different to her too. Or maybe . . . I scratch my cheek and turn away.

I feel her fingers on my chin. She tries to turn my face toward her, but I jerk my head away.

"It's not that noticeable. Honestly, I'm not just saying that." She raises her fingers.

I block them with my hand.

"I'm sorry," she whispers.

I have this weird feeling she's about to ask me about it. Like how it happened. "We see whales here in the summer. It's pretty cool," I say.

"Wow, that must be awesome. I've seen them from boats but never from shore."

"They're pretty far out and you need binoculars, but it's still cool. You should come by during the summer, and I'll show you." *It's September, retard. She'll hate you by Halloween.*

She doesn't say anything, which convinces me that what I just said was totally stupid. She's staring at my face again, but I can tell she's not looking at me. She's looking beyond me. Like I'm one of those 3-D drawings, and she's waiting for a hidden fairy-tale castle or werewolf to emerge. As much as it feels like she's not seeing me, I have this itchy sensation she's seeing more of me than anyone ever has. Even me.

Wynona's really pretty, but not the kind of pretty you see in magazines. It's not like she's goofy-looking or anything, but her face is long, and her eyes are far apart, and her eyebrows are thick, and her nose is skinny, and her lips are puffy, and her chin sticks out. I know I'm not describing her good because now it sounds like I'm lusting after an orangutan, but she really is pretty, just in a not-so-perfectly-balanced kinda way.

Her face is radiating all kinds of colors and flavors. Caramel cream and emerald ice and frosted pearl and mango dew. Holy hell, I sound like some éclair-pounding, Bavarian cream–spraying pastry puff or something.

My ocular malfeasance is tingling me a prickly pineapple passion right in the ol' fruit basket. I hope she doesn't take a gander south and see my rising tide. *Chubbalubbadingdong.*

Her eyes blink, her face melts, and she sighs. The next thing she says almost blows me off the cliff like a hurricane gust.

"You're very handsome, Cricket."

The nerves in my head fizzle, and my dingle tingles.

My carbonation must be obvious, because she cocks her head. "I'm serious. I've never looked at you up close before. You're always so far away or buried under that hood of yours." Her mouth opens. "I can't believe I just said that out loud. Sorry."

I know I should say something, but my mind is cramped. I can't say I think she's pretty in a crooked, out-of-whack way, like I was just thinking.

I sense something behind me. My chest tightens, my

mind whirs, and an alarm shrieks. "More likely the ocean air fucking with your vision," I say, jerking a glance behind me.

"Why do you say that?"

She suddenly looks different. Real different. Like the old Wynona. The angry, crazy, screaming bitch in La-Chance's waiting area. Kernels in my head start popping, and the tiny door in my Great Wall slams shut.

How could I have been so stupid to have fallen for her bullshit apology? Obviously she's up to something. She's setting me up. Jesus, I'm so friggin' stupid. She's Pitbull's girlfriend. He's probably right behind me in the bushes getting ready to hurl me off the cliff. Fuck!

I jump to my feet and back away from the cliff. "Don't fuck with me, Wynona. I'm not a mental midget like Pitbull."

She stands and hugs herself like she's cold. "What are you talking about?"

Panic knots every muscle in my body. I spin to see who's charging, but no one's there yet. I can feel Pitbull's presence in my gut, and it makes me nauseous. I slowly back away from Wynona and the rhododendron trail. That's where he must be. I slither along the narrow ledge of boulders. It's a good place to ambush someone. I gotta get to the grassy lawn, but that's a few hundred feet away.

"Cricket, what's wrong?"

I keep working my way along the boulders. Finally,

I turn and sprint. I need to get as far away from the cliff as possible. Once I'm on the grass, I drop to my knees to catch my breath. I can't see Wynona. I wonder if Pitbull's alone or if he brought friends. Damn, pretty ballsy of him to come after me so soon. His stitched-up head must still be wicked sore.

Goddamn it, Wynona! You lying fucking whore. I shoulda pushed you off the cliff when I had the chance.

If he's alone and on the path, I can enter from the driveway side and surprise him from behind. If he's packing a weapon, I wouldn't get in trouble for beating him senseless. No one could argue that wasn't self-defense. It would prove my case to Principal LaChance and Mother Mary. And Wynona.

I search the ground for a weapon. I grab the first thing I see, a thick piece of driftwood with spiky roots on one end. I race toward the parking lot. Wynona's bike is still there. They're probably hugging, laughing, and scheming out phase two. My chest feels like it's gonna explode.

I round the corner onto the trail at full speed and don't notice Wynona running toward her bike until it's too late. I slam into her hard and we both go down, but I don't let go of my cedar sword. I spin to my feet and get ready.

"Where is he? Where the fuck is he?" I'm screaming 'cause I'm scared. Not scared, but you know.

Wynona's still on the ground. She has one hand on her cheek. "Where is who?"

"Your boyfriend, asshole. Where's Pitbull?"

She gapes at me with a frightened expression. "What are you talking about? Buster isn't here."

"Yeah, right! How fucking stupid do you think I am?"

Wynona lowers her hand. It's covered in blood. She has a long scratch on her cheek. Her fear has morphed into terror.

Oh, shit.

She runs toward her bike.

I look up and down the trail. There's no sign of Pitbull anywhere. I run toward her. "Wynona."

"Leave me alone."

I stop at the edge of the trail. *Oh my God, no fucking way. Was she really here alone?* "Wynona . . ."

She dabs her cheek with a tissue.

Fuck, fuck, fuck, fuck, fuck.

She jumps on her bike.

"Wynona."

She rides away.

Wynona, please.

And then she's gone.

I sprint back to the boulders, hoping that if I run fast enough, I can reverse time. Wynona's not there. The waves roll and laugh. It's windy. Or was it windy before, and I just didn't notice? I imagine a giant gust whooshing me up and carrying me far, far away. So far I'll never make it back, no matter how hard the guilt tugs. So far I'll never see this place, this life, or Wynona again.

I look over the edge. The waves crash on the rocks. Again and again. Again and again. They're relentless. They'll never stop. Never.

I glance at my driftwood battle-ax. My gut twists. My body cramps. My head pounds. My heart rips.

I don't scream until the sharp wooden point is halfway down my chest. I throw the weapon over the cliff and grab my chest. My fingers are wet and sticky.

CHAPTER 16

Caretaker keeps a first-aid kit in the boathouse. I douse my wound with hydrogen peroxide. It bubbles pink and foamy and stings like a futhermucker. I'm scared it might need stitches, but that's just my vagina talking.

I run downtown in the hopes of finding Wynona. Maybe she didn't go straight home. I'm grounded, but I don't care. I look for her bike outside the pharmacy. I check the emergency entrance to the hospital. Maybe she went to Pitbull's. Maybe I drove her back to him.

Something inside me needs to find her. Needs to know if her cheek is okay. Needs to try to explain. *You see, the thing is, I'm psychotic.* Nutseekookoo *is the technical term. Yup, one swan dive away from permanently relocating to the Everlasting Land of Nod. Wanna grab a soda? How about dinner and a movie? We could see* Psycho. Donnie Darko. Fatal Attraction.

Yeah, right.

I scan every shop and parking lot on Main Street. Her words echo in my head like a horror movie trailer. *It's not that noticeable. You're very handsome. I've never looked at you up close before. You're always buried under that hood of yours.* She saw me. Saw me from afar. Saw me buried under my hood. She saw *me*. And she came to the Prison. My home. Wynona Bidaban came to *my* home to see *me*. To apologize to *me*. She almost cried when she thought about the names she called me. She was sorry. Really sorry.

I crisscross every inch of Black Cove Park. She's not there. I sit on a bench and gaze at the blank slate of sea. She's not the girl I thought she was. She's so much more. She likes Monty Python. She likes God Art. She knows she shouldn't be with Pitbull. She *paaahh*ed him. She actually *paaahh*ed him. And I ruined it. I ruined everything. Ruined everything forever.

I look around to make sure no one's nearby and light up a joint. I take a couple hits, snuff it out, and stuff it back in my wallet.

I take one more pass along Main Street but don't find her. Maybe I should just forget the whole thing. Forget everything. Wynona, my chores, everything. Just go to Grubs's apartment and get wasted. But I'm already in pretty deep with Mother Mary. I start walking back to the Prison, then freeze on the sidewalk. If I don't find Wynona, I won't see her for another week on account of my suspension. *Shit!*

I walk the downtown strip one more time, then head to Grubs's apartment. His car's not there. My chest's throbbing with pain, and I feel lightheaded. I look up and down Main Street, trying to decide what to do, where to go. I feel lost. The town looks eerily unfamiliar. I suck in some deep breaths but can't seem to get any air into my lungs. My brain feels fuzzy and my stomach's in knots. I spot the miniature lighthouse on the corner of Naskeag Road. The road to the Prison. My road. I sprint home.

Mother Mary's standing on the front porch when I run up the driveway. I try to think fast, but my brain's still lost in Wynona Hell.

Mother Mary's face is tight and red. "I'm tempted to say 'strike three,' but we're probably up to three thousand and three by now."

"I had to, um . . ."

"Don't even try, Cricket." She goes inside and slams the door.

I spend the rest of the day doing chores. Every movement rips at the stinging gash in my chest. Bending, lifting, sawing, weeding, raking, hauling, throwing. I see Wynona's face in everything I touch. Her glow, her laugh, her smile, her skin, her fingers on my chin. Her grimace, her terror, her cut, her shriek, her fingers on her cheek. Her scared eyes—that's the worst. She came here to apologize, and I scared her. Her initial instincts were right. I am a freak. A freak of nature.

I'm still thinking about Wynona at dinner. It's like the feeling of a nightmare that clings to you with hazy images and cloudy fears even though you can't remember what the dream itself was about, except I remember every detail of this dayscream. In my gut I've got a maggot-infested tumor denser than one of Sister Eliza's bran muffins, reminding me every second exactly what it's about.

I can't believe I freaked out like that. I felt so certain she was bulldozing me into a mushy pile so Pitbull could drop-kick my ass into the briny deep. Why else would she talk all that crap about me being good-looking and stuff? I know I'm an ugly fuck. I know my scar freaks people out. First expressions don't lie.

But if she wasn't setting me up, why was she buttering me up like some tasty stud muffin? There's no way she can really think I'm a hot tamale or anything. Her eyes seem to work fine. She walked right to the edge of the cliff without falling over. *Monkey nuts—what gives?*

I'm halfway through my peach cobbler when Mother Mary taps me on the shoulder and finger-twirls me to the tower. At first, I'm like, *How the hell am I gonna mind-spin happytime tales with this nightscare bottlenecking my brain?* But then, I'm like, *No, this will be good, clear my head, get me to stop skull-mashing the Wynona gashing.*

The Little Ones follow me to the tower and settle in. I ask them where I left off.

Gregory Bullivant's pudgy cheeks drift at me from starboard. "Apollo Zipper didn't die when the ferry sank in the English Channel, Mr. Cherpin."

Even though the Little Ones call me Mr. Cherpin all the time, something freaky happens when Gregg-plant Parmesan says it. I suddenly feel older. Like I really am Mr. Cherpin and not just on account of a bunch of kids way younger than me calling me that. Maybe it has something to do with Mother Mary telling me I can't live at the Prison after I turn eighteen.

Whatever the reason, the feeling makes it seem like my driftwood antics with Wynona happened a long time ago to someone much younger and much different. I know that sounds wacky because obviously I'm not old-er, and I'm not different. I'm just me. Me, the storyteller. Me, the orphan. Me, Mr. Cherpin.

I suddenly know what I have to do. It hits me square in the forehead like a stiff jab. I have to stop listening to the music and face it. I have to find that little girl I scratched on the face and apologize. I have to apologize to Wynona.

Holy gutloads of mayhem and dismayhem, Batman.

How the hell did all that emotional hullabaloo kitty-cat my snugglepuss so lickety-split on account of one midget toad calling me Mr. Cherpin? Man oh man, the braineroo is one funky organ. I mean, turn and face the strange ch-ch-ch-ch-changes, Mr. Bowie.

The Little Ones are staring at me like I have three heads, so I'll have to finish brain-scrambling this Freudian omelet later.

"Right, Apollo Zipper. The ol' Zipperoo. Zip, Zippy, Zipster." The Little Ones have no idea I'm killing time trying to pull something out of my ass. "The Zipmeister. The Zipinator." I dim the lights and rub my hands together. Damn, even my hands feel older. Rougher, more callused. Probably just from the yardwork. "Well, Apollo Zipper did not die on that fateful ferry fiasco back in eighteen girdedy-nerner."

"Eighteen seventy-five." It's Billy Kopin, who never speaks, speaking.

I give tough-guy Billy a thumbs-up. Huh, maybe I ain't the only one transmogrifying in this magical power tower tonight.

I tell the Little Ones more about the phantasmagorical adventures of Apollo Zipper. Like how he survived the ferry debacle by floating on the ship's steering wheel, and how he washed ashore on a tiny island in the North Sea, and how the island was inhabited by runaway orphans who traveled the rocky trails on the backs of domesticated wolves. The Little Ones nearly bust their little lungs cheering when I tell them there were no adults on the island, which meant no homework, baths, bedtimes, or Brussels sprouts.

Just as I'm telling them that the rogue wave that sank the ferry was not an accident and was caused by evil adults who enslave children in underground diamond mines, the door to the storytorium swings open and Mother Mary Mistiming enters, clapping her hands. The hot air from the Little Ones' groans warms the room. They line up and file out.

I stay behind, munch some leftover popcorn, and think about Wynona. I have to find her and apologize. But how? And where? And what will I say? I can't do it at school. Too many people around. I can't do it here. There's no way she'll ever step foot on this hallowed ground again. I can't do it at her house. Too many parents around. Plus, I don't even know where she lives. And even if I do find her and get her alone, chances are she won't stick around long enough for me to squeak out an apology.

I gaze at the dark, distant sea. The ocean looks motionless from this far away. Unlike the way it rock-'n'-rolls a head-banging vertigo from up close. Funny how that is. How things are so calm and peaceful from far away, but up close that surreal scene cartwheels your nutsack like a pebble in the surf. Maybe that's why people like Man Art more than God Art. A painting of a tsunami can't obliterate your ass the way a real one can.

I head to my attic asylum to drown my sorrows. I'm like Rooster Cogburn in *True Grit*. We both *love to pull a cork.*

CHAPTER 17

I drank too much last night, so breakfast is a bear. I'm sweating more than the plump Jimmy Deans on my plate. But greasy chow is the best thing for a hangover. And ain't no one better at dishing up greasy chow than porky nuns.

The only thing tougher than sitting up straight and keeping your elbows off the table when you're hung heavy is Sunday Mass. And that's next.

My limbs feel waterlogged, like they're nailed to the pew. Tough to pay attention to some ignoramus preaching a bamboozling folly when your pores are secreting a boozeoozling jolly. I'd like to crawl up to the altar and chug the priest's wine to exorcise my way to a miraculous healing. One of them *hair of the dog that bit ya* deals.

One cool thing about church is that you can close your eyes and snoozadoozle and the priests and nuns figure you're praying extra hard. Well, I'm praying extra hard that I can summon up the courage to knock on Wynona's front door when something the priest says drips a mystical intravenous prophecy into my pounding veins. It's from Psalm 26, in the pre-Jesus section of the Big Black Book.

Expect the Lord, do manfully, and let thy heart take courage.

Holy guacamole, Batman! Did God just call me a pussy? Ain't that a kick in the circumcised love staff? I hate to sound all religiously douchenozzled, but heck if the Old Man isn't ordering me to grow some nads and get my ass over to Wynona's house to apologize. At least, that's the way I figure it.

But how can I get away? How can I escape my forty years in the desert of chores? How can I Moses my ass out of Egypt while Mother Maraoh Pharaoh has me chained to a wheelbarrow and rake all day? *Mother Mary Mothballs, let thy orphan go!*

Later that morning, the good Lord floats a solution from on high while I'm raking the backyard.

Humbly heeding the Lord's merciful command, I lean my rake against the sacrificial boulder, gaze into His cloudy face, raise my boot heel to the heavens, and smite my mighty footwear upon the consecrated handle, thus snapping it in twoeth. *The Lord hath spoken.*

Oh my goodness. Whatever shall I do? I am rakeless in the Garden of Should and Needful. How in Heaven's name shall I complete my chores like the repentant soul I am without my trusty garden staff? O Lord, why hast Thou forsnookered me? But wait. I hear the Lord guiding me again through the darkness of my trials and tribulations.

Driveth thee Prison vaneth to the raketh-changers in the Hardwareth Temple, sayeth the Lord, and pur-chaseth a neweth tooleth with the nuns' sacred cardeth of credit.

The only problem is, I need the Lord to thrice bless-eth my holy asseth because I don't know where Wynona liveths. But I know someone who does.

Grubs is sitting in a lawn chair outside the auto repair shop when I pull up. He's drinking a giant Dunkin' Do-nuts coffee, which, knowing Grubs, probably doesn't have a drop of coffee in it. His slippery grin confirms my suspicion.

"Nice van, Reverend Cricket. You come to convert me?"

"Even God's given up on you."

"You got that right." He takes a huge sip and tosses a crooked glance at the orphanage van. "Must be tough to score chicks in that rusty hunk of shit."

"It belongs to the Catholic Church. Chicks ain't the objective."

Grubs laughs and spits out some "coffee."

A car pulls up to the pump. Grubs lumbers to the shiny silver Audi and jams the handle in the fill hole. He leans over to flirt with the middle-aged woman while the pump clicks. I can tell by the way he's shifting his head around that he's peeping down her blouse. After she drives away, he grabs his crotch and flicks his tongue like a lizard. That's the universal gas station attendant signal for romantic interest in an attractive female customer. He sits down and chugs his drink.

"Wouldn't mind taking that little MILF up to the love loft for a roll in the hay," he says.

"Yeah, I'm sure she'd be impressed. Maybe afterward you could treat her to a corndog in the restroom."

"Fuck you, Rockefeller. At least I got my own place."

"You live in an attic above a garage."

"You live in an attic above a cult of frigid nuns."

I laugh. "Touché."

Grubs gets up and goes inside. Probably to add more caffeine to his coffee.

I'm dying to ask him where Wynona lives so I can go see her before I lose my nerve, but I don't wanna just blurt it out. Fortunately, I have a plan.

"Hey, that dude Billy Jo Bidaban lives around here, don't he?" I ask when Grubs returns with a fresh "coffee."

"Nah, he's up in Bangor at community college."

"Oh, yeah. But he used to live down by the ballpark, right?"

"Nah, he lived in that piss-yellow farmhouse near the sledding hill on Granite. The one with the big horse barn and shit."

"Oh, right." I feign interest in watching an old lady wrestling her walker down the sidewalk.

Grubs kicks my ankle. "What gives? You got something going on with Billy Jo behind my back, bro? You better not be motherfuckin' me, dude. He ain't around much, but he's still my best customer."

Shit. I don't want him thinking I'm the kind of slimy prick who'd scam deals under the table. Guess I gotta let the fat out of the hag. "Hell no, I wouldn't pull that shit. I'm trying to hook up with his little sister."

Grubs starts *aaaaaahhhhhhhh*ing and banging his fist on his thigh. "No way. You tapping that ass?"

"Not yet, but I'm planning on it." I'm not planning on it, but what am I gonna say? To be honest, the way he says it makes me wanna knock his fuckin' head through a gas pump. But I know he doesn't mean anything by it. He's just being Grubs. Plus, what the hell do I care what he says about her?

"That little bitch is a hot hunka meat. I wouldn't mind boarding that red caboose for a midnight ride to Brownsville Station." He cracks up at his own joke.

Okay, that was a little much. "Easy, dude."

"What the fuck, faggot? You soft on this bitch or something?"

"Shit no. She ain't nothing to me."

The brakes in my gut screech when I park the van in front of Wynona's house. There's no way she'll talk to me after what I did. She'll probably slam the door in my face before I can utter a single sorry. No, she won't do that. She'll punt me in the pigskin and then slam the door.

Her house is this wicked old farmhouse perched on a hill near downtown Naskeag, with Death Wish sledding hill on one side and a giant cell phone tower on the other. It's pale yellow with brown shutters. A gross color combination if you ask me.

There's a screened-in porch across the entire front of the house, which I realize I'm gonna have to enter to knock on the door. *Damn.* Her dad's landscaping truck is parked in the driveway. *Double damn.*

One thorny splinter of hope keeps prickling my potato, though. She came to the Prison to apologize. She didn't come for some flaky get-in-touch-with-nature walkabout. She came to see me. Now, maybe at first it was just to apologize, but there were definitely moments of sticky eye-canoodling between us. I didn't imagine that.

Every time I think of that cut I sliced in her face, my stomach somersaults. There's no way I can knock on that door. What if her stepmom answers? Or worse, her father.

Wynona, sweetie, the gentle lad who filleted your face is at the door. How do you do, Cricket? So nice to meet you. Would you like to come in? I have a lovely set of stainless-steel steak knives in the kitchen. Perhaps you'd like to lop off one of my wife's breasts?

Oh man, I'm in Troubletown. But I gotta go. Face the music. Take my lumps. Be a man. Just like Mother Mary Maturity said. Grow up. End it before it starts. Exactly. That's exactly it. No matter how bad it goes, at least I will have done one tiny thing right in my stupid, pathetic life. *Do manfully, and let thy heart take courage.* Jeez Louise! What the hell is that Holy Roller hullabaloo doing tickling my jigglies a Jehovah-loving mischief?

I jump out of the van and shake off the sillies like some epileptic vampire. The house sways as I get closer. *Nuckfuggets.* The whole family's probably hunkered down beside a window watching me schlep my crazy ass up the gravel walk. For all I know, Mr. Bidaban's unlocking his gun cabinet at this very moment.

No matter. Just apologize and go. Say sorry and bolt. Ding-dong, sorry, see ya. That's all. Nothing more. Nothing more.

The front steps are enormous pink and gray granite

slabs that look like they were dumped there by a passing glacier. I tiptoe up them and open the screen door. It squeaks. I wince and freeze. I'm pretty sure I hear a pump-action shotgun being loaded.

I step forward. My fingers shake as bad as my legs, but I don't stop. I press the doorbell. Like I'm pressing the On button to the electric chair I'm strapped into.

Please be Wynona. Please be Wynona. Please be Wynona.

A statuesque man opens the door. He's huge and square, like the house. His head is bald and shiny, like a bowling ball.

He doesn't say a word or budge an inch while I struggle to get my words out. He's got Bluto forearms that could knead my noggin into a spinach quiche. I finally murder the frog choking my vocals. "Excuse me, sir, is Wynona home?"

He looks mad. "Who may I say is inquiring?"

"Cricket Cherpin."

Now he moves. Not much, just a head twitch. Man, if I had a dime for every head twitch I got when I said my name.

"I'm sorry?"

I squeak out my name again.

He stiffens. "One moment, please." He closes the door in my face.

I breathe for the first time since I got out of the van.

The door opens and Wynona appears, decked out

in frilly Sunday fineries. All white and warm and whip creamy. Seeing her so clean and pretty makes me realize I'm wearing my work grubs. *Shit, I should have cleaned up and changed.*

Then I see it. The Band-Aid on her cheek. It's not as big as I feared. I was expecting her whole head to be wrapped in gauze or something. A stratosphere of air vents from my chest.

Wynona's staring at me. I can't tell if she's happy, mad, sad, or all of the above. Her dad musta taught her that expression 'cause she's got it down pat. I better speak fast before I lose my chance. And my nerve.

I try to sound manly and confident, but the words leak out mangled and prissy. "I came to apologize."

She crosses her arms over her chest.

I try to remember the words I'd been practicing all morning. "I'm sorry I freaked out like that. It's just when you said what you said, I was sure you were messing with me, and it hit me that you're Pitbull's girlfriend, and I thought maybe some kind of revenge thing was going down."

Her head tips a teeny bit to one side. "I told you I broke up with Buster."

"You never said that. I mean, you did that *paaahh* thing, but . . ."

"But what? I was lying to you? You think I was lying to you?"

"Jeez, you're saying it like no one's ever lied to you."

Her eyes drop and she unfolds her arms. "No, I've been lied to."

There's a white bracelet on her wrist with little red roses that look real, like they grew there. A tiny vine squeezes through a tiny crack in my Great Wall. "When you said what you said . . . about . . . you know . . . I just . . . I was sure you had to be messing with me."

She raises her head and wrinkles her forehead. "You mean when I said you were handsome?"

I nod.

"But you *are* handsome. Why would you think I was lying? I can't be the first girl who's ever said that to you."

It's hard to explain the feeling that consumes me when she says that. The only way I can describe it is this. There's a fifty-million-horsepower vacuum cleaner hanging over me, and I have a vacuum port on the back of my neck, and someone jams the vacuum hose into my port and turns the vacuum on, and every molecule inside me is instantaneously sucked out, and my port is plugged. Shrink-wrapped, I think they call it. That's how I feel. Shrink-wrapped.

I must *look* shrink-wrapped, too, because Wynona steps onto the porch and touches my forearm. "Are you okay, Cricket?"

I can't answer. I don't know how to say it. Only one

thought remains after all the sucking. "I'm not handsome. I'm . . ." I can't say it out loud.

Wynona steps closer. She smells like coconut. "Cricket, listen to me. If you don't know you're handsome, then you're the one who's lying to you."

For a split second, my mind slips and unshackles and swells and—holy shit—I almost let pussy tears dribble out of my eye sockets, but I get ahold of myself. I still can't think of anything to say, so I just stare at Wynona's pretty face.

She's staring at me good. Her lips have shifted a little, and she looks a bit happy. That makes it easier to keep my eyes locked on her. Truth is, it isn't hard at all to keep my eyes locked on Wynona and not just because of her prettiness. She has this way of staring that makes it okay to stare back. It's freaky. I've never stared at anyone so good and long before, let alone a beautiful girl.

And then it happens. If you had asked me to guess what would happen next, I wouldn't have guessed it in a million guesses.

Wynona kisses me. She friggin' kisses me. She leans in, tilts her head, and kisses me. With her eyes open. And I ain't talking no chicken-lipped peck. She kisses me a real kiss. I mean, she doesn't jam her tongue down my throat or anything, but she actually kisses me a real kiss right on the lips. She holds the back of my head and mashes her lips all over mine. I mean, she goddamn friggin' kisses me!

I think I kiss her back — or at least try — but my head's so dizzy I have no idea what I'm doing with my own mouth.

When she pulls away, she has an even bigger smile on her face. I must have the look of the living dead, because she giggles a guilty giggle and touches my lips with her fingers like she's trying to wipe away my goofiness.

Unfuckingbelievable. Wynona Bidaban kissed me. I should sprint to the cliffs and skydive into the Briny Hereafter, because nothing in life can ever get any better than this. Nothing. Ever.

But it does get better.

"You wanna come in and have lunch with us?"

There are only two problems. One, I'm dressed like her dad's lawn slave, and two, I'm completely sober. I don't even have a mini nip in my pocket to take the edge off. And eating at the same table as the Bald Terminator is going to be an edgy situation at best. But what other option do I have? Run away again? Slice up the other cheek and head for the hills? Which makes me realize there could be three problems.

"What about, you know, your injury?" I raise my hand toward her cheek. "Do they know it was me who . . ."

She grabs my fingers and squeezes. Her hand is soft and warm. "I told my dad the truth. I ran into a tree branch."

She smiles.

I smile. "By the way, how is it?"

"It's fine. Just a scratch."

"Sorry 'bout that, too."

"No biggie. Just another flesh wound." She's staring at my face, and I watch her eyes drift to the left. Eyes always drift to the left, eventually. She raises her hand.

I back away before her fingers touch my face.

"I'm sorry," she whispers.

I don't answer. *What's she got to be sorry about?*

She slips on some phony bubbles. "So what do you say? Will you have lunch with us?"

I look down at my clothes. "I don't know. I look like shit."

"You look hard-working. My dad will respect that."

How Wynona got me to enter that house, I'll never know. That's a lie. I do know. It was her eyes. Okay, that's a lie too. It was her luscious tatas. Okay, that's a lie too. It was her museum-quality ass. Okay, that's a lie too.

It was her kiss. She could have asked me to do anything after that kiss. I would have jumped into a flaming friggin' volcano to retrieve a rusty can of Spam for her after that kiss. It was that delicious. I don't need booze to make it through one stupid lunch fiasco. I'm still high from that friggin' kiss. Okay, that's a lie too. A swig or two of happy juice would come in damn handy right about now.

Wynona's house is unlike any I've ever seen. Right in the middle is a gigantic room that's a combination kitchen, dining room, and family room. I duck when I enter because the ceilings are low. I raise one arm and press my palm against the plaster.

Wynona shrugs. "Built in 1784. People were a lot shorter back then."

I raise my other hand and hold it next to her forehead. "Just back then?"

She slaps my hand. "Hah, hah, very funny." She tickles my armpits and I drop both arms.

Everything in the room is made from dark wood. Trim, beams, floors, cabinets, furniture. The support columns are tree trunks. The rear wall has three enormous sliding glass doors that overlook an evergreen forest, while the front windows overlook the downtown. It's weird, like the house is teetering on some invisible boundary line between two completely different worlds.

Floor-to-ceiling bookshelves crammed to capacity line the side walls. They remind me of the Naskeag Public Library.

I search the room for a booze cabinet, hoping there's

one tucked away in a corner so I can nonchalantly stroll by for a stealthy swig. No such luck.

For a millisecond, I worry about getting in trouble for not returning the van immediately as Mother Mary Maharaja had ordered, but are you kidding me? Like I'm gonna pass up this once-in-a-lifetime opportunity 'cause it might cost me some extra pussy willow pruning or whip me up a saucy side of nun-tongue? *Phuuuuuuh, right.*

Wynona loads me up with plates and bowls. She grabs glasses and silverware. We set the table together. I breathe in the heavy scent of her home—garlic, onion, lemon Pledge— and it drips from my nose to my toes. I feel grounded, like I live here or something.

Every time Wynona passes a certain place setting, her face tightens and she slams the dishes and utensils down. I'm guessing that's her stepmom's seat.

Mr. Bidaban comes in and ties a white apron with giant strawberries on it around his waist. He walks to the stove, jams his beak into a steaming black pot, and *mmmmm*s. He sprinkles some spices in and stirs it with a wooden spoon. Seeing this big-ass dude smile and hum in a girly apron as he stirs his stew makes me feel less fruity about the cooking I do at the Prison.

Wynona and I sit on one side of the table. She smiles. "Thanks for helping me set the table."

"You're welcome." The nuns say thank you all the

time at the Prison, but it's a different kind of thank-you. My insides bubble, steamy and delicious, like the insides of that big black pot.

Mr. Bidaban carries the pot to the table and sets it on a big square piece of ceramic tile that looks like it fell off someone's bathroom wall. He walks to the staircase on the opposite side of the room and hollers up. "Roxanne, lunch!"

Wynona leans over and her shoulder touches mine. "It's almost noon. Time for Sleeping Beauty to get up."

A few minutes later, a tall woman with short blond hair comes down the stairs. She's wearing a long white skirt and a long orange T-shirt that goes halfway down her butt. She has big boobs, though maybe they just look big on account of her shirt being so tight. I look away when Wynona pinches the bridge of her nose and sighs. I guess her stepmom gives her nasal congestion.

Mrs. Bidaban stops at a chair opposite us and stands beside it. For a moment, I think she's deciding whether she wants to dine in my presence, but then Mr. Bidaban pulls out her chair and she sits. *Damn, I wonder if I was supposed to do that for Wynona.*

She folds her hands together and looks at Wynona. She tosses me a quick glance, then looks back at Wynona.

Wynona exhales loudly. "Roxanne, this is a friend of mine from school, Cricket Cherpin. Cricket, this is Roxanne."

I stand and extend my hand like the nuns taught me.

Roxanne eyes my hand like I'm trying to pass her a hunk of moose shit. She finally shakes it, but only with her fingers, which is good because her hand is so soft and delicate, I'd probably crush it.

She pulls her hand away, tilts her head, and glares at Wynona. "Cricket Cherpin? Nice try, Wynona."

"Roxanne!" Wynona snaps. "That's his real name. Apologize right now!"

"Oh, please," Roxanne grumbles.

"Dad!"

"Well, Wynona, it's not like you haven't done it before," Mr. Bidaban says as he unties his apron and hangs it on a hook. He looks at me as he sits down. "Roxanne was calling Wynona's friend Alison 'Emma Royds' for months."

Wynona laughs.

"It's not funny, Wynona," Roxanne snaps.

Wynona turns to me. "We got caught when I told her Alison's boyfriend's name was Hugh Jass."

I pretend to wipe my mouth with my napkin so Roxanne doesn't see me laughing.

Mr. Bidaban picks up Roxanne's bowl and starts ladling. She stops him after one ladle. He fills mine to the tippity top, which I'm happy about 'cause I'm starving. He reminds me of me serving the Little Ones at the Prison.

It's seafood stew in a red sauce like marinara but thinner. There's fish and scallops and mussels and a few other oceanographic crustaceans I don't recognize. Wynona digs in, so I do too. I discover a few miniature octopuses backstroking in my briny porridge and they're chewy as hell, but their taste isn't bad. Actually, there's no taste at all, except for the sauce the eight-legged wonders are swimming in.

It's scrumptious. This rough-and-tumble Hulkamaniac can cook.

Every time Roxanne takes a spoonful or adjusts something on the table, Wynona winces and shakes her head.

"Where do you live, Cricket?" Mr. Bidaban asks.

Wynona stops chewing.

"At the Naskeag Home for Boys," I say.

Roxanne snaps a glance at me, then surveys the table like she's counting the silverware.

"That's one prime cut of real estate," Mr. Bidaban says without looking up from his bowl.

I'm not sure what he's talking about, so I don't say anything.

Roxanne slurps a spoonful. Wynona blows out a lungful of air.

"You lived there long?" he asks.

"Eight years."

"Eight years? How long's that place been open?"

"Eight years."

"No kidding, huh? So you were one of the first boys there?"

"Yes, sir."

"Don't worry about the *sir* part, Cricket. I appreciate the sentiment, but it's not necessary. You can call me Roger."

"Really?" *Shit, that came out squeaky and surprised.* I lower my voice and try again. "I mean, okay, Roger." *Jeez Louise, that was weird.*

Mr. Bidaban is talking to me like I'm a real person, like I'm someone he invited over. Like the way Caretaker talks to me in the boathouse. Most adults are assholes when they talk to you. They'll toss out a question to sound superior and sophisticated but never stick around for an answer. So Mr. Bidaban is either pretty cool or he's the best phony-baloney actor I've ever seen. I mean, serve me up a Long Island Iced Tea Inside the Actors Studio, Mr. Lipton, 'cause this guy's flipping talented.

As much as I like the way Mr. Bidaban's talking to me, I wish it was just me and Wynona having lunch. Maybe she'd kiss me again if we were alone. When she sets her napkin on her lap, she squeezes my thigh and my crotch rocket jumps. I feel my face flush.

Roxanne picks up her empty glass and waves it in front of Mr. Bidaban's face.

"Oh gosh, sorry." He hustles to the counter and grabs a pitcher.

Roxanne just sits there like she's at a restaurant.

"You need help, Dad?" Wynona asks, glaring at her step-bitch.

He kisses the top of her head when he returns. "No, thanks, sweetie. I got it." He fills all the glasses with lemonade so pulpy it looks like there are seeds floating on top.

Mr. Bidaban digs a mussel out of his bowl with his hands. "Did you know it used to be a prison?" he asks me.

"Yes, I heard that."

"The nuns do a good job with the boys there," he says with a mouthful of mussel. "You're evidence of that, Cricket. Polite, hard-working. Not like most of the teenage dipshits we have wandering these small-town streets."

"Dad."

"What? I didn't name names."

"Well, it's kinda obvious."

"I said teenage dipshits. Not football dipshits."

"Dad, stop it."

I chuckle.

"It's no secret in the Bidaban household how I feel about Buster. I hope you're not friends with that cretin, Cricket."

"No, sir . . . I mean, Roger. Far from it."

"Good, good. You ask me, that obnoxious ignoramus got what he deserved when he got the tar kicked out of him. Hopefully, whoever it was knocked some sense into his thick head, but I doubt it."

"Dad, Cricket . . ."

I touch Wynona's leg with my fingertips.

She turns to me, surprised. ". . . does the landscaping at the . . ." She hesitates, like she's embarrassed to say the word *home* or *orphanage* in front of me. ". . . at the property," she continues. "You should see the gardens. They're magnificent."

Roger Bidaban smiles big and sincere at his daughter. It's obvious he loves her a shit-ton. "I've seen them many times, my dear. I try to bid that darn job every year, but the nuns have never subbed the work out as far as I know. Heck, why would they when they've got a pro like Cricket on staff?"

My insides warm. For the first time in my life I feel proud to be from the Home. I lean over my bowl, afraid my face is movie-reeling my feelings.

I spoon in more of the tasty subaquatic concoction, then reach for my flaky croissant. Just as I'm about to slap a wad of butter onto it, I spot Mr. Bidaban slopping his into his bowl to sop up the scrumptious juices, so I follow suit and use my doughy delight like a sponge.

Mr. Bidaban inhales his roll. "Apparently, a lot of

folks in town were against the church opening that or-phanage. Can you believe that? They figured kids from broken homes would be broken kids. I mean, Christ al-mighty, we're talking about orphans, not juvenile delin-quents. Well, those nuns sure taught the townspeople a thing or two. Every boy I've met from the Home is cour-teous and good-natured. And that's saying a lot, consid-ering the circumstances most of them come from. I've heard some of the backgrounds. Why, without a place like that, you'd have a lot more child criminals roaming the streets, and that's a fact." He points his licked-clean spoon at me. "Agree or disagree, Cricket?"

"Well, I . . ."

"It's okay if you disagree. Go ahead, speak your mind."

"Well, I wasn't going to disagree. The nuns are strict. They run a tight ship. Ever since I was little I remem-ber them preaching at us about how we should act in town. They used to say we were . . ." My throat con-stricts. I have a sudden case of brain freeze, except the frost is in my gut. I suddenly understand where the chills are coming from. I'm speaking about myself and my life to a complete stranger. My legs shake and my forehead sizzles.

Mr. Bidaban leans in. "Representatives? Ambassa-dors?"

"Something like that," I choke out.

"Well, good for them. A lot more than most of the parents do around here. Kids today never stop to consider how their actions might bring shame and pain on other people. On their parents. Their brothers and sisters. Their family name. It's a good moral to instill in kids. To teach them that their actions have consequences on others. Kids today are selfish. Hell, what am I saying, kids? Most of the adults around here aren't much better."

"Dad, please. I didn't invite Cricket in so he could hear one of your famous 'Kids of Today' speeches."

Mr. Bidaban's words are bubbling a spicy bouillabaisse in my gut, and not 'cause I'm worried about bringing shame upon my crackhead parents or foster whore. But my options for life are full of nothing but shame and pain. Drug dealing, boxing, or that third option I don't like to think about 'cause it makes me sick to my stomach. Checking out of Hotel Life would bring a boatload of shame. And pain. To me and others. One other in particular. And a bunch of Little Others. Jesus, how the hell would Mother Mary explain that to the Little Ones? And what would stop them from doing it themselves once they got old enough to realize how much life sucks?

"I don't hear him complaining."

"He's too polite to complain. That's why I'm complaining for him."

"Look at him. Look at his face. That is not the face of a complainer. That is the face of a thinker. See? See that expression? He is seriously pondering what I just said. That is a sign of intelligence, Wynona. If Buster were here, he'd be scratching his ass."

"Dad!"

"Of course, for Buster, that is a form of thinking, since that's where his brains are located."

"Dad, stop it!"

Mr. Bidaban's rumbling laughter yanks me out of myself. I notice Wynona's bowl is empty, so I suck down the rest of my deep-sea stew.

Mr. Bidaban wipes his mouth and stands.

I scramble to my feet.

He throws his napkin down with unnecessary force and extends his hand. "It was a distinct pleasure meeting you, Cricket."

I shake his hand. It's rough like tree bark. "Thank you, sir."

"We'll clean up, Dad."

"Thanks, sweetie. I gotta make the rounds and check on my crew. Make sure they're not sleeping on the job."

Mr. Bidaban slaps his belly and leaves. Roxanne leaves the table without saying goodbye. She barely said a word during the meal. Just made weird sucking sounds with her tongue after each swallow.

After Wynona and I clean up, we head to the front porch with lemonade refills. I hadn't noticed before, but it's furnished with these ratty old chairs that look like they came from the Salvation Army. We sit down and I sink about ten feet into the cushion. Damn, this old hunk of junk is comfy. I could fall asleep in this bad boy.

From this hilltop elevation, I can see the whole town and the ocean beyond. It makes me feel like I'm looking at a miniature train set with Styrofoam hillsides, plastic train trestles, and tiny people I could pick up and plunk down wherever I want.

"Did you like lunch?" Wynona asks.

"Yeah, it was awesome. But I guess I coulda done without the octopus testicles."

Wynona giggles. "Tentacles."

"No, I'm pretty sure mine were testicles."

"You're gross."

"Your stepmom's sweet."

No answer.

I look over. She's staring at the town like she's thinking about moving some people around.

Whoopsadaisy. Back pedal engaged. "I was just joshing. What's up with her?"

No response.

"I guess that's the Roxanne you wrote about in your English paper?"

"Yeah, that's her."

I follow her gaze to see if I can figure out what she's staring at. Her eyes are pointed toward the church steeple, but I think that's just so her face will be pointed away from me. Maybe she's crying. Jesus, what the fuck is up with this world? Even people who've got it all get stabbed in the heart for no reason whatsoever. This whole world ain't nothing but one giant Kick in the Nuts factory.

It makes me realize what a waste of time hanging out with Wynona is. What a dangerous waste of time. I'm chasing my heart in circles like a stupid dog chasing its tail, as if I don't know that once I catch it it's gonna chomp me a molary malfeasance. What the hell am I doing here? Dragging my ass out of the mud to play tea party in Candy Land. My gut tightens. I stand. "Hey, I gotta go."

Wynona whips her head around. "What? Why? I'm sorry. I was just thinking about my mom. I didn't mean to be rude."

"No, it's not that. I was supposed to have the van back like two hours ago."

"Oh." She looks away but not as far.

"Thanks for the food. It was really good."

She looks up at me and opens her mouth like she's gonna say something, but then closes it.

I set my glass on the wicker table and leave. I wonder if she's looking at me as I lumber down the gravel walk. Probably not. I wonder if she knows I don't want to leave but have to. Probably not. She's probably looking at that faraway place again and thinking the same thing I'm thinking. What a waste it is to spend time with me. What a waste I am.

I don't look at her house as I drive away. I'm too scared the porch will be empty.

Mother Mary's sitting in the foyer reading when I slip through the front door. *Shit, I forgot to go to the hardware store and buy a new rake.* I throw my hands in the air. "The hardware store was fresh out of rakes, so I had to drive around to a bunch of other places looking for one, but no luck."

Mother Mary holds her giant paw out and I hand her the keys. "I understand," she says flatly. "Surprising that Home Depot, which is only twenty minutes down the road, doesn't stock such a common yard tool."

"Oh, right, Home Depot. I didn't think about going there."

"Don't think about going anywhere in the foreseeable future, Cricket." She stands and clicks off the lamp.

"When I didn't find you in the backyard, I looked for you in your room. Not finding you there got me thinking. Perhaps it was premature to give you your own room. You are clearly not mature enough for such a privilege. Perhaps it would be easier to keep tabs on you if you were back in the bullpen with the boys." She turns and walks into her office.

Shit, I hadn't thought about her playing that card. Man, that would suck major league balls.

Raking leaves with a good rake is bad enough. Try raking with a busted one held together with four rusty roofing nails and fifty feet of duct tape. I don't care. Wynona Bidaban kissed me.

But man, this head-heart tug-o'-war is tussling me a rope-burning mischief. All I know for sure is, no matter which side wins, I'll end up facedown in the mud.

I really like Wynona. I like being with her. But when I'm with her, I feel like I'm on a tightrope tethered between two skyscrapers about a mile in the air, and any second a giant gust of reality is gonna typhoon my clowning-around ass headfirst into Never Never Land. And I've been around long enough to know there ain't no safety nets in real life.

It's sad about Wynona's mom. I wonder what happened. That snooty-toot her dad picked up at the

Stepmom Swap Meet is a sorry replacement. Not that I'd know, but what could be worse than that shrivel-pussed prima donna?

Adults are wacky. Even the sane-seeming ones. Guess it could be worse. Wynona's dad really seems to love her. Not like my crackhead creators.

Shitnuggets! What am I gonna do?

Sam and Archie come running up to me, pushing a wheelbarrow of weeds that's teetering side to side because they each have a handle.

"We have a plan." Sam gasps, panting. He's wearing hand-me-down denim overalls that are three sizes too big, so the crotch droops to his knees.

"A plan for what, Mr. McGregor?"

"A plan for tag-teaming the girls we like," Archie says between breaths.

I probably should have used a different phrase. "Oh yeah, what's your plan?"

"Tina Gopi plays on the basketball team, so Archie's gonna try out for the boys' team 'cause the boys and girls practice at the same time after school. Archie's really good at basketball, so he'll probably make the team easy."

"Wow, that's a smart plan."

"Yeah, and since tryouts aren't for a few weeks, we're gonna steal a basketball from the gym storage room and

Archie's gonna carry it around school so Tina sees and knows he's into basketball."

"That's an even smarter plan." The boys beam. "Just make sure you steal a ball that doesn't have the school name written on it so you don't get caught."

The boys look at each other. "Oh yeah," Archie says.

"Don't worry. If you can't get one from the school, I'm sure we can get our hands on one somewhere."

"If this works and Archie gets to be Tina's boyfriend, he's gonna ask her to talk to Emily Stemple for me about my microscope and the algae slides I made all by myself, 'cause she's in Science Club."

My head tingles and my eyes get watery. "That's a damn good plan, boys," I say, patting them on the shoulders.

They smile wicked wide smiles and run off with the wobbly wheelbarrow between them.

I wipe my eyes and wonder why I'm getting all emotional. I think it's 'cause Sam and Archie seemed so normal just now. Just a couple of goofball kids scamming ideas on how to meet girls. They didn't look like abandoned orphans at all.

I drop my rake and walk to the edge of the cliffs. I sit on a boulder and look out over the endless sea. I imagine the water turning light pink and spinning, spinning, spinning until there's nothing left but a bright white porcelain floor.

I wish my baby brother, Eli, had lived so I could have been a big brother to him. I think I could have been a pretty decent big brother. Defending him from assholes and talking to him about girls.

I watch the dark waves roll toward me like they're carrying years on their crests. I wish I had an older brother. Someone who could have defended me from assholes and talked to me about girls. Or even an older orphan. How come I have to be the oldest kid here? The nuns say everything happens for a reason. I don't believe that. But someone has to be the oldest. Maybe when the Little Ones are older, they'll be happy I was around to defend them from assholes and talk to them about girls. Any one of them could have died just as easily as little Eli. But they didn't. They lived. And I lived. And now they're here. And I'm here. At the Prison. The oldest orphan. Their older brother.

I roll onto my side. The stone is rough and cold against my cheek. I imagine my scar slipping off and slicing the boulder in two. The granite gash swallows me whole. I fall and fall until I finally hit the center of the earth and incinerate into nothingness like a feather in a furnace.

My Silky Jets jetty is extra windy tonight, the herbaceous puffdiddle is extra smooth, and the spiked lemon cider is extra sour. Just like I like it. I slide into my dolomite recliner and let the gravity of the sea drain my churning jambalaya. The moon's shining bright on my inspirational *escritoire*. I grab a notebook and pencil from my backpack and scribble Reason Number Two of my Dear Life letter.

Dear Life, You Suck
Reason Number Two
By Cricket Cherpin

THINGS AIN'T WHAT THEY SEEM.

This make-believe home ain't a home. Plunking a pearly gate on hell don't make it heaven. This place ain't nothing but a wallpaper prison pretending to be a home on account of none of us have homes. But no one says that out loud. Everyone goes along to get along because what's the alternative?

This make-believe family ain't a family. Four dozen derelicts snoozing under the same rafters and extricating bran muffins into the same crapper don't a family make.

See, here's the thing. This ain't normal. Don't take no rocket scientist to figure that out. Like sometimes the nuns will try to sweet-talk you into thinking we're a family, but the bottom line is, family ain't the exterior stuff you can rattle off in a speech to a scared little dude who's just been dumped on your doorstep. Family is the invisible junk only someone in a family can see. Not that I've ever seen it, but some stuff you don't have to see to know it exists. Like wind and heat and cold and pain.

But home and family ain't even the big stuff. It's just the obvious stuff. The big stuff ain't never talked about. Like why we're still here. I know the score. Every kid in this place knows the score. Sure, we all play mind peekaboo and pretend the truth disappears when we cover our eyes, but we know what's going on.

Life's about getting picked. For kids and adults. By an apple pie mumsy or a musclehead quarterback or a moneybags boss or a sexytime squeeze. The game never changes. Only the prize. At some point, you just gotta accept that the milk jugs are nailed to the platform so no matter how many balls you throw, you ain't gonna knock that Jug of Gibraltar off the shelf and win the stuffed leprechaun. 'Cause the game's fixed against you.

It's like the piece-of-shit foster whore they put me with in Boston before sending me here. Took the idiot social workers forever to figure out my new caretaker was a shorthair shaker. Took me nine seconds. She'd been hooking for years but had pulled the lambskin over Social Services' eyes. From the way the crack-toking moms and dragon-chasing dads in the neighborhood talked, Social Services were the only folks in all of ASSachusetts who <u>didn't</u> know Chastity Cocktrumpet didn't reside anywhere near Innocent Street.

She tried to keep me from spilling the beans by spilling my genes with a little rub-a-dub-dub bald stiffy in a tub, but I never finagled that bagel. That's messed up when you think about it. Not that I ever think about it. It wasn't like she was my real mom or anything. Just another scheming grownup trying to score green from humans or clean from God by pretending to give a flying fuck about the miniature hostage tossing and turning on the pee-stained mattress in the basement.

Guess the canker sores on her lips and mannaise on her forehead didn't tip the professional progeny-placers off. She said it was on account of the cold weather. Yeah, snow squalls will detonate a pussy eruption on Herpes Mountain. So will grease drippings from a rancid sausage.

I swear, I ain't never seen anyone slower on the uptake than phony-baloney goody-two-shoes do-gooders. Especially when the intake is so close to home. They got no problem mind-juggling storytime tittle-tattle about life two thousand years ago, but good luck getting them to notice the dog shit on the bottom of their shoe. Never stops 'em from blaming the smell on someone else though.

So let's be real. Is it really such a good thing the sun will come out tomorrow, or is Annie a lying ginger whore?

CHAPTER 18

I have plenty of air pockets popping my gut a carbonated dysentery on my first day back at school. The tacked-on notoriety of being the only student at Naskeag High to ever be suspended twice in the first two weeks of school doesn't help. I mean, that's probably some world record in the *Guinness Book of Dirtbag Records.* The kids at school already stare at me crooked-headed as it is, so I can imagine the FU glares I'll get now.

Unless I get a surprise hero's welcome like in the Prison commissary. Doubtful, though. Pitbull's popular, and as much as kids detest him behind his back, they'd never cross him to his face. Spineless pussies. No, it will be a zero's welcome for sure.

Stress factor number one is Pitbull. Although I pummeled him into a blood-gushing pile, there's always the revenge factor. I may not have completely beaten that impulse out of him. And now since he knows he can't whup me on his own, he won't come at me alone.

That's why I have an enormous carving knife stuffed down my pants. You think I'm kidding? I ain't. Don't worry. I have it professionally situated so it won't fillet me a transgendering mischief. I actually created a rather clever concealer. I sewed the mighty scabbard's leather holder inside my pant leg. See, knowing how to sew comes in handy for numerous manly situations. I cut a hole in my front pocket for the handle to poke through. It's a pretty sweet setup. I can get the knife out lickety-split, and it's not noticeable 'cause my 1990s cargo pants are extra baggy.

Stress noose number two is Foxy Moxie. During my suspension, the teachers emailed me homework assignments, and Moxie superhighwayed me numerous reminders to complete my written responses to her comments on my letter. I emailed her Reasons One and Two over the weekend, and I'm nervous about how she's going to react. Not that I care what she thinks or what grade I get, but the last thing I need is more mind-mashing sessions with the school shrinkadink, Dr. Merewether.

Stress tab number three is Principal LaChance. He's just looking for an excuse to give me the permanent boot. And if I get booted from here, the Diocese will kick me out of the Prison even before I turn eighteen.

Thinking about getting booted from the Prison gets

me thinking about the deepest stress mess of all. It's not school-related, but it's haunting me worse than any of this Drama Club claptrap. What the hell am I gonna do on the morning of my eighteenth birthday? The tragic day is only eight months away. I can't stay at the Prison, and I'm not sure I wanna be promoted from collecting money for drugs to dealing them. I got no problem screwing up my own life, but I ain't interested in helping other kids screw up theirs. And I definitely don't want to fight for a living.

Option three trickles down my spine like icicle icemelt. Skipping out on paying my bill at Life's Front Desk is a nerve-racking consideration, to say the least. I mean, it'd be nice to make all my problems disappear in one fell swoop, but the thought of actually performing that fell swoop freaks me out. I ain't afraid of swallowing pain from a dude's fists, but I ain't real keen on feeling that final mind-bashing blow on account of I might actually feel it.

And then there's the risk factor. Every exit method I've read about carries a *frying pan into the fire* consequence if you fail. I mean, shit, I complain about how bad things are now, but I'd be super-duper double pissed if I screwed up my exit and wound up in a wheelchair sucking SpaghettiO's through a straw and struggling to remember the words to "Itsy Bitsy Spider."

Of course, if I skydive off life's skyscraper now, I'll

never get to kiss Wynona again. Those luscious lips are worth a lifetime of torment.

I haven't seen or spoken to Wynona since last Sunday. Not like it's been ages or anything, but a week feels like a year after a heart-thundering kiss. I thought about going to see her a million times and even started walking to her house a few hundred times, but my brain always did a U-turn before getting too far. During my Prison chores, I couldn't go more than five minutes without glancing toward the driveway in the hopes of seeing her bike.

The reason my mind keeps about-facing my body is because I'm Nostradamus. I'm serious. I can see into the future. And standing directly in front of me is a heart-shattering earthquake that's gonna register a 9.9 on the Rectum Scale. Wynona doesn't know me. She said it herself. She's only seen me in Kibbles-n-Bits. Once she gets a glimpse of the whole enchilada, she'll lose her appetite. I'm like an eclipse. Not safe to stare directly into.

None of it matters anyway. It's all fairy-tale tomfoolery. Wynona got all hot and bothered on account of I pounded Pitbull, or she I-Spied a few things we have in common, or her father thinks I'm a thinker, or some other nonsense, but none of it's more than a thirty-second sound bite that suckered her into the Newfangled Dude Store for a new wave Cricket doll. But that purchase will get stuffed to the back of the closet once she gets bored playing in Cricket's Dysfunctional Dreamhouse.

Things look pretty normal at school. The Prison van drops us curbside, so we have to cross the crowded courtyard to get to the entrance. The Little Ones huddle tight around me, a gang of homeless midget Crips.

A whirligig spins inside my head as I wonder who will be confrontation number one. Pitbull and his buddies? LaChance? Foxy Moxie? Doc Merewether? Wynona? I stuff my hand in my pocket to make sure the knife's still there, which of course it is, but that doesn't stop me from checking every five seconds.

Okay, here we go. I have my answer. Stress factor number one is barreling straight at me with a grizzly bear glare. He's alone, which means either he wants to make up, or he has a weapon. *Hmm, which could it be? Shit. The Little Ones.*

I start shoving them toward the doors. "Go on, get to class." They don't move until they see Pitbull, then they scram.

Crowds of kids have spotted Pitbull heading for me and are pointing, nudging, and whispering.

The Little Ones clump together near the front door of the Lower School.

"Inside. Now!" I yell, but they don't move.

Pitbull's coming strong. I can see the cuts and bruises on his face from here. If he has a gun, I'm screwed.

Then a funny thing happens. A gooey warmth flushes me. Similar to my post-whup-ass fuzzies. Every particle of stress and fear dissolves. Pitbull's gonna solve my problems for me. I stuff my hands in my pockets and savor my final breaths.

This won't be a bad way to go. I'll die a hero. Clint Eastwood–style. I hope Wynona's watching. It'll be a full-blown *Romeo and Juliet* murder-in-the-courtyard love scene. If she kneels beside me while I'm dying, I'm gonna say it. My final three words. *Sweet.*

I glance back at the Little Ones. They look terrified. Oh, if they only knew my happy truth.

Pitbull's ten feet away now. His hands are in his pockets. *Where's the gun? Why hasn't he drawn?* He's closer, closer, closer. *Jesus, he's massive.*

Five, four, three, two, one. He slams into me with his shoulder. Hard. So hard it knocks me to the ground.

And then . . . he's gone.

What the fuck?

The Little Ones sprint to my side.

"You okay, Crick?"

"How come you let him shove ya?"

"How come ya just stood there?"

"Are you gonna go after him?"

"Are you gonna pound his face again?"

My warm fuzzies evaporate, leaving my insides dry and brittle.

I yell louder than I should. "How many friggin' times do I gotta tell you idiots I don't fight unless it's self-defense? He fucking bumped into me. Big deal."

Before I walk away, I glimpse their twisted faces. *But we gave you a standing ovation in the dining room and you didn't yell at us then.*

At the high school entrance, I turn. They haven't moved. I yell to them. "Go on, guys. The bell's gonna ring."

They head inside. That's when I see her. She's been there all along. Watching. Waiting. Thinking. Probably rehearsing her escape speech. I can't tell which Wynona it is. The pissed-off one or the kissing one.

My legs calcify as she approaches.

"You really care about them, huh?"

The inside of my head is Niagara Failing, so I crank down hard on the shut-off valve. "I'm a bad example."

"Not from where I'm standing." She stares into my eyes, and the two sides of her melt together like a grilled cheese sandwich. "I guess my dad was right about you. You are a thinker."

Jesus, she's pretty. I hope every asshole in the courtyard is staring at us. I feel guilty for letting her think I'm something I'm not. "I'm nothing, Wynona."

Her gaze tears me apart. *Why can't I see what she sees?*

"I don't think you're nothing," she says softly.

In the hallway, the bell rings for class. Wynona slides her hand around my waist. I feel lifted. Like my feet aren't touching the ground.

At the end of English class, Moxie Lord saunters to my desk in a sky-blue dress swimming with tropical fish. She looks like an aquarium. I'm surprised she's not wearing tortoiseshell sandals. This lady is one singed-crust banana nut pie.

I'm still here because before class Foxy slipped me a note asking me to stay after, which means either she's gonna tear me a new one about my Dear Life Reasons or we're gonna play a nice game of Statutory Hide the Salami. I hope there's a lock on the door. Or maybe we'll go back to her place. She probably lives in a 1960s Volkswagen van. She'll be thrilled to know I have a freshly rolled herb wand in my wallet.

She swings a chair around and cowboy straddles it, which is frightening on account of she's wearing a dress. She leans in and our shoulders touch. Her breath tickles my forearm. She smells like pineapples. A tingle scrubwiggles my nutsack.

I pretend to look at the papers she's dropped on the desk as I stare down the front of her dress. Her bra is papaya green, and she has wrinkly folds between her boobs like Shar-Pei puppy skin. Wrinkles and freckles. *Eebyjeebyville*.

She yanks my hood down. "Explain yourself."

At first I think she's bagged me for ogling her suck sacks, but then I realize she's talking about my Dear Life Reasons. "What?"

"Where has the author of Reasons One and Two been residing for the past three years?"

"What are you talking about? I wrote those."

"I know you wrote them."

"So what's the beef?"

"The beef is, why have you been feeding me frozen cowpie since freshman year when you're obviously capable of grilling up filet mignon?"

She's not looking at my papers. She's looking at me, right at my face. But I can tell she's not looking at my scar. I can always tell when someone's staring at it. Like I have dead skin sensors or something.

"I don't know what you're talking about."

"Bullshit."

I tilt my head and look at her. She's got her granny glasses perched on the tip of her nose like a pigeon on a ledge. She's not as easy to stare at as Wynona, but easier than usual on account of her saying "bullshit" like a regular person instead of being a tight-ass teacher. It dawns on me that she's giving me a compliment.

Foxy Moxie pinches the bridge of her nose and speaks with her eyes closed. "I watched an interesting documentary Saturday night on bird migration. Did you happen to catch it?"

"No, I missed it. Hopefully you recorded it."

She harrumphs a laugh and opens her eyes. "Scientists have discovered traces of a mineral called magnetite in the brains of migratory birds. Near the upper beak. It's an iron oxide that is apparently extremely magnetic. The deposits give birds the power to sense the earth's magnetic field, and they can navigate by it during migration. Birds can actually sync themselves with the earth's magnetic field to find their way for thousands of miles even when they're young and making the trip for the first time."

"Cool." It actually does sound cool.

"Yes, my sentiments exactly." She looks in my eyes with an expression like she's about to tell me I'm her adopted alien son or something. "Cricket, if a creative writing mineral exists on earth, you have a large deposit of it in your young brain."

A warm stickiness slithers from my ears to my hips. I thought my writing would piss her off. Or at least offend her, since she's an adult. Instead, she's giving me a big slippy-slap on the back for being a dickhead with words. Damn-o-damn, where the hell's that upside-down cake factory when you need it? I think I'll go there after school and apply for a job in the assumption-flipping department.

She leans in. "Writing the way you do can't be taught. It's spontaneous, original, and honest. It doesn't just flow—it overflows. And you let it follow its own course. You're a natural, kid."

Her words overflow me. Caretaker used to say I was a natural when I first started working out with him in the boathouse. When he taught me the basics of boxing. He was the first person in my life to ever tell me I was a natural at something. The first and last. Until today. Eight years later. *Jesus, eight years.*

I can't think of anything to say on account of I don't have much experience in the compliments department. Maybe I should stab her in the face with a tree branch and run away. I rub my fingers over some boobies a perverted predecessor carved into the desk. I can't get my eyes to move, so I don't know if she's looking at me. I'm scared to see her expression. What if it's cream-corny? What if she's expecting a thank-you or a hug? What if it's smug like she thinks she just saved my friggin' life or something?

She rolls the papers up and raps them on the desk. "What are you doing after you graduate?"

I picture myself in a Bar Harbor alley in a knit cap and sunglasses, slipping a bag of powder to a teenage crackhead. "I don't know."

"Have you applied to college?"

"Naaah."

"Why not?"

"What, are you kidding me?"

She scrunches her face. *"Naaah."*

Hmm. Slightly humorous. "Why the hell would I go to college? There ain't nothing I'm good at except cracking numbskull skulls."

"Apparently, you didn't comprehend the metaphorical depths of my bird migration analogy?"

"What the hell am I gonna do with fruity writing? Whip up dead granny cards for Hallmark?"

Mademoiselle Lord leans back and pops me an open-mouthed glare like I just shit on her sandals. "Are you joking, Cricket? You read novels, don't you? You watch movies. Who do you think makes up all those fabulous tales? The story fairy? Haven't you ever thought about creating a story all on your own? Completely original. Completely from scratch." Foxy has a wicked gleam in her eyes.

I'm tempted to tell her about my Prison tower story-time, but I don't. "No, I've never thought about it."

Moxie doesn't bite. "Oh, please. Give me at least some credit. I'm not nearly as stupid as I look."

Books and movies. Apollo Zipper would be famous. *Apolloblanca. Gone with the Zipper. Apollo of Arabia. The Zipper Mutiny. Apollo-Hur. Rebel Without a Zipper.*

"If you don't go to college, what are you going to do with your life?"

Slightly less humorous. Do you not recall the ominous message in my Dear Life, You Suck letter, Lordy Lordikins? "What life?"

"Oh, right, I forgot. You're planning a retreat via the escape pod when no one's looking. Leave the rest of us here to go down with the ship."

I'm not sure if I should be offended or amused. I flash Moxie one of my best pre-fight glares.

She's not intimidated. "Why would you want to jump ship now? The ride's just about to start getting fun."

"Oh, really? How's that?"

"You're graduating high school. You're getting away from all of us pain-in-the-ass teachers who've been ordering you around and making you write stupid letters. You'll be an adult. You'll be able to do whatever you want. You'll be free."

I have to admit, her comments gush some sticky juices outta me like a machete slicing a ripe watermelon. I never thought about it that way. I've only thought about how the freedom's gonna freak me out when I get kicked out of the Prison. I've never thought about how the freedom's gonna free me. Of course, I can't let her know her words have tickled me a mischievous fancy.

"Yeah, right, free." I serve it up with an extra dollop of sarcasm.

"Why haven't you applied to college?"

"Why would I?"

She jabs me with her own pre-fight glare. *Not bad.*

"I wouldn't get in, and even if I did, I couldn't pay for it."

"I've seen your transcripts. You could get in. And most kids can't afford college but they figure out a way. The question is, how can you afford *not* to?"

I lift my head and gaze around the room.

"What are you looking for, Cricket?"

"The poster you just read that platitude off of. It must be here somewhere."

I feel her smile. "That one's been hanging in my head for a very long time. Anyway, you pay for college the same way everyone does. Beg, borrow, and steal. It's the way of the world."

"You don't understand my world."

"I understand it more today than I did last week."

Shit. Maybe I dripped out more personal ickies in my Reasons than I should have. I never thought we'd be talking about them. I just thought she'd scratch me an F and call it a day. "I ain't got the dough to mail in an application, let alone buy books and pay for room and board and all that other crap. There's no way."

"There's always a way. But forget money for a moment. Would you like to go to college if you could?"

"I don't know. I've never thought about it."

"I find that hard to believe."

Damn, this tripping Janis Joplin wannabe is good. I slip her a sideways glance. Her expression's serious, but her eyes are giggly. I can tell this ain't no typical shooting-the-breeze bullshit conversation. She's after something. Something about me. Something for me.

Foxy Moxie stands and slides her chair under a desk. "Think about it. If you decide it's something you want to explore, see me after school on Monday. I'll give you some suggestions on schools with good writing programs. Then we can connect with Miss Regan about financial aid and scholarships. She's a wiz at all that. She can probably finagle a way for you to attend college and get paid to do it. But don't wait too long. Last thing you want to do is miss the scholarship deadlines and be stuck in this frosty hellhole for another year." She winks and walks away.

Huh, how do you like that? She hates this place too.

CHAPTER 19

I'm under the big oak tree near the tennis courts at one o'clock, as requested. I ain't skipping out of school. It's a half day. Skipping after being back only two days would not be good. Not that I wouldn't have done it for a date with Wynona. That's what this is. A date. At least that's what she called it this morning when she asked me. I don't know what we're doing, but I don't care. Ain't that a smooth sailing tack in the udder rudder? I don't care one rat's nut what we do. Just to be with her is enough. Holy fruit-swizzled pirouettes, Batgirl. I sound like a friggin' Portuguese love sonnet.

I see her coming. The way she's glowing and grinning, I'm expecting an avalanche of words to tumble out when she gets to me, but she just says hi. She grabs my hand and pulls me toward the main road. I glance over my shoulder to see if any of the kids in the courtyard are watching, and they are, so I'm psyched. Their faces aren't scrunched and tilted like usual. More open-mouthed and gawky. *Sweeeet.*

We walk for a while without talking. She's squeezing my hand like she's afraid I'll bolt if she lets go. Like I'm a stray dog she's rescued. Our palms are sweaty, but she doesn't seem to notice. I feel fruity holding her hand in the middle of town, and I'm praying no one like Grubs or one of the guys from Duckies drives by. I'd never hear the end of it. Even though I'm feeling like a Tinker Bell balloon floating down Main Street in the Thanksgiving Day parade, I don't let go. It's worth the risk. She's worth the risk. Her fingers feel like the end of an electrical wire wrapped in soft cloth. The current's zapping my hand, energizing my arm, and singeing my chest. There's a hazardous sensation coursing through my veins too, on account of I know any second a bolt of reality might electrify my ass. Truth is, I like the feeling.

I don't realize where we're going until she yanks my arm a sharp left toward her driveway. *Oh, shit. I hope we ain't doing another eat-'n'-greet with Sergeant Superdad and Madame Step-Snob.*

"I already ate lunch," I grumble.

"Cool, me too."

At the top of the driveway, we turn onto a gravel path that curves around the house, which is a relief because I like being alone with her. Maybe she's taking me somewhere for a secret smooch session. The sound of gravel crunching under our sneakers makes me realize we haven't spoken during the entire walk. Just a few hints and glints between our sweaty palms.

The trail slopes downhill toward a big barn that's tilting so much it looks like it's about to tip over. A small corral built from wooden pallets is attached to the barn. There's a watering trough and one of them crossbeam things that's used in old Western movies to tie up horses. I'm just waiting for John Wayne to waddle out. *Where'd you find this peckerwood?*

When we get to the barn, the smell of horseshit slams me hard in the face. And I thought scrubbing seagull shit off the boathouse roof was bad. Pterodactyls couldn't shitzkrieg turds this huge.

Wynona unlatches a bungee cord lock and slides the giant door open. "Wait here," she says, stepping inside. A few minutes later, she walks out leading two horses.

I cross my arms over my chest and glare.

She beams at me. "What?"

"I hope this date don't involve me hauling my skinny ass onto one of them giant goddamn Pegasus bastards."

She feigns a frown. "Arabella and Mingo do not have wings. And I resent the implication. They are purebred Appaloosa." She steps forward and loops the reins around the tree-trunk crossbeam.

Oh, Jesus nut-crushing Christ. I'm doomed. I've never been on a horse, and I definitely don't want today to be my circus clown debut. Me bouncing and bashing the ol' family jewels a galloping mischief is not good first-date material. Afterward, we'll sip lemonade on her front porch while I apply an ice pack to my nutsack.

I watch her saddle the horses, all the while trying to think up some excuse that will get me out of this death-defying debacle.

Wynona finagles her sneaker into the loopy footholder thing and swoops onto the bigger horse like he's a playground seesaw. She merry-go-rounds me a grin like she's expecting me to do the same.

I flick her a crooked stare.

"What?"

"What do you think, what? I ain't scaling my ass up that friggin' four-legged skyscraper."

Wynona scrunches her face and sticks out her tongue. *Damn, she's cute.* "Don't tell me you're scared of a little horse?"

"I ain't scared of him. I'm scared of the big-ass boulder he's gonna buck me into."

"She."

"What?"

"Mingo's a she, and she's a sweetheart. She wouldn't hurt a flea."

Just then, Mingo jabs her head at me and snorts like she's agreeing.

Wynona laughs. "See?"

"I don't know."

"Oh, please. You can fistfight a guy as big as a horse, but you're afraid to ride one?"

Her saying that pushes me over the edge. I'd rather get thrown off a horse to my death than have Wynona think I'm a pussy. I step up to Mingo and notice that my saddle has a giant handle like I'm some Special Olympics equestrian. I'm surprised she's not making me wear a football helmet.

I jam my foot into the loop and grab the handle. Mingo starts walking, forcing me to hop on one foot to keep up. I try to push off the ground, but before I'm halfway up she lunges forward and I lose my grip and land on my ass.

Wynona's cackling under her hand, which for a split second bubbles a rage in my gut like right before a fight, but then I notice something unusual in her sparking eyes. She's looking at me differently from the way most glaring eyes do. She's laughing like we're at the cinema together watching a Monty Python flick.

I jump to my feet and fake a laugh, but I can feel the red on my face. "Wouldn't hurt a flea, huh?"

"Just relax," Wynona says through the giggles. "You're making her nervous."

"Maybe we should shoot her up with some equine ecstasy."

Wynona smiles and my insides swoosh. I walk over to Mingo and jump onto her like I've done it a million times.

I don't know if it's the elevation or the view or the giant body twitching between my legs or Wynona's applause, but something immediately lifts me to a place I've never been and transmogrifies me into a person I've never seen. Like all of a sudden, I am a horseback rider. Mingo must sense the change, because she nods and blasts me a nostril-flapping thumbs-up and trots off like I ESP'd her a *ready, set, go.*

Wynona gallops past me with a solemn expression, as if my ass-over-teakettle tumble never happened. I'm bouncing pretty good, so I press down on the foot holders and the ride smoothes like the feet things are control pedals. I let go of the handle and hold the reins like Wynona, except I use two hands. I feel balanced.

We pass through a gate into an enormous field and the tall tan grass swaying in the wind makes me feel like I'm riding through a wheat ocean on a dirt jetty.

Wynona fades into the scenery like she's painted there.

Mingo's head is tick-tocking like a metronome. Even though I can't see her eyes, I can tell by the way she's holding her head up that she's proud of me and proud to be carrying me. She's snorting me *attaboy*s and being extra careful with her footing and speed. This probably sounds corny, but I sense she's looking out for me. Like she actually cares about me.

I suddenly feel like Mingo is carrying me into my future. It makes me feel old. Older than I've ever imagined myself getting. Like ninety or a hundred. So old the memories aren't memories but parts of me, like limbs. Real parts of a real person. So old I can see more stuff behind me than in front.

I'm sitting at an enormous oak table talking to a skinny, scared, dirt-encrusted kid. I'm explaining to him how horseback riding isn't about skill, but trust. I'm explaining to him how horseback riding is about more than him. I tell him about the horseback ride I took that day with the beautiful girl in the beautiful field beside the beautiful ocean and how the beautiful wind made my ugly eyes cry. And I tell him about how that horse saved my life.

Mingo snorts me back to the present. The tall, tan grass sways beneath me. The warm wind dries my eyes.

My eighteenth birthday suddenly feels very far away.

Mingo catches up to Arabella as we enter a tunnel of trees. It reminds me of the rhododendron path at the Prison, except this trail smells like the pine-scented disinfectant I scrub the toilets with. Mingo trots alongside Arabella as if she has a secret to tell her, and my leg bumps Wynona's. She smiles without turning, makes a clicking sound with her mouth, and jabs Arabella in the sides with her heels. They gallop away.

The tunnel dumps us onto a sandy beach littered with leaves and limbs like a hurricane hit it. I wonder if they washed over from the Prison.

Wynona turns Arabella smoothly toward the ocean like the reins are a steering wheel. Mingo follows.

Wynona gazes at the ocean as if it's her first time seeing it. I'm right next to her, but she doesn't see me. Her gaze is intense. And familiar. The courtyard. The day I pummeled Pitbull. After the fight, when she was kneeling beside him and glaring at me with that look of . . . what was it? Not fear. Not anger. Determination. Except today I'm the pummeled Pitbull, and the ocean is me. *Freaky deaky*.

I'm happy she likes God Art more than Man Art.

She turns to me when her conversation with the ocean is over. "You're a natural."

Jeezy breezy lemon squeezy! Being called a natural for the third time in one lifetime.

She inches Arabella closer and leans her face into mine, and my face does the same without me telling it to. Her kiss feels like a feather landing on my lips. She keeps leaning until her body is sliding down Arabella like some equestrianated stripper move.

I dismount with far less grace, and we meet at Mingo's ass. *Romantic*. Mingo flicks her tail and catches me in the eye. Wynona laughs. The horses stand at the water's edge as if she ordered them to. I step back, and Wynona steps forward and grabs my hips and keeps walking until she bumps into me and hugs my waist, and I stumble backwards and fall on the sand, and she lands on top of me, which I guess was her plan all along because she's giggling an evil giggle.

Her eyes are glowing green like they're plugged into something, but I don't get much time to appreciate them on account of a distracting crotch rigor mortis that boinks me south of the border. Normally, I wouldn't care about a little beach time chubitation, but the way Wynona's positioned, her hoo-ha sensor's gonna set off a warning alarm with the slightest twitch.

I try to mind-wrestle the blood flow with thoughts of nuns, bran muffins, and horse manure, but Wynona shifts her hips and the friction is too much, and it happens. Cricket Junior repositions himself. He's like, *Hey, what's going on up there?*

Now there's blood rushing to my face as fast as other places, and I'm waiting for Wynona to jump up and slap my cheek, but she doesn't. Instead, she presses her chest hard into mine and starts kissing me hot and heavy with tongue and everything. *Oh, shit, this is trouble. Definitely not gonna slow the flag-raising ceremony down in Stiffytown.*

Suddenly, she pulls her lips from mine and stares at me hard and cold.

I brace for the impact.

Then she says it. "I'm a virgin."

That's what she says. *I'm a virgin.* You believe that secret-slipping hullabaloo? I'm expecting to get tally-whacked across the face, and she tells me something all personal and intimate like that.

I'm so shocked and relieved, I respond without thinking. "Me, too."

Her face crinkles. "Yeah, right."

Shit, maybe I shouldn't have leaked that. Do girls think that's faggy and lame? Damn it, why did I say that?

"You're joking, right?"

Shit, what do I do? Lie? Make up some steamy story? Spin some freaky shit about some chick I hooked up with in the walk-in cooler at Duckies? As I'm scrambling for a juicy lie, my crotch rocket shifts again, but this time in a deflating direction. My mind runs out of fuel, and my imagination deflates too. *Fuck it. I'm a horseback rider now.* "Sorry, no. I've never done that."

Her face softens. "Why'd you say sorry?"

"I don't know. You had this expression like you ex-pected me to be all experienced with girls and shit."

Then the strangest thing happens. She lowers her body onto me like she's tired. She starts kissing my chest through my shirt and unbuttoning a few buttons, and it feels really good what she's doing, and I'm really getting into it and so is Cricket Junior, who's preparing backstage for another surprise appearance, when Wynona suddenly sits up and screeches like Captain Jumptoattention poked her in Naughtytown.

"What the hell is that?" she screams.

Jeez Louise, I didn't think the mini ironman was that powerful. Then I realize she's pointing at my chest.

I peer at my wound through the gap in my shirt. No wonder she screamed. It looks gross. It hasn't scabbed over much on account of I think it's infected. It's red and raw, with a damp scab that's like six inches long. I try to lighten things up. "Just a flesh wound."

"Jesus, what happened?"

"It's just a scratch. From yardwork and stuff."

"Yardwork, my ass. That thing is friggin' huge. Did you get in a knife fight or something?"

"No, seriously, it's from a tree branch."

"Bullshit! Tell me the truth. What happened?"

"I didn't get in a knife fight, I swear."

She crosses her arms over her huffing chest. She looks like she did that day in Principal LaChance's waiting area.

"I cut myself on a tree limb that day after I scratched your face."

"What do you mean? Like on purpose?"

"No. Sorta, but no."

Her face starts to shake.

"It wasn't on purpose, I swear. I'm not like some . . . It just happened. I was so freaked out by what happened . . . by the cut on your cheek . . . I was just so pissed at myself for hurting you. I just freaked out. But not on purpose. I think I was just trying to . . . even things up."

Tears start dripping down her face. "Even things up? My cut was an accident."

"I know. This was too, I swear. It just . . . I just . . ."

Her tears start coming faster. She opens my shirt and looks more closely at the gash. Her face scrunches, and the tears become a waterfall. Some of them land on the wound. I imagine them miraculously healing it like in a science fiction movie, but they mostly just sting.

She dries her eyes and stares into my face. "Can I tell you a secret?"

I nod.

"I don't like fighting, but I was secretly rooting for you."

I take her head in my hands and pull her lips to mine. Her heat melts into me like sunshine.

We kiss some more and ride some more and kiss some more and ride some more. We don't do anything more than kiss, which I'm happy about. I'm nervous about the sex thing because I really like Wynona, and I don't want to make some rookie sex mistake that might make her stop liking me. I mean, she likes me now, and we're not doing anything more than kissing, so if she's cool with it, why mess it up? One of those *if it ain't broke don't fix it* deals Caretaker's always rambling about.

At the end of our date, I walk home really slow to savor the hot-cocoa-in-my-bloodstream sensation. My feet feel like they're in stirrups.

CHAPTER 20

Dinner that evening is my all-time favorite. A Monte Cristo sandwich. It's ham and Swiss cheese stuffed between thick slices of French toast sprinkled with powdered sugar and served up with raspberry jam. *Sweety eaties.* I'm super hungry, so I eat two portions. I can put away food like a pregnant rhino. I probably have a parasite or something.

After dinner, we clean up and head to the storytime tower. The Little Ones settle in all comfy-cozy with pillows and blankets and ginormous bowls of popcorn. The room smells like a movie theater. If you didn't look too closely, you might be fooled into thinking this was a real family room and the Little Ones were real family.

It's easier than usual to slide into Storyland tonight, probably on account of that's where I've been all day. I grab my notebook and flip it open. I scan my scribbles to refresh my memory. This is the first time I've ever written one of my stories out instead of just jotting down notes. Maybe I'll show it to Moxie.

I tell the Little Ones more about the island Apollo Zipper got stranded on, which I call Kef. Like how the Kefian kids stay underground during the day because on Kef, sunshine makes kids grow older.

I've never seen the Little Ones listen so intently. They're staring at me the same way Wynona did on the beach today. Like they're seeing through me. A strange foreboding scrubwiggles the back of my neck, and I turn. There's nothing behind me except my bright reflection in the black glass. My face morphs into an image of Wynona surrounded by a wheat-field frame. Her face is glowing like it did on Arabella today. She's smiling her calm, confident smile. I feel the corners of my mouth rise. Her face disappears and my reflection returns. I'm wearing her calm, confident smile. I almost don't recognize myself.

I hear a sniffle behind me and turn. The Little Ones are still staring. Maybe I look different to them, too. Or maybe it's what I said about the Kefian kids wanting to stay young forever. Maybe they're wondering if they'd want to stay young forever. Maybe they think the Kefian kids are crazy. Who in their right mind would wanna stay an orphan forever? Maybe they want to change too, and grow up under the singeing glare of the brilliant sun.

The silence rumbles like thunder. I place my hand on my chest. It's not thunder. It's my heart.

I tell the Little Ones how the Kefian kids work together to gather food and cook and clean, and how at night they go swimming in an underground grotto that's warmed by an enormous bonfire. I tell them about the beautiful island girl Apollo meets, Wanony, and about her plans to steal a ship and sail far away from Kef, and how Apollo asks her if he can come along, and how she says yes.

The Little Ones sit perfectly still like they're frozen in place.

The story room floods with light when Mother Mary enters. The Little Ones don't get up right away, and Mother Mary doesn't rush them. She sees they need to defrost before they can move.

After the Little Ones leave, I gaze at the dark, distant sea. I think about Apollo and Wynona. They both feel so real and yet so make-believe. I wonder what would happen if I believed in them. I wonder if believing in them would help me escape my island.

I recline in my fire-escape lounge chair and stare at the stars. A buried Dear Life Reason has been prickling my gray matter. One I never thought I'd write about. But that bumpy horseback ride jarred it loose from my underground vault, and it's been bouncing around in my head like a ticking time bomb. I gotta get it out before it explodes.

Dear Life, You Suck
Reason Number Three
By Cricket Cherpin

IF CHRISTMAS SUCKS, WHAT HOPE IS THERE FOR THE OTHER 364 DAYS?

I was eight years old. It was Christmas Eve. I only discovered it was Christmas Eve when I was led outside by the social worker and saw the sign in the liquor store window. CHRISTMAS EVE SPECIAL! RUM EGGNOG! $7.99! At first, the only blinking lights I saw were the ones on the police cars and the ambulance. But then I saw the colored lights in the upper-story windows of my apartment building and the lit-up Christmas tree on the fire escape. I couldn't see any of that stuff from our apartment because we lived in the basement and didn't have any windows. I knew Christmas was coming. I just didn't know when.

Christmas music blared through the paper-thin walls from the apartment next door.

Silent night, holy night
All is calm, all is bright

Dad didn't have money for a tree, so he dug up
a shrub in the playground across the street. It didn't
need a plastic base because the dirt and roots held it
up. The asshole had money for drugs and booze but
not for a Christmas tree. It didn't have any lights or
ornaments. Mom and Dad got high and decorated it
with shit they found around the apartment. Broken
crayons, empty beer cans, plastic straws, razor blades.
A spoon bent into a Z with a bronze burn mark on the
bottom. The special ornaments, like my Matchbox cars
and Eli's pacifier, hung from shoelaces on the higher
branches. At the peak of the Christmas shrub, five
hypodermic needles were taped together in the shape
of a star.

On the glass table beside the electric heater, Mom
and Dad left Santa a few powdery lines and a cocktail.

The music from next door was so loud, it felt like it
was playing inside my head.

> Round yon Virgin Mother and Child
> Holy Infant, so tender and mild

Eli screamed in the bathtub. Mom screamed
back. Eli screamed louder. Dad couldn't hear any of
it over the bubbly sweet crackle of his pipe. I usually
volunteered to give Eli his bath when Mom was high,

but I didn't volunteer that night. I didn't want to leave the Christmas shrub. I knew it was only a shrub decorated with trash, but there was something magical about it. I thought maybe something magical would happen in my life if I knelt beside it long enough.

It was the silence that made me go to the bathroom. Silence scared me back then. I was used to crying and screaming.

The only sound besides the silence was the loud music playing in my head.

> Silent night, holy night
> Shepherds quake at the sight

Eli floated facedown in the tub. It was one of those old, white porcelain tubs with feet that look like lion paws. A giant, headless, hollowed-out porcelain lion.

The water was pink. Eli's tiny bum looked like two bars of soap. His hair drifted like seaweed. I could hear the water draining. Mom had pulled the plug and was sitting on the toilet, waiting. What was she waiting for? I ran to the tub but her backhand stopped me.

Mom wasn't crying. Her face was pale and hollow, her skin so taut it looked like her bones were about to rip through. The air in the bathroom was heavy. Heavy like that tub. White porcelain heavy. Pink water heavy.

I asked God to fix things. Change things, reverse things. Something. Anything. God didn't answer —He just kept swallowing that heavy pink water.

The music played inside my head.

Holy Infant, so tender and mild
Sleep in heavenly peace

I didn't hate her. I wasn't mad at her. I hated me. I was mad at me. I never should have believed in that shrub. Why did I believe in that shrub? Maybe if I hadn't believed in that shrub . . .

"What do you imagine awaits you on the flipside?"

Eli awaits me on the flipside. I wonder if he's still a baby. I wonder if babies grow in heaven. I wonder if I'll recognize him. I wonder if he'll recognize me. I wonder if he'll be mad at me. I wonder if he'll forgive me.

Violent night, unholy night
All is gone, all is fright

CHAPTER 21

I'm up early considering it's a Saturday. I still have chores from Mother Mary's list to finish before Grubs picks me up at noon. He said noon, which means one. He wanted to do the collecting tonight, but I told him I have plans.

I have another date with Wynona. Unlike our last date, I know what we're doing this time. Well, partly. We're gonna chow some eats at Pizza Palace downtown and then catch a movie, except I don't know what movie. It's sure to be something out of date on account of the cinema downtown has been around since the era of silent movies, and the flicks it plays are almost as ancient. Kids in school joke about going to Naskeag Theater like *Omigod, this wicked scary movie just came out about this killer shark on Cape Cod.* Or *Omigod, let's go see that new movie about the cute little alien who can phone home using his finger.* There's a big cinema complex at the mall with about ten theaters, but I've never been.

I'm still grounded, but Mother Mary and Sister Elizabeth are in Bar Harbor for the weekend at some religious hoedown, so I should be in the clear unless one of the other nuns finds me missing and rats me out.

Another reason I'm up early is so I can raid the petty cash box in the walk-in pantry. All I have in my wallet are a few dead moths and a few live moocahs. I need to pinch some dough, otherwise I'll be drinking a glass of Parmesan cheese for dinner and making Wynona pay for her own slice. I know she knows I'm not rich or anything, but I can't get the image out of my head of her standing at the pizza counter thinking, *Jesus, you can't even scrape up enough cash to snorkel me a slice of pepperoni, you cheapskate.*

The sun's barely up, and I'm in the east garden with my broken rake. It's a giant circle of wild rose bushes with an enormous red maple tree in the center that's surrounded by prayer benches. Mother Mary Meditation sends me in here often. *Think about what you've done, and ask the good Lord for forgiveness.* On days when I don't need forgiveness, she sends me in to rake. It's not bad on account of the roses smell super sweet, except they're big and bushy and they block the view of the briny deep, which I like to gaze at when I'm contemplating my existence. Which is what the red maple is for.

I commence my ascent. The view from the peak of this Scarlet Delight is magnificent, but the sway glories my soul a splendiferous agitation. If one branch snaps, there's a lot of air between me and ground zero, and that landing's gonna end my tree-climbing days permanently. Makes me wonder if catching glimpses of sublimitacious grandeurs is worth the risk.

The sun's at that height where it looks perched on the horizon. It's casting a jetty of light across the surface of the sea from it to me, like it's daring me to leap aboard and run for my life toward the engulfing flames. Speaking of which . . .

Chick stuff is tricky. When I'm with Wynona, I'm bamboozled into feeling that maybe it won't end. Our relationship, I mean. When we're staring at each other, or holding hands, or kissing, it feels detached from reality, and my mind weakens and starts whispering to my soul like, *Who knows, maybe.* But I know that's just mushy fairy-tale gobbledygook.

The reality is, we're graduating in the spring, and there's no way Mr. Incredible is sending his only daughter to the Naskeag Institute of Cosmetology. Hell, she'll probably go to college in Alaska or Hawaii to get as far away as possible from Roxanna the Hun. Before her first semester is over, she'll meet some *GQ* cover model who can buy her the whole Pizza Palace instead of one stupid slice.

Going on another date with Wynona is stupid. I should cancel. Do it nice and friendly so I don't hurt her. Maybe be totally honest and tell her all the stuff I'm feeling. No, that wouldn't work, because they're not feelings, they're fears, and I'd come off sounding like a pussy.

Then again, if I know it's gonna end, and I know *how* it's gonna end, and I know it's gonna hurt, and it's inevitable anyway, why not just float as far as the hypnotic helium carries me and let the crash happen when it happens? I'm already floating in the clouds anyway, and the drop won't be much greater, so what the hell? I feel like Professor Marvel in *The Wizard of Oz* right before he sails off in his hot-air balloon. *"Frightened? You are talking to a man who has laughed in the face of death, sneered at doom, and chuckled at catastrophe. I was petrified."*

During a break on my favorite boulder, I hear footsteps approaching, so I snuff out my joint on my boot heel.

"Don't worry, I ain't gonna rat you out, you juvenile delinquent." Caretaker stands beside me with his hands on his hips.

I don't know what to say. He knows I party, but he's never caught me in the act.

"You should cool it with that shit, though," he says. "Ain't you ever seen them TV commercials? It fries your brain like a sunny-side-up egg."

"Good. People will have something to eat at my funeral."

Caretaker chuckles. "You got a twisted sense of humor, Cricks." He sits down beside me and stretches out his long legs. "You give any more thought to my idea about you boxing professionally to pay the bills?"

"Nah, some goody-two-shoes teacher at school is trying to finagle me into college."

"Hmm, interesting," he says. "Cricket Cherpin goes to college. Sounds like the title of some old Capra movie."

"More like a Three Stooges skit." I look at his face. His skin is wrinkly, in a smooth, low-tide sand ripples way. "I'll keep training, though. Just in case they give me the boot." He smiles and raises his left eyebrow. I wait for him to say something he thinks is funny.

He doesn't. Just slaps my knee and climbs to his feet. "You got time to give me a hand fixing that broken storm window in the dormitory? That ocean wind's blowing mighty cold at night and it's only gonna get colder."

"Yeah, sure,"

He extends his hand and pulls me up. Jesus, he's strong.

I jump into the death seat beside Grubs. Before I can close the door, he floors it, the tires squeal, and the door slams on its own.

"Shit, dude, you almost took my leg off."

Grubs laughs and takes a pull on his forty. He stuffs the bottle between his legs and hands me a small wooden box. "Wanna bump?"

"Nah, I'm good." I slide the box onto the dashboard.

He looks at me like I pissed in his beer. "Really? It's primo Peruvian."

I don't answer.

He pulls a joint from his shirt pocket and waves it in my face.

"No, thanks."

"What the fuck, dude?"

"I'm just chillin'."

"Since when does the psycho Cherpin chill without the influence?"

I gotta feed him an answer or he'll never shut up. "I'm hung, dude. Partied hard last night." That's a lie. I stayed in and read and then watched *An Affair to Remember*. Didn't party at all, actually, which is rare. I don't know why. I couldn't get Wynona out of my head. Not like I was trying. I like having her in there. Sometimes. Sometimes I kick her out and stomp her into the dirt. I can't get that memory of her saying she's a virgin out of my head. Every time I replay that reel, I feel her warm mound squished against Mr. Happy. To know she didn't funk any monkey business with Pitbull is a relief.

"Suit yourself, faggot. Leaves more for me."

The whole situation with Grubs is fucked up. Here's this drug dealer speeding around this tiny-ass town burning rubber and running red lights with blow in a box and weed in his pocket and booze between his legs, and he never gets in trouble on account of he rats out bigger drug dealers speeding around bigger towns with bigger stashes in bigger trunks. Meanwhile, I pop an asshole a few righteous shots in the noggin and I get kicked out of school for a week. I'm tellin' ya, chain me to an Uneasy Bake Oven inside the upside-down cake factory.

On Main Street, we get stuck in traffic, which is unheard of in this pissant whistlestop. I see a limo parked in front of Saint Mary's and a crowd of fancy-schmancy folks stream out of the church.

"Oh, for the love of Christ!" Grubs yells, slamming the steering wheel.

"Someone musta just tied the knot."

"More like tied the noose." He chuckles.

"If Toni gets her way, you two will be next."

Grubs swings his arm and slams me in the chest. "Don't even fuckin' joke about that, dude."

We see men in suits loading a casket into the back of a hearse.

"Oh, shit," Grubs mumbles.

We ride around for a couple hours making collections. Everyone pays up, so I don't have to get out of the car once. Which gives me plenty of time to think about collecting with Grubs. I don't want to do it anymore. And I definitely don't want to deal. I'm gonna tell him once we're done for the day.

He pops open his third forty and fires up a joint.

"Hey, why don't you let me drive home," I say.

"Fuck you, I'm fine."

"You're all over the fucking road, man."

"I'll take Roller Coaster Alley so we go undetected."

"Oh, great, that'll be safer."

Grubs coughs a laugh and blows smoke in my face.

Roller Coaster Alley is this curvy street that loops around the landfill. They call it Roller Coaster Alley 'cause it has wicked steep drops that give you belly tingles like a roller coaster.

I'm not too worried, 'cause Grubs knows the Alley like the back of his hand, and he's driven it in worse condition. Plus, the Alley's almost always deserted, so it's safer than going through downtown.

At the top of the Alley, Grubs jams the gearshift into first and revs the engine. He grins at me with his teeth clenched, like he's trying to show me how white they are. "Ready?"

I grab the dashboard and look down the first steep drop. I feel like I'm at the peak of a roller coaster at that split second right before the car nosedives down the track. "Yeah, just take it easy. You're drunk."

He revs the engine again and the car shivers. I feel the vibration in my feet, thighs, and back.

"I ain't drunk. I'm at that perfect place. Just beyond

buzzed but just before shitfaced. I'm like one of them religious yogis."

I look at Grubs and can't help laughing. He's got a shit-eating grin on his face like a kid who just farted in church.

"Just take it easy, Yogi Bear."

He laughs and revs the engine. "Here we go, Boo-Boo."

He pops the clutch, the tires squeal, and we lurch forward. All of a sudden, we're flying down the steepest section of road at seventy miles an hour. Grubs is clutching the steering wheel like it's a poisonous snake and grinning his crazy, teeth-clenched grin.

We hit the first bump and I fly out of my seat. I get a wicked flutter of tingles in my belly. I'm pretty sure the tires left the road. We hit the second bump and I don't get the tingles as bad 'cause I'm expecting it, but the car swerves wildly to the left when we land. Grubs doesn't overcorrect, just snaps the wheel a little right, then a little left, and taps the brakes. I'm shocked at how well he controls the car considering his condition. We're still going something like fifty, but we're past the bumps and almost to the bottom of the road where it meets Route 6. I breathe, for the first time since the top of the hill.

Grubs lets out an enormous sigh and reaches for his beer. "Oh, shit," he says, looking down at his tipped-over beer and drenched crotch.

We both crack up laughing.

He grabs a handful of napkins from the glove compartment and starts dabbing his crotch.

I glance back at the road and see a dump truck barreling onto Roller Coaster Alley from Route 6. He's clipped the corner, so he's in our lane and only about fifty feet away.

"Grubs, look out!"

Grubs looks up, and his face wrenches. He slams the clutch, downshifts, and yanks the steering wheel sharply to the right. We start to fishtail, and for a second I think we're gonna spin out of the truck's way and be flying in the opposite direction before it hits us, but then I see the truck's headlights smash into the driver's side window. Grubs raises his hands and screams.

That's the last sound I hear. Grubs's girlish scream. And the sound of the truck's headlights smashing through the glass. Two thoughts screech through my head before everything goes black.

Shit, the Little Ones. What will they do without me?

Shit, Wynona. She'll think I stood her up.

CHAPTER 22

Blessed are the poor in spirit: for theirs is the kingdom of heaven.

So, Heaven's actually pretty sweet. Confusing, but sweet. The sweetest slice of upside-down cake I've ever chumpadiddled. God doesn't want to toboggan your ass down a black diamond of despair too fast and furious, so He eases you into the helter-skelter hereafter slow and steady by submerging your senses with the familiar. For me, it's my Silky Jets. Not a bad place to spend eternity, if I may say so myself. He hasn't poured me a stiff one or fired me up a bambalacha Buddha, but I imagine that's coming soon enough. Saint Peter will stroll down the jetty in a tuxedo with a maxi pad draped over his forearm and silver-platter me all manner of jolly juices, herbalicious sizzle sticks, scallops wrapped in bacon, and apricot tartlets. God's a wicked serious munchies connoisseur.

Blessed are the meek: for they shall possess the land.

It's a woman's voice. I don't hear the words so much as feel them. Inside. Her voice is gritty and worn. Is it . . . ? Impossible. How did she find me? When did she get out of jail? What the hell is she doing here?

And what's all this crap about the meek inheriting the earth? The meek don't inherit shit. Except beatdowns and bruises. The Little Ones are proof of that.

I gaze at the sea and see clouds. I gaze at the sky and see waves. I look down to see if I'm standing on my head. No, I'm right side up. It's this place that's upside down.

Blessed are they that mourn: for they shall be comforted.

Southern Comforted, hopefully, 'cause this place is freaky. Not at all what I expected.

What do you imagine awaits you on the flipside?

Well, Moxie, it sure as hell wasn't this. Not this sunny darkness and straight-as-an-arrow confusion. I mean, I got the job done, no thanks to me, without the long, drawn-out pain of the experience, but now that I'm here,

I don't know if it's a good thing or a bad thing. What was all that hocus-pocus about *all will be revealed?*

The black sun sets into the surf. Psychedelic colors burst from the clouds like fireworks. Talk about God Art. I feel like I'm inside a painting. A skinny stalk of a boy on a million-acre jetty beneath a zillion-gallon ocean.

An image of Wynona floats in front of a cloud. The scenery darkens. A wave crashes inside me. I'll never see Wynona again.

Blessed are they that hunger and thirst after justice: for they shall have their fill.

I look around for my thermos. It must be here somewhere. Jesus liked to pull a cork.

Whitecaps roll across the sky like storm clouds. The silence is deafening. There's not a single sound. Except it's noisy as hell. The noises are muffled. Dings, beeps, murmurs, and squeaks. Rolling over me like a distant thunderstorm. One sound is distinct. Her voice.

Blessed are the merciful: for they shall obtain mercy.

The merciful. Mother Mary Merciful. I should put in a good word for her with the Big Guy. If I can ever get a word in edgewise. Boy oh boy, God sure does talk a lot in the Bewildering Beyond.

Blessed are the clean of heart: for they shall see God.

I guess that's why I ain't seen Him yet.

Wait a minute. Why am I thinking He's a Him? It's a woman's voice I'm hearing.

I gaze down at the sky and up at the sea. Then it hits me. This ain't Heaven! It's HELL! All has been reversed! And revealed! Why was I thinking this was Heaven? What the hell would I be doing in Heaven? Whatever made me head-hanker the nebulous notion I'd be heading north for the winter of my discontent?

But if this is Hell, why's God speaking to me? What the devil is She doing here? Then it really hits me. That ain't God tongue-wrestling my ears a deafening fancy. It's Satan! God ain't a chick. Beelzebubbies is! Holy vaginal variations, Phatgirl.

Now ALL has REALLY been REVEALED.

Blessed are the peacemakers: for they shall be called children of God.

Children of God.

Then it really, really hits me. Harder than anything ever has. And I've taken some hard-ass hits. I know why I'm here.

I scan the cliffs for his little body. Is he here? Fuck, no, why would Eli be here?

That's when I decide to lie on a boulder and call it a day. And by *day* I mean *eternity*. I start crying and can't stop for anything, but I don't care 'cause I'm alone.

Blessed are they that suffer persecution for justice's sake:

Blessed are they that suffer persecution? Are you fuckin' shittin' me?

I step to the edge of my Silky Jets and take one last look at the noble sea swaying above me like a vast, watery veil. I look down, pick a cloud, and jump.

I fall and fall.

For theirs is the kingdom of Heaven.

Shit, the Little Ones. What will they do without me?

*LutherHarrySheldonCameronRobertJeffThomas
IanJayDanteJohnChristopherJackAldenMizu
FrankArnoldBillyStephenRichardPaulNic
EugeneMattBrianDrewAlexTimMark
RyanJakeMichaelBobbyJames
ConnorRileyTannerDale
JustinArchieSherman
GregoryAaronSam
AndrewBernie
Charlie*

I land in the sea. Darkness swallows me. The pressure crushes my skull. The salt water burns my eyes. The pain brightens in the blackness.

I hear Her voice one last time.

Because this my son was dead and is come to life again, was lost and is found.

CHAPTER 23

Everything's gray and fuzzy. My tongue's furry. I'm thirsty. I pry my lips apart and try to speak. No words come out, just a groan. A black figure looms over me. The pain in my head makes my eyes water. I close my eyes.

"I'm thirsty."

Mother Mary's eyes are bloodshot, and her face is chalk white. She's propping up a scared smile with cracked lips, clutching a Bible to her enormous breast. She opens it and starts rifling through the pages.

Oh, no, please. Water, not parables.

She clears her throat. Her voice is gritty and worn. "And when Jesus was come into the house of the ruler, and saw the minstrels and the multitude making a rout, he said, 'Give place, for the girl is not dead, but sleepeth.' And they laughed him to scorn. And when the multitude was put forth, he went in, and took her by the hand. And the maid arose."

I croak my words. It hurts to talk. "You calling me a fucking girl?"

Her face collapses. Then explodes. She squeezes the Bible to her breast. "He's back!"

A nurse hands me a cup but yanks it away after only two sips.

"What the frig?"

"You have to go slow. You've been out a long time."

My stomach flutters. *A long time.* I feel like Christopher Walken in *The Dead Zone.* "*When I woke up, my girl was gone, my job was gone, my legs are just about useless. Blessed me? God's been a real sport to me!*"

"How long?" I croak.

"The doctor will be here in a minute."

I try to grab her arm, but my arm won't move. I turn to Mother Mary. "How long?"

She looks at her watch. "Fifty-eight and one-half hours, my son." She sniffles and leaves the room.

I drop my head back and sigh. *Shit, that ain't nothing.* I was afraid it was gonna be like ten years, and the next news was gonna be that Wynona's married with three kids or something.

There's a commotion in the hallway. Mother Mary's talking to some cops, and there's a bunch of other nuns from the Prison and a bunch of administrative people from the school, who I recognize on account of being sent to LaChance's office so often. There are some teachers, too, and Dr. Merewether. I see a flash of black and wonder if it's Caretaker. Principal LaChance is out there too. He probably came to expel me for missing fifty-eight and one-half hours of school.

I suddenly remember why I'm here. Grubs. I look at the bed next to me. It's rumpled but empty. He probably got out already.

My insides feel like they're being twisted like a wet rag. I yell to the nurse. "Nurse Ratched, can I get some drugs or something? My body's killing me."

She scowls. "The doctor will be right in."

Bitch. What the frig is she so pissed about?

The doctor comes in. He looks about twenty years old. "How are you feeling, Cricket?"

"Like shit. Can I get some pain pills or something? Everything hurts wicked bad."

"Your body has experienced a great deal of trauma, Cricket. Cracked ribs, a broken arm, bruised bones. And we sewed up your head with twenty-two stitches. But even with all that going on, a great deal of the discomfort you're experiencing is from the muscle spasms. They're tensing to protect the bones and organs."

"Thanks for the anatomy lesson, Doc, but can I just get some friggin' drugs?"

The doc smiles. "We already have you on a morphine drip and a muscle relaxant, but we can up the dosage and see how you feel." He rattles some technical mumbo jumbo to Nurse Poleupherass, and she injects some juice into my pain cocktail.

"Hey, Doc, how's Grubs?"

The nurse yanks the needle out and glares at me like I pinched her ass.

Heads in the hallway turn, and Mother Mary walks in. The doc looks at her like he's asking her something with his eyes, and she nods.

Oh, shit. How many times have I seen that exchange?

The doc steps to the side of the bed and puts his hand on the rail. "I'm sorry, Cricket. Gregory Dillar passed away before the ambulance got him to the hospital. I'm very sorry." He pats my shoulder and leaves the room.

I don't feel anything right away. My head's woozy, but that's probably from the drugs. I immediately start running reels of memories of all the shit we did together in the hopes of building up enough pressure to blow the lid off my emotions basket. The memories fill me up but just make me feel nauseous. No explosion.

Mother Mary puts her hand on my shoulder where the doc's was, like she's trying to stop some bleeding.

Grubs is dead. I can't get the words out of my head. *Grubs is dead.* And I was with him. I reckon that's why all the cops are hanging around. Speak of the devil.

"Good afternoon, Mr. Cherpin," a mean-looking cop says. "How are you feeling?"

The extra juice is starting to kick in, so the edgy part of the pain is gone, but everything still throbs with a dull ache. "Fine."

"Are you up to answering a few questions about the accident you and Mr. Dillar were involved in on Saturday?"

My gut shrivels.

"You're not in any trouble. We're just hoping you can fill in some of the blanks."

I don't trust this slick-haired douchebag. "Do I need a lawyer or anything like that?"

"We're not charging you with anything, Mr. Cherpin."

Mother Mary steps to the other side of the bed and jabs a chubby finger in the cop's bony face. She looks pissed. "I'll be holding you to that, Tommy. If there's any funny business down the road and you press charges after questioning him without a lawyer, you'll be answering to me and the attorney general. You hear me, Tommy? I'll have your ass."

Holy shit, look at that. She looks like she's gonna wallop him.

"Yes, ma'am. I assure you we have no intention of bringing charges of any kind against Mr. Cherpin."

"Fine. Go ahead, Cricket. Tell him what you remember." She squeezes into a chair beside the bed. "You don't mind if I listen in, do you, Tommy?"

"No, ma'am, not at all." The cop's voice is shaky.

That cracks me up. Mother Mary can scare the shit out of anyone.

I tell the cop everything I remember about Roller Coaster Alley and the dump truck, and Grubs trying to save us. I don't say nothing about the beer or the drugs, but the cop probably already knows about that. He writes everything down in a fairy-sized notebook and asks me a bunch more questions. I can answer some of them. Some of it's just a blur. Not the part about the headlights coming through Grubs's window, though. That son-of-a-bitch is crystal.

The cop leaves. Mother Mary smiles a sad smile and follows him.

The folks in the hallway stream in and out of my room like a funeral procession, blabbering greeting card messages like "Get better soon" and "We're all rooting for ya" and crap like that. Their crinkled grimaces make me realize I must look pretty fucked up, which makes me think two things. One, I have no interest whatsoever in checking myself out in a mirror, and two, Mother Mary didn't flinch at all at my appearance.

The ladies from the school front office cry as they bring me a giant purple plant, and Sister Gwendolyn fights back tears as she squeezes my unbroken arm. Even

La-di-dah LaChance pats me on the shoulder and tells me to hang in there. Funny how no one wanted me to hang in there all them times I was sitting in LaChance's waiting room.

Once the platitude parade has passed, I crook my head to improve my view of the hallway. *Is she out there? Why isn't she out there? If it was her in here, I'd be out there.*

Then she appears. In the doorway. Like an angel. Like a vision. I know that sounds corny, but that's how she looks in her cloud-colored clothes with the bright light behind her and her face so pretty, it doesn't look real. She's bawling like crazy. Her eyes are red, and her face is soaked, but there's joy beaming through the sadness like sun streaks through tree branches.

She runs at me with this look on her face like she's gonna leap onto the bed and grumble me a hot and horny tumble right here and now in front of the nurses and cops and nuns and God and everyone. She screeches to a halt beside the bed and buries her wet face in my chest.

I cringe from the pain but don't move. I think I'm smiling, but I'm not sure.

The doc must have dripped some sappy, sinister fairy dust into my IV bag, 'cause my eyes are swelling like I'm friggin' Tinker Bell.

I catch a glimpse of Mother Mary in the doorway.

She's got one hand over her mouth, and her eyes are glossy.

After Wynona shakes and shivers all her tears out, she lifts her head and glares into my moist, stupid, faggot eyes. "I was so scared," she says. That's all she can get out before she starts bawling again. She drops her head on my shoulder and cries into my ear. I can hear all the gurgly hacks and sniffly snuffs real good, and it's kinda gross but okay. I wipe my eyes with the sheet when she's not looking.

Her crying gets me thinking. I ain't never had anyone cry over me before. It's always been the other way around. And she's not bothered by my messed-up face either. She's snuggling up to me like I'm the cutest little huggy bear in the world, when in reality I must look like friggin' roadkill. I think I'll check out the hospital cafeteria to see if they have upside-down cake on the menu.

Just then, Moxie Lord pushes through the crowd and enters the room. She's wearing a purple dress with giant yellow flowers on it. She looks like she just flew in from Bermuda. Once she's close enough to get a good look at my face, she freezes. She crosses her arms over her chest and scrunches her mouth like she's about to send me to the principal's office. Her voice is chalky. "If you think this little stunt is going to get you out of meeting with me about those college applications, think again, wiseass." Her face starts to shake, so she pretends to scratch an itch on her forehead. She reaches into her pocketbook and yanks out a folded piece of paper. She steps forward and thrusts it at me. "I want this homework assignment on my desk by Friday. I don't care if you have to dictate it to your better half here. I want it by Friday."

Wynona takes the paper from her and unfolds it. Then she reads it to me. "Write a letter to someone you've always wanted to thank for something but never had the nerve."

I look at Mademoiselle Lord. Her eyes are puffy and her face is pale. I raise my unbroken arm.

"Yes, Mr. Cherpin."

"What about teachers?"

Foxy Moxie flashes me a slippery grin.

Damn, Lambikins Lord wants me *baaaad*.

She points a quivering finger at me. "Friday." Then she turns and leaves.

I watch her squeeze her way through the crowded hallway. *The crowded hallway*. I mean, I know some of them are here for legal shit on account of Grubs dying, but not all of them. Not the teachers and administrators and nuns. I mean, why would they come if they didn't care? At least a little.

Caretaker walks into the room and stands beside Wynona. He doesn't flinch at my appearance. He extends his hand and I shake it. Before he lets go, he pats the back of it with his other hand. He's never done that before. "How you holding up, Shirley?"

"Fine," I grunt.

He raises his left eyebrow. "You look like you went twelve rounds with Mike Tyson."

"No, it was twelve rounds with your wife."

Caretaker chuckles and throws a pretend punch at my head.

I introduce him to Wynona.

He gives a little bow when he shakes her hand. "What in tarnation is a pretty young woman like you doing with a juvenile delinquent like Cricket?"

"I'm a delinquent in disguise," Wynona whispers.

"Lord, help us," Caretaker bellows, laughing and slapping his legs. "It's the modern-day Bonnie and Clyde."

The drugs are pirouetting fruity thoughts in my head, so I don't catch all of Wynona and Caretaker's discussion, but I can tell from their tone that they're getting along swell.

"Well, I'm gonna hit the road, Cricks. Them Prison chores ain't gonna complete themselves." He nods at Wynona. "Try to keep this boy out of trouble if you can, beautiful."

"I'll do my best," she says.

At the door, Caretaker turns. "Cricket, you probably noticed that I held my tongue from dishing you out a well-deserved 'I told you so.' I did that on account of your fragile condition." He gives me a salute and walks out, then pops his head back in the doorway for a second. "Cricket."

"What?"

"I told you so."

Wynona looks around to make sure the room's empty, then slips something into my hand. It takes a few seconds of rubbing to figure out it's my old friend Ignatius Podiddle. At least I can sneak some tunage while I'm here.

She touches my cheek and smiles. She's looking at me the same way she looked at the ocean that day we went horseback riding. Like she's seeing deep, deep beneath the surface of the waves.

I smile. I'm having trouble keeping my eyes open. I feel Wynona's lips on my cheek. Then I feel Wynona's love in my heart. Then I fall asleep.

When I wake up, the room is darker. And empty. The hall is deserted. I hear a sniffle beside me. Wynona must still be here. I turn.

It's not Wynona. It's Nurse Bitchalot. She's crying into a mountain of tissues.

I grumble a hi and startle her.

She jumps up and starts to leave.

"'Sup?" I ask.

She stops. I'm confused on account of I don't know her from anywhere, so I can't figure why she's all busted up about me being all busted up. Then it hits me. "Were you guys friends?"

She nods into her tissues. "My name's Toni." She blows her nose. *Gross.* "Did Gregory ever talk about me?"

Shit. Toni. Grubs never said she was a nurse. "Yeah. He liked you a lot."

She sniffles. "You're lying."

I remember something Grubs told me one night when we were getting high in the state forest. Something he had supposedly said to Toni when they were having this serious discussion about life and marriage and shit like that.

So I tell her. "Grubs told me once that he didn't think he'd make a good husband or father on account of all his partying and dealing and staying out and shit. He said he was scared about fucking up a good thing and, maybe worse, fucking up a kid. He said if he wasn't so scared of them things, he'd hunker down and marry Toni."

It's obvious from her reaction that he really did say this to her 'cause it completely demolishes her, but in a good way. It makes me feel happy because at least she knows I wasn't lying about Grubs, and she knows he really did like her a lot, and if there could have been one special chick for him, it would have been her. That probably sounds like some psychological horseshit, but that's what I feel as I watch her exorcise them pain demons.

After all the crying and moaning, she leans over and kisses me on the forehead. It's a long kiss, like she's trying to press something into my mind through her lips and wants to make sure it sticks. She hands me a piece of paper and leaves. I squint at it under the red glow from the heartbeat machine. It's short and sweet and to the point. Grubs to a T.

Last Wilted Testicle of
Gregory "Grubs" Dillar.

I ain't got shit but my ride, Crick, so if I
bite it early it's all yours.
You need all the help you can get with the
chicks anyway, faggot.
If there's any stash in the trunk help
yourself. But the fuzz have probably
snatched it by now if you're reading this.

Enjoy the ride my friend.
G

I fold the letter, stuff it under my pillow, and jam my earbuds in to drown out the sound of my crying.

CHAPTER 24

I've been in the hospital for two weeks. I would have been out sooner, but a hunk of metal that harpooned my thigh was rusty and germed me up an infectious calamity. It freaked the doctors out for a few days on account of they were worried about the juices leaking into my bloodstream and killing me off.

Except for the constant ache from being on my ass all day, I don't mind it. It's peaceful. No responsibilities, other than scarfing down three squares a day and getting poked, prodded, and sponged down. I like the sponged-down part. Usually it's Toni who scrub-a-dub-dubs me sweet and gentle, which is cool 'cause she's wicked nice to me now and even teases me a little with a naughty grin as she sponges up my thigh higher than she's supposed to. She never sponges all the way to Naughtytown, but she knows she's getting me all hot and bothered. I mean, it's kinda obvious. Every now and then this fat old bitch nurse washes me down, which sucks balls on account of she's dick-shriveling gross to look at, and she scrubs me raw like she's scraping burnt cheese out of a lasagna pan.

After the first week, teachers started bringing me homework assignments. I didn't mind. It helped kill the time. Moxie Lord brought me a bunch of college brochures and scholarship applications. Holy higher education enemas, Riddler. Me in college. Pass me another slice of upside-down cake.

I have a bunch of other reasons for my Dear Life letter, but I'm not in the mood to scribble them into fruition. Finishing the letter doesn't feel as important now. I guess I have what they call writer's cock.

Today Mother Mary's bringing a gaggle of Little Ones to the hospital for a storytime visit. She says they've been hounding her something silly about when I'm coming home so I can finish the Apollo Zipper story. She told me about it yesterday, so I've been scribbling notes on the back of the prescription pad I lifted from Doc Hollywood's coat pocket.

Toni wheels me into the rec room, where the Little Ones are waiting. I don't get a hero's cheer because Mother Mary warned them to keep their little yaps shut while in the hospital, but their goofy grins and jittery waves are good enough for me. I gotta find out what the hell they put in the oxygen here on account of it does a number on my eyeball glands. I tamp down my emotions hard and fast and wheel myself down a path between their little bodies to a spot by the window.

I scan their anxious faces. "Jeez Louise, I finally get away from you noisy numbnuts and you find me anyhow." The Little Ones laugh under their little hands. My head feels like a hot-air balloon that's about to pop.

"So, you wanna hear what happened to our old pal Apollo, eh? Well, I guess it's fitting that I finish the story here in the Naskeag Hospital on account of this is exactly where Apollo wound up after his transatlantic journey with Wanony and some of the other Kefian ruffians. In fact, I found out from a nurse here that the room I'm staying in is the exact same room Apollo stayed in after his ship reached the coast of Maine back in 1875."

The Little Ones *oooooh* and *aaaaah*.

"Now, Apollo knew that they were in for a long and treacherous journey, so he took Wanony aside to explain the risks to her and make sure this is what she wanted to do. She told him that she didn't care how dangerous it was. She wanted to sail far away from Kef, because she didn't want to stay a kid forever. She wanted to live under the bright glow of the sun, even if it meant growing old and dying."

I pan the sea of little heads peering up at me. Their faces radiate a calm excitement. It makes me think that this is what little faces should look like all the time.

I tell the Little Ones how Apollo, Wanony, and ten other Kefians stole a ship from a neighboring island and set sail for America. I tell them all about the long and difficult journey and how they survived by snorkeling with spearguns and shooting birds out of the sky with slingshots. And how, after three months at sea, they finally spotted land and Wanony was so happy, she kissed Apollo right on the lips!

The Little Ones groan in unison. *"Eeeehhhhrrrr."*

"Big, wet, and juicy! With tongue and everything."

"Eeeeeehhhhhhhrrrrrrrr."

I tell them how Apollo sailed their ship straight into Naskeag Harbor and how they used the timber from the ship to build a giant house right on the shore.

"And guess what that house is today?" I ask.

"Our house," little Andrew hollers.

"Our house," I say quietly. "And the Kefian kids grew older and bigger and stronger now that they were living above ground instead of beneath it. And Apollo and Wanony got married and had kids, and their kids grew up and got married and had kids, and so on and so on, and guess who one of their descendants was?"

Gregory Bullivant jumps to his feet. "Zachary Zipper! The old man from the library!" he screams.

Mother Mary rushes over and shushes him.

"Exactamundo, Greggplant. And the Zipper family lived happily ever after in the lovely state of Maine for many generations to come."

The Little Ones jump up and clap and cheer until Mother Mary and the other nuns get control of the ruckus and settle them down.

"Oh, and by the way," I say softly. "Save those seashells I gave you on the day I started the Apollo Zipper story. They're from the island of Kef."

Toni's with me on checkout day, helping me get dressed and teaching me how to walk on crutches and change my bandages and stuff. She keeps getting teary-eyed and hugging me.

While I'm packing, I find the Bible Mother Mary was hugging the day I woke up. "Does this stay here?" I ask Toni, waving the Bible at her.

"No, that belongs to that big fat nun. The wicked mean one."

I smile.

"She was like a friggin' crazy person with that Bible," Toni says as she stuffs get-well cards and drawings the Little Ones did for me into a Salvation Army bag.

"What are you talking about?"

Toni brushes a few straw-colored wisps off her face. She's pretty in a rough-and-tumble kinda way. "We all knew you couldn't hear her, but she wouldn't quit. We were like, 'He's in a friggin' coma, weirdo.'"

"What do you mean? She was reading it to me?"

"All day and night while you were out. Over and over. It was friggin' annoying."

I open to a page marked with a yellow sticky. The Beatitudes. I read a few lines. I get a freaky déjà vu feeling.

Toni sets the bag on the bed. "Yeah, that first day she refused to leave when visiting hours were over, and she raised such a ruckus that Mrs. Barrett finally told us to bring in pillows and blankets so she could sleep in the bed next to you. I ain't bullshitting about her being crazy, either. Some of my shifts are overnighters, and I swear to God that psycho witch was up all night reading that stupid book out loud. It got to the point where we all knew the lines by heart and were repeating them to each other in the hallway. *Blessed are the poor, blessed are the hungry, blessed are the thirsty.*" Toni laughs. "It was wicked funny."

I turn to the window so Toni won't see the tears.

CHAPTER 25

Tomorrow's my first day back at school. I'm anxious to get back. I don't know why. Maybe on account of I'm a celebrity from surviving a deadly car crash. Or maybe I want to see Wynona in a normal-life setting. Or maybe I'm curious to see if my cracked Great Wall of China will hold up outside the Prison. They're tiny cracks, but still. Or maybe I just want to get busy so I can stop thinking about Grubs.

I probably shouldn't be so anxious to go back. I'm sure Pitbull's got an elaborate revenge plan figured out by now. Maybe I'll get lucky and he'll be content with the ass-knocking he gave me the other day in the courtyard.

I hobble to the cliffs with the cane Caretaker lent me. I hate using it, but my ribs are still wicked sore, and I can barely walk to the bathroom without something to lean on. I'm supposed to use crutches, but leaning on them makes me feel like a pussapalegic. I crash on a nice flat boulder and take out my pen, notebook, and thermos.

I have one final Dear Life letter to write. This one's for my eyes only. I take a sip of lodka and venomade and start scribbling.

Dear Life, You Cut
The Story of My Ring
By Cricket Cherpin

I was seven. My dad took me on a drug deal with him. He always took me along so he could hide drugs in my socks and underwear. He told me never to take them out until he gave the thumbs-up.

We were in this ratty warehouse with a bunch of guys he'd never done business with before. They pulled guns and knives on us and told my dad to hand over the stuff or they'd slice me up. My dad said "Fuck you," and the guy cut me. Cut me bad. Dragged that shiny silver blade down the right side of my face. It hurt more than anything in my life. Blood gushed out like crazy. I was sure I was gonna die. I screamed and cried, waiting for my dad to flash me the thumbs-up.

He never did, so the guy cut me again.

My dad still wouldn't hand the stuff over, so they beat the shit out of him and dumped us in an alley.

When we got back home, my dad gave me his ring
for being brave and not ratting about the drugs. He
couldn't take me to the hospital 'cause he didn't have
money or insurance, so the cuts scarred up pretty
noticeable.

The letters on the ring are my father's initials. BC.
Boone Cherpin.

Why do I keep the ring?

He told me I was brave.

Why do I think about that day so often?

He was proud of me.

In my younger years, I thought the ring had magic
powers. I'd aim it at my head and memories would
disappear. I'd aim it at people and they'd avoid me. I'd
aim it at my opponents and they'd collapse. BC. Brave
Cricket.

As I got older, the ring lost its magic powers.
Memories returned. People persisted. Opponents fought
back.

Why do I still believe that ring can protect me?

Compared to knives, what can fists do?

I need to find a new source of magic.

I put my pen down, grab my thermos, and walk to
the edge of the cliff. The sky is dark, the ocean wild. I
take a long swig.

A memory of Dad's ugly face yelling "Fuck you" at the drug dealers flashes in my mind.

He chose drugs over me.

I look at my ring. *BC. Broken Cricket.*

My head swells, but no tears drip out. Only sadness. Hate. Confusion.

Maybe I kept the ring to distract myself from the real scars I got that day.

I gaze at the endless sea. Churning, churning, churning. Forever and ever and ever. That sea will never stop churning. No amount of magic will ever stop that sea from churning.

I look at my ring. *BC.*

I look at the sky. *Believe, Cricket.*

I step closer to the edge of the cliff and throw my ring into the ocean.

CHAPTER 26

Mother Mary's on her knees in the second pew with her forehead on the seatback and her palms up like she's catching rainwater. I sit in my usual place in the last row and watch her boulder-like body heave in supplication. I wonder if her prayers will be answered. I wonder if they already have. What in the world possesses a woman to become a nun? I mean, jeez, of all the shit you could do. I'd rather follow a circus elephant around with a pooper-scooper.

I remember the first time I saw her praying like this, slumped over, all still and silent. I thought she was dead. It was when I first got here, and I ran to my room and hid under my cot on account of I figured I'd get blamed.

I lie down on the unforgiving wood, rest my feet on a stack of hymnals, and close my eyes. I think about Apollo Zipper. I wonder if the ending I told the Little

Ones was the right ending. I wonder what will really happen to Apollo in his new world. I wonder if he'll really grow up now that he's living in the sunshine. I wonder if he and Wanony will really fall in love. I wonder if she'll outgrow him the moment the sun strikes her pretty face. I wonder what she'll do when she grows up. I wonder what Apollo will do. Maybe he'll write a novel about his tragic oceanic adventure and smuggle the manuscript to a civilized city where people hurl words instead of fists. Maybe he'll have an epiphany about the ferry tragedy freeing him into the arms of a long and happy Down East life.

"An interesting position of beseechment, Mr. Cherpin." Mother Mary looms over me like an enormous storm cloud.

I pull myself up. "Sorry."

"*No worries, mate.* Besides, it looks comfortable. I'd try it myself if I thought I could fit."

I follow her to her office.

She steps to the window and opens the drapes.

It's dark outside. There's moonlight, so I can see the ocean in the distance. And myself, closer. My reflection in the window is faint. I can't see my scar.

"I was wondering why . . . in the hospital . . ." I can't finish the sentence.

Her reflection comes into focus, beside me, hovering over the desert of black.

"I made a choice years ago, Cricket. Just like you will make a choice soon. I chose to give my life to God. I knew what the sacrifice entailed. As a woman, I knew." She puts her hand on the glass like she's trying to touch some faraway thing. "The extraordinary thing is that God figured out a way to bless me with what I sacrificed. I don't know how I'll ever repay Him. Of course, I know I can't. None of us can. But I'd like to. I often wonder if that's what Jesus meant when he said we must lose ourselves to gain ourselves. That we must give up everything to gain everything."

I look at the back of Mother Mary's hand. At the veins and wrinkles. Something about her powerful hand makes me feel less confused. I don't know why. It's as if her hand is covering up a confusion keyhole.

I think about Mother Mary reading Bible verses to me in the hospital. I wonder if she was doing that as a way of trying to repay God for what He gave her. "What did God give you?"

Mother Mary turns. "He gave me a son, Cricket."

My eyes swell. I want to look away, but Mother Mary hasn't, so I can't. If I look away first, I'll lose. I'll really lose.

She walks to her desk. "Principal LaChance called me today."

"What the hell? I haven't even been in school!"

She smiles. "He didn't call to reprimand you."

I flash her a crooked glare.

"Have you been coaching the Little Ones about ways to deal with bullies at school?"

"I don't know. Maybe."

"There was an incident today."

Oh, shit.

Mother Mary lifts a piece of paper off her desk and looks at it. "There is a new senior at school named Ezekiel Turgeon. They call him Zeke T. Apparently, he's even more obnoxious than Buster Pitswaller, if you can believe that."

"Impossible."

"He was picking on Gregory Bullivant in the courtyard before school, and our little Charlie led a gang of Little Ones in revolt."

"No shit."

"During the confrontation, a senior named Madison Connors came to their aid and verbally accosted Zeke T. with such . . . unladylike . . . language that she earned herself an after-school detention."

"Good for her," I say, smirking. Madison Connors sits in front of me in English class. She's a spindly redhead who always wears tight jeans and tall black boots. She smiles at me sometimes, but we've never spoken. I'm glad she stepped in to help the Little Ones.

She waves the piece of paper at me. "What's this all about, Cricket?"

"I don't know. I guess the Little Ones just decided to take matters into their own hands."

"Bullspit." She glares.

"I just told them that they might have better luck dealing with bullies as a group instead of one on one."

She tosses the paper on her desk. "I see. So you suggested that they confront their problems as brothers instead of fighters."

"Yeah, sorta."

She taps her chin with her fingertips. "Well, good for you, Cricket. Maybe there's hope for you yet."

"I wouldn't go that far."

She smiles.

We make two cups of tea in the kitchen and carry them outside. We don't talk for the longest time. We just walk the trails and listen to the wind whistling through the tree branches and the waves crashing on the rocky shore. Mother Mary takes a break on one of the prayer benches in the rose garden.

There's a ton of shit I want to say to her, but every time the words slip from my brain to my tongue, they bottleneck. It doesn't matter. She knows what I want to say. She always knows.

I finally break the silence. "I think God paid me a visit while I was snoozadoozing in the hospital."

"Oh, really? Did He have anything interesting to say?"

"Well, not in words exactly. But I think He told me that what happened to my baby brother wasn't my fault. That it's not one kid's fault what the mom does to the other kid no matter what the first kid did on account of he's just a kid."

She looks at me. Her face is calm. Calmer than I've ever seen it. "King Solomon couldn't have said it better himself, Cricket."

"I don't feel so guilty about it now."

"Good. Guilt sucks. And you certainly have no reason to harbor guilt over that tragedy."

"I always knew in my head it wasn't my fault, but I could never convince my heart."

"Unfortunately, that's where guilt roots the deepest."

"I guess God did some weeding or something."

Mother Mary doesn't respond. Well, that's not exactly true. She says a lot with her eyes. The way she's staring makes me realize she's never looked at my scar. Not once in all these years. Like it's invisible to her.

I grab a thick limb on the maple tree and dangle my lanky legs. "Moxie Lord thinks I might be able to get into college for my writing."

Mother Mary nods.

"Not that I could friggin' pay for it."

"Don't look at me, Cricket. I took a vow of poverty a long time ago."

"Maybe I could ask the pope for a loan."

She blows out a loud *puuuuugh*. "Yeah, right. Get in line." She slaps her hand to her mouth. "Whoopsadaisy." She crosses herself and kisses her fingertips.

We leave our empty teacups on a bench and walk to the cliffs. It's windy and cold. I watch the ocean churn. Something's missing.

"Goodness, the tide's high," Mother Mary says, peering over the edge.

I gaze at my Silky Jets and realize what's missing. My jetty is completely submerged. "Jeez, it sure is. I ain't never seen it this high."

"That's one thing you can always count on in this place. High highs and low lows. No way around that."

A strong onshore wind blasts my face as if the ocean agrees.

"It's on account of the full moon," I say. "Did you see it last night?"

"No, I missed it. Us old fogies don't stay up as late as you, Cricket."

"What are you talking about? My curfew's ten."

Mother Mary blasts out another *puuuuugh*.

"What?"

"Oh, please. That fire escape's seen more late-night action than Mary Magdalene after a Sadducee bake sale."

I chuckle and step closer to the edge.

"Be careful, Cricket."

The ocean is stunning. Crystal reflections dance on

the surface. I gaze up at their source. The sky's plastered with a zillion sparkling stars. Wispy clouds decorate the foreground. Like a baby's been finger-painting on God's blank canvas.

"Full moons push and pull the tides much more powerfully than at other times," I say.

"That they do," she says quietly.

"Thank you," I whisper.

Mother Mary pats my back, resting her hand there for the briefest moment. Long enough, though.

"We going to Salivating Arny's tomorrow to get the Little Ones some new duds?" I ask.

"That we are."

I know I'm gonna walk tall on that sidewalk tomorrow. For Mother Mary. And the Little Ones. And me. The thought makes me smile.

I turn to ask what time we're going, but she's gone. She's walking away from the cliffs with her arms extended, her palms up, and her head tilted back. Somehow I know she has her eyes closed. She sees better that way.

Thank You

In Order of Appearance

(What can I say? I like old movies.)

Mom

For brainwashing me into believing I can do anything I set
my mind to.

Family and friends

For love, support, laughs.

Liz Bicknell

For having a sense of humor.

Carter Hasegawa

For advice and critique (without a contract) that was instrumental in taking the manuscript to the next level.

Lisa Borders

For book doctoring that healed gaping wounds.

Critique Group Cohorts

Michelle, Kristy, Peter, and Frank. For encouragement and
harsh words delicately delivered.

Michelle Cusolito

For being an optimistic and insightful writing ally and seeing beneath Cricket's scars very early on.

Rubin Pfeffer

For guidance, wisdom, and honesty. For being an exceptional agent, but more important, an exceptional person.

Jeannette E. Larson

For taking on a diamond in the extreme rough.

Adah Nuchi

For lifting Cricket out of the slush and falling in love with him from page one. For passion, patience, vision, and calm, despite my constant objections and whining. For helping me make the story everything you always knew it could be, so much more than I ever imagined. And most important, for your gentle stubbornness when you knew you were right, which was pretty much most of the time.